# BROKEN
## ∀NGEL

**Center Point
Large Print**

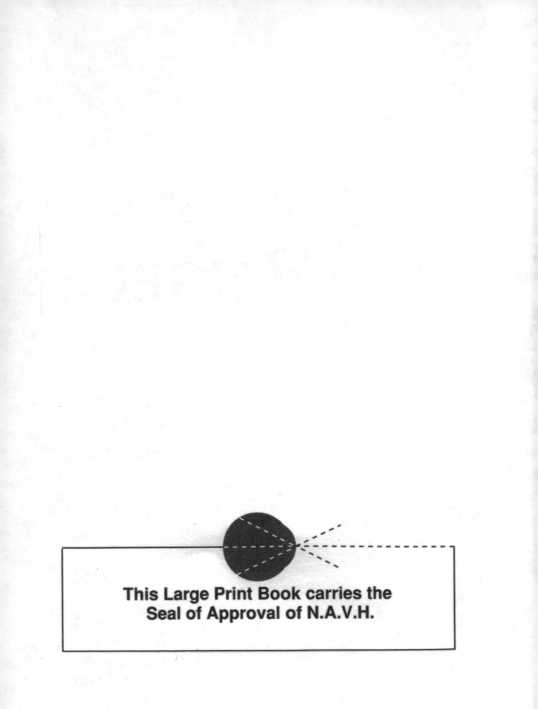

**This Large Print Book carries the
Seal of Approval of N.A.V.H.**

# BROKEN ANGEL

## SIGMUND BROUWER

CENTER POINT PUBLISHING
THORNDIKE, MAINE

This Center Point Large Print edition
is published in the year 2008 by arrangement with
WaterBrook Press, a division of Random House, Inc.

The text of this Large Print edition is unabridged. In other
aspects, this book may vary from the original edition.
Printed in the United States of America.
Set in 16-point Times New Roman type.


ISBN: 978-1-60285-270-9


Library of Congress Cataloging-in-Publication Data

Brouwer, Sigmund, 1959-
    Broken angel / Sigmund Brouwer.--Center Point large print ed.
      p. cm.
    ISBN: 978-1-60285-270-9 (lib. bdg. : alk. paper)
    1. Fugitives from justice--Fiction. 2. Large type books. I. Title.

PS3552.R6825B76 2008b
813'.54--dc22

2008019709

*To Cindy and Olivia and Savannah*

*Always, as big and forever as the sky.*

*We had agreed—the woman I loved and I—that as soon as you were born, we would perform an act of mercy and decency and wrap you in a towel to drown you in a nearby sink of water.*

*But in the motel room that was our home, the woman I loved died while giving birth. You were a tiny bundle of silent and alert vulnerability and all that remained to remind me of the woman.*

*I was nearly blind with tears in that lonely motel room. With the selfishness typical of my entire life to that point, I delayed the mercy and decency we had promised you. I used the towel not to wrap and drown you, but to clean and dry you.*

*As I lifted your twisted hands and gently wiped the terrible hunch in the center of your back—where your arms connected to a ridge of bone that pushed against your translucent skin—I heard God speak to me for the first time in my life.*

*He did not speak in the loud and terrible way as claimed by the preachers of Appalachia where I fled with you. Instead God spoke in the way I believe he most often speaks to humans—through the heart, when circumstances have stripped away our obstinate self-focus.*

*Holding you in your first moments outside the womb, I was overwhelmed by protective love. Even in the circumstances that you face now, believe that my love has only strengthened since then.*

*I do not regret the price I paid for my love for you. But I do regret what it has cost you, all your life. And I have never stopped regretting all that I've kept hidden from you.*

*My confession begins with how I deceived you the day after your sixth birthday. You may still believe that we went to the surgeon to help the dove, the one you named Angel.*

*It was a lie. If only that were the worst of my sins . . .*

In the afternoon of the day after Caitlyn's sixth birthday, the waiting room had been quiet, without the coughing or groaning found among those down the hall waiting for a general physician. The physician, an Appalachian like them, had determined their ailments were ones to be treated by a sharp scalpel, and he'd sent them here to see the Outside surgeon, who spent a week every month inside the Great Fence.

Standing beside Papa, Caitlyn felt self-conscious among these strangers. She held a small wooden box with her white dove inside, lifting the lid occasionally to whisper encouragement to it, glad to find its black eyes still bright and attentive.

She'd found Angel below a window and had given her care for a week already. Papa had promised Caitlyn that a surgeon might fix the dove's broken wing, and she had prayed all the way from the collective that God would allow it.

To ease her nervousness, she used her tongue to wiggle a loose tooth back and forth. She had already lost four and was proud that she had learned not to cry at the quick pain that came when Papa helped her pull them loose. She wore the red shoes she'd been given for her birthday but couldn't fool herself into believing they made her look pretty for these people. She held Papa's hand for comfort and kept her back pressed against the wall. She wore a loose jacket but still felt as if all these strangers knew that her back was not like the backs of other girls.

Once, before they'd settled at the collective, she and Papa were at a church gathering in a small town along an abandoned railroad, deep in one of Appalachia's hundreds of valleys. Children had been playing around the adults, who stood in a tight group to discuss the weather and the morning's sermon. Caitlyn had made friends with another girl who was tiny like her. They wandered among the boys, who were rough and tumble and pushed Caitlyn to the ground. Her new friend helped her up and patted Caitlyn on the back. A question was asked, and Caitlyn began to shed her coat, innocently. Papa ran toward them, shouting.

He arrived soon enough to prevent other adults from seeing, but three of the children had already glimpsed Caitlyn's mutated arms—terribly thin and long, dark with shaggy and coarsened hair. They screamed in horror, and Caitlyn never made the mistake of playing with other children again. Not because Papa warned her against it, but because she finally understood she was different. She didn't like being different. It made Papa sad.

When Caitlyn's name was called, Papa stood and took her by the hand to a small private room where the surgeon waited.

The surgeon had his back to them when they entered. He turned, holding a clipboard. He wore a mask but had pulled it down so his entire face showed. He had short brown hair and dark brown eyes.

Caitlyn sensed the same thing in the man as she did in Papa. She couldn't put it into words, of course, not even in her thoughts, but she understood the aura of sadness and kindness about the surgeon. Others often recoiled from her, but he knelt and put his hands on her shoulders.

"Hello," he said, looking directly in her eyes.

"Hello," Caitlyn said. She felt safe with this man, like she did with Papa. "Papa said you might be able to fix Angel and help her fly again. I call her Angel because she is so white."

She opened the box. The surgeon studied the white dove with great seriousness. He asked permission to lift the dove out of the box. Caitlyn liked that. Other grownups would not have been that nice.

"I've never seen such a beautiful bird," the surgeon said.

Caitlyn shook her head. "Me neither."

"I'm told you are not a physician interested in politics," Papa said to the surgeon. "That is the only reason we are here. We have a little angel who needs help."

"I'm from Outside." The surgeon still looked into Caitlyn's eyes. Smiling, but still with sadness. "What happens in Appalachia is not my business."

"We need to trust you," Papa said. "I can't even tell you why or how important that is."

The surgeon set the dove back into Caitlyn's box.

He consulted his clipboard. "Jordan, right? This need is why you wouldn't let the general physician prepare the x-rays?"

"Feel my daughter's back," Papa said. "Between her shoulder blades."

Caitlyn stepped away instinctively, but Papa told her it would be all right. He helped her remove the loose coat. Caitlyn stared at the floor and shivered as the surgeon's soft, gentle hands ran along her coarse skin. Why did she have to be such a burden for Papa?

"Very atypical," the surgeon said. "Not only her back. But her fingers. Her hands. Her thin arms. I'd like to do a medical history. Maybe there is some hormone treatment to—"

"She needs your help," Papa said. "A simple operation on her back. Help. Not questions."

The surgeon raised a questioning eyebrow.

"In my other life," Papa said, "I had considerable medical background, but I'm not a surgeon."

"Your other life?"

"My daughter would not have been able to cope, Outside. That's why we are here."

Caitlyn wanted to pull on Papa's hand. He and the surgeon had forgotten about the box. Although Papa had taught her to be polite and not interrupt adults, she couldn't help herself and held the box toward her father. "Papa, don't we want to help her fly again?"

Papa smiled and kissed her forehead. "Yes, my love. Sometimes adults talk about things that aren't interesting to a little girl. Forgive Papa."

Caitlyn studied the doctor's face. Papa said he could help them, and she was terrified he would refuse. It was such a beautiful bird. She loved it. She wanted it to fly.

"After the x-rays," the surgeon finally said, "we'll need blood samples."

"Just x-rays," Papa said. "Samples become part of medical files. The x-rays, I can take with me."

The surgeon was quiet for another long moment. He looked at Caitlyn again, and his sad smile surfaced.

"X-rays that you can keep, then," the surgeon said. "If possible, surgery later today. Whatever you are trying to hide is on your conscience. I want to help the girl."

"Thank you," Papa said.

Caitlyn wiped away tears. The surgeon had agreed to try to help her beautiful broken bird and she was happy.

The surgeon nodded at Caitlyn, as if he understood the reason for her tears. "X-rays first."

Papa held Caitlyn's hand while she stood in front of a strange machine. She was forced to wear a heavy gown. Papa wore one too. The machine made a chunking noise. She was asked to stand sideways. Another chunking noise.

"This will help?" Caitlyn tried not to move the box in her hands.

"Yes. This takes a picture of bones to see what is wrong. Hold the box still, my love."

After, they waited in the small room until the sur-

13

geon returned with black and white sheets. He held the sheets against a board of light on the wall.

"Amazing," the surgeon said. "This bone structure. The formations are like—"

"No questions, please," Papa said. "For the sake of the girl. Once surgery is complete, she will be free."

The surgeon studied the x-rays. Caitlyn was fine with the silence. When they were away from others, she and Papa often sat together, content, saying nothing.

"No," the surgeon finally said. "Too dangerous."

"You said what happens in Appalachia is not your business."

"I don't care that you're illegal. The surgery is too dangerous."

The surgeon put his finger on one of the sheets. "Here. You can see the growths. That means extra blood vessels and the nerves at the spine too. If I go in there now, at the base, there's a very good chance that she will be paralyzed."

Papa was silent for so long that Caitlyn wondered if he was feeling ill. When he had a cold or a fever, she liked to tend to him. To fuss over him and bring him water to drink. It was so little compared to all he did for her, but it seemed to make him happy.

"You can't fix my broken bird?" Caitlyn asked.

"Outside, there are facilities for specialized surgery." The surgeon spoke past her. "I can make a recommendation. With the right people and equipment, it should be possible to make a complete removal. You know that Bar Elohim grants mercy visas for medical visits to Outside."

"No. It would destroy her."

"But these are spinal specialists. They wouldn't paralyze her."

"It would destroy her life," Papa said. "She cannot return Outside."

The surgeon froze and stared at Papa. "Return? You've considered escape?"

"That was another statement of trust. What can you do to help?"

"Will these grow as she matures?" the surgeon asked, tapping the sheet again. "I ask because you seem to know more than you want to say. For someone with a medical background."

"In Appalachia, it's wisest to say little," Papa answered.

"There will be future growth?"

"Yes." Papa spoke so quietly that Caitlyn could barely hear him. This tore her heart.

"When you are confident that the growth has stopped," the surgeon said, "come back to me. I will cut them off away from the base, far enough from the spine that we don't risk paralysis. What remains won't be too difficult to hide with the right clothing."

"The growth will continue until after puberty. Something needs to be done now."

"Surgery every time there's another few inches of growth?" the surgeon snapped. "Is that what you want to do to her?"

"No." Papa looked at his shoes.

Caitlyn fought tears again. "We have to wait to fix the bird?"

"Yes," Papa said. "I promise, even though it can't fly, we'll take very, very good care of it."

# DAY ONE

*I am not a man that women look at twice.*

*Yet she did, the woman I loved. Caitlyn. The name I would give to you in honor of her memory.*

*She was a dark-haired beauty. She saw beyond my shy conversations and saw something in my eyes perhaps, a loneliness of soul that touched her. At first, our eyes held contact longer than necessary. On my later visits we exchanged smiles, our first tentative conversations. A touch of fingertip to fingertip.*

*Our love grew until we pledged to seek a life beyond the prison that held her. She was six months pregnant when we escaped, became man and wife, pledging together to be parted by nothing short of death.*

*Our pledge lasted until the end of her pregnancy, when you were thrust into this world among the echoes of your mother's death. You did not kill her, Caitlyn. By taking her away from any medical help, I was responsible.*

*And although I knew then that someday I would have to pay the price for my love for you, it has arrived far, far too soon . . .*

## ONE

With late sun spreading an orange glow, wind carried the chorus of baying bloodhounds to Jordan and Caitlyn. They had climbed to the top of the mountain and reached the barren and stunted scrub pines, which grew at awkward angles from crevices in the rock.

Jordan consulted his vidpod and assured himself that the GPS coordinates were correct. He glanced around.

Below, on one side, was the valley where the bounty hunters followed their dogs. The trail that Jordan and Caitlyn had taken up the mountain from that valley was a snake of betrayal, with the bloodhounds roaming free, picking up their scent on bushes and across the long grasses.

Jordan had seen Appalachian bear hunts and knew this would be the same, the noise of hounds galvanizing the killing lust of the Rottweilers straining against leashes, waiting for the bounty hunters to release them once the prey had been sighted. To the Rottweilers, there was no difference between bear or human. Nor, probably, any difference for the bounty hunters.

The other side of the pinnacle was a drop of hundreds of feet where a waterfall fed an ancient rift of stone that widened into a valley, with the occasional bounce of sunlight off curves of the stream far below and a panoramic view of other mountaintops.

They were trapped.

Jordan put his arms around Caitlyn, as if protecting her from the noise of the hounds. He was a tall man in his fifties, thin and muscled from years of repetitive labor. The wind plucked at his untrimmed, graying hair.

"Papa," Caitlyn said, leaning into his chest, the wind rocking them slightly.

*Papa.* One gentle word.

It had been three days since they had fled the collective, with bounty hunters in pursuit. Jordan had taken them half the length of Appalachia and was exhausted. He knew he could contain the exhaustion enough to hide it from Caitlyn and hold it off long enough to do what was needed. His sorrow, however, was so overwhelming that he didn't know if he could trust his voice.

He stepped back and took her face in his hands, desperate for time to stop. Through the years, it had been too dangerous for the luxury of photographs. Jordan's scrapbook of Caitlyn's childhood was a series of different moments committed to memory, moments where he was far too aware that it would all be taken from him someday.

This day.

Without her cloak, lying on the ground beside them, Caitlyn's slenderness was striking. To Jordan, the beauty in her face gave her a dignity that far outweighed her lack of size. The pupils in her eyes were eerily large, her fingers like long claws. He had learned to love those fingers and hands, the unnaturally thin delicacy of her legs and arms and torso. He'd long stopped noticing the coarse hair on the hunch centered between her shoulders.

Caitlyn smiled back at Jordan. A small, hesitant smile that betrayed the fear she tried to hide from him.

"This is my fault, Papa," she said. "I am so sorry for what I've done to us. Whatever it is, I didn't mean to do it. Tell them that. You don't need to be punished. You've done enough, never leaving someone like me."

Her words almost broke the last of his strength and composure. But Jordan knew what she meant. She wondered if she had inadvertently broken a law. If she had triggered something that the Elders needed to punish. Had she been seen without her coat or said something that was reported?

"No," Jordan told Caitlyn. "You did nothing wrong."

He wanted to hold her again. But it would be a comfort of deception and shame. His shame. He should tell her that they were paying for his sins, not hers.

Hiding during the day, traveling the dangerous paths through the valleys at night, he'd been snatching moments to write the letter that would explain. Because she would despise him later, he wanted his final memories of her to be untainted by the horror of comprehension that would come with truth.

It was not the time to confess his sins. It was time instead to send her into the abyss.

21

Jordan could not hope for a sacrificial ram to appear, but he understood what it must have been like for Abraham to climb Moriah to the place of sacrifice with a trembling mixture of faith and hope and sadness that was a far heavier burden than any physical weight. In her trust, Caitlyn, like Isaac, had been totally unaware of the purpose of their climb. Isaac's ignorance could have only deepened Abraham's sorrow, as Caitlyn's did for Jordan's.

Yet Abraham wouldn't have seen in Isaac's eyes what Jordan saw now in his daughter's.

The wind and the height, as it always did, awakened an instinct in Caitlyn. On other days like this, all through her childhood, Jordan had taken Caitlyn to places where they could be alone and quiet, often at the edge of a cliff to give them a view, with Jordan hiding from Caitlyn how badly he was trying to suck the marrow out of each second together.

That sweet poignancy of those picnics had always intensified as he observed little Caitlyn marvel at the hawks soaring below them, their shadows flashing across the tops of the pines of the valley. Caitlyn had watched with unknowing longing, the way God's touch makes human souls instinctively yearn for a place unseen.

Despite the baying of hounds, a constant reminder of the danger, Jordan hoped that this same longing had returned to her.

In the last few months, triggered by puberty occurring far later than in most girls, changes had rapidly forced themselves on Caitlyn's body. She'd become voraciously hungry, especially for milk and meats. The hunch between her shoulders had grown like a cancer, spreading down her back in slow ripples, shiny and swollen until near bursting. The coarse hair draping her shoulders and upper back and arms became thicker than straw, and the outer layers of what had once been hair became dull with a sheath of dead, flaky skin. Her fear at a first menstrual cycle Jordan had been able to explain. As for the growing bulge, he did little except assure her that it was what her body was meant to do. Anything more would have meant revealing the horror that he was too cowardly to expose, except by letter.

Jordan wore a hip pack. He unbuckled it and squatted as he reached inside. When he stood again, he offered Caitlyn a piece of clothing.

"You need to wear this."

She frowned. To her, it was obviously far too small. Jordan knew better.

"A microfabric," he said. "It will stretch."

She ran the shiny, smooth black material across her face. "Microfabric?"

All her life, her clothing had been rough cotton. She'd never seen material like this. "From Outside," Jordan explained, although this answer alone would raise a dozen more questions. Before she could ask, Jordan spoke again.

"You'll need to shed all your other clothing. Step into it, and pull it up your body."

He faced the other way to give her privacy, although her thin body had few curves to suggest womanhood. Perhaps the microfabric wasn't needed, but he wasn't going to send her into the abyss naked, like an animal.

"Papa," she said, "at the back. I can't reach."

He turned to her.

The microfabric emphasized her sleekness. It was sleeveless and would not restrict her arms. She spun to show him her back. The shiny black suit was open in a long slit, and the monstrous bulge of her back protruded partway through.

Jordan was satisfied with the tailoring. The suit was worth the money and risk of getting it smuggled into Appalachia. "Leave me your blouse," Jordan said. "Put the rest of your clothes back on. The cloak too."

He didn't have to tell her why she needed the cloak. To hide what set her apart.

"Remember everything I've taught you about Outside." He'd always let her believe they would be escaping together.

He took a shoelace from his pocket that he'd kept in preparation and tied it through a buttonhole of the blouse.

"Papa, what is happening?"

Through the years, he'd suffered her anguish at any reminder that she was so different. How much easier it would have been to show her a cocoon discarded by a butterfly, explaining the purpose of her hideous hump and what joy could be ahead of her. But it would have led to the other questions that he had never wanted to answer. So again and continuously, he'd been a coward. Not explaining.

He placed the vidpod in her hands. "Unregistered. Use it for navigation. I have one too."

"Unregistered!" All Appalachians knew the sentence was five years in the factory for anyone caught in possession of an unregistered vidpod.

"That's not important." Jordan uncoiled a rope from the hip pack. Thin, nylon, lightweight. "Below us is a stream. Follow it upstream to a cave behind a waterfall. Inside, you'll find instructions. Hurry out of the valley. Travel tonight. I don't know how long I can delay them."

She blinked hard. "No, Papa!"

"You have to make it Outside." Jordan spoke as he tied one end of the rope to the trunk of a stunted tree.

"Nobody makes it Outside. Please, don't leave me."

"There is a man named Brij. Among the Clan. He's waiting for you."

"The Clan!"

"Caitlyn, you've been taught not to fear the legends."

"I can't go without you."

"We can't both make it." Jordan threw the loose end of the rope over the edge of the cliff. He had full confidence she could climb down with ease. She was light boned. Muscle and sinew. Unnaturally so, and unnaturally strong. "This will get you to a ledge below. You'll find more rope to help you climb down."

"Not without you." She wept.

"Listen to the hounds," he said. "We don't have much time."

"Why didn't you tell me earlier this was your plan?"

He tested the rope again, looked over the edge and swallowed back the feeling of vertigo. He knew Caitlyn didn't share that fear. "I can only ask that you trust me."

"I won't leave you."

"You have no choice," he said, shaking off the spinning sensation. "You can't be taken, dead or alive. You must not fall into their hands."

"Who are they?" She reached for him. "Tell me what this means! Papa, I'm afraid."

He stepped back. It hurt, not to reach for her. "Trust me, Caitlyn."

"Papa!" He'd never rejected her before. But if he held her now, he would lose his resolve and keep her in his arms until the dogs arrived.

"Caitlyn. I love you as big and forever as the sky." That had been their game.

*"Caitlyn, how much does Papa love you?"*

*"As big and forever as the sky, Papa."*

He squatted and reached into the hip pack again. The letter. His confession. He walked around her again and slid it between the microfabric and her body.

"Take the rope," he said. He spoke in such a way that she wouldn't fight him any longer. "Now."

He helped her over the edge of the cliff.

"Papa," she cried. "Papa!"

He steeled himself to ignore her, acutely aware at how little her delicate body weighed. He waited until her weight was no longer on the rope, then untied it and eased it down the cliff.

"Papa!" Wind brought her plaintive cry up to him. Then she was gone.

Jordan leaned forward and whispered it again. "I love you as big and forever as the sky."

Then he took the lace that he'd tied to her blouse. He began to walk quickly, dragging the blouse behind him. The longer he could keep the hounds pursuing her scent, the better the chances that Caitlyn would make it Outside.

At best, he'd stay ahead of the hounds another half hour. Long enough to make it difficult, if not impossible, to backtrack and discover where Caitlyn had escaped.

The dark of night would be a mercy of sorts. He'd hear the hounds, but in the final moments, they'd only be a frenzy of shadows, throwing themselves upon him.

Then, finally, his guilt and grief would end.

# DAY TWO

*For years, you and I were safe, simply because the greatest empire the world has ever known was as dependent on water as any primitive culture. But when the Water Wars ended, the military machine went back to previous tasks. My desertion of the machine was once again relevant, and the agency resumed its pursuit.*

*Caitlyn, I did not regret trading the freedoms of the civilized world for the theocracy of Appalachia. Others may have their memory bank transfers in lieu of vacations, their biological insertions of computer chips to efficiently monitor body functions. They may prefer the constant noise and sensory overloads. I prefer a fire on a starlit night, the sounds of insects like a blanket over us.*

*I do regret that even the isolated valleys could not keep us safe. Cautious as I was, I underestimated the all-seeing power of Bar Elohim. I only wish they would have arrived a month later. A week later. A day later. Even hours later.*

*Because I write this as we are on the run, the hounds are never far away, and there is not enough time to finish this letter as it should be written . . .*

## TWO

Mason Lee was no handyman, but he took pride in the terror he could generate with duct tape and a few specialized articles of hardware.

His appearance and reputation helped in this too. He had long curly hair and a waxed mustache and, except for the eye that he couldn't change, was vain about his features, but anyone who commented on his obvious attention to appearance suffered for it. Although he was only medium sized, much larger men who knew him always gave him plenty of room, knowing he was as good with a knife as he was unpredictable. Those who didn't know him gave him room too; his milky left eye, the one he hated to be reminded of, drifted to one side and made it difficult to tell where his eyes were focused, giving him what he knew folks described as a spooky, even cruel appearance.

Still, much as he enjoyed the perception about him, it meant little unless a man could back it up.

Like now, for example, just before dawn, in an ordinary, small-town hotel room. Low-wattage lamp. Lumpy mattress. Side table. Straight-backed chair. Cheap plastic shower curtain.

With pride in his creativity, Mason had rearranged the room with a simple goal. To inflict pain and terror as efficiently as possible. Folks said he had no imagination, but they only had to see what he'd done in the hotel room to understand otherwise.

First, he laid the shower curtain on the floor at the foot of the bed like a pull rug. He'd placed the straight-backed chair on top of the shower curtain, facing away from the bed and close enough that when he sat on the edge of that lumpy mattress, he could lean forward and reach the chair without straining. The side table sat in front of the chair, where the lamp illuminated his specialized articles of hardware: a metal bucket and blowtorch, the Heretic's Fork, and a thumbscrew. Below the table, atop the plastic shower curtain, a small cage imprisoned two rats, and a burlap sack rippled with movement. The sack let the victim wonder exactly what animals it contained.

Mason thought as he surveyed the room that a man could travel light, and except for the effort it took to capture the rats and snakes during the day, a setup like this only took a couple minutes and worked just about anywhere in Appalachia.

On this occasion, all Mason had left to do was wait, and he wasn't good at that, even with the flow of anticipation. Much more fun hunting his prey; at least, this morning, he expected a punctual victim.

Sure enough, Mason had hardly taken his spot on the wall beside the door, a roll of duct tape in hand, when he heard footsteps in the hallway. The soft-heeled footsteps of a man in expensive shoes.

Mason peeled back a few inches of duct tape and clenched it between his teeth, letting the roll hang from his jaws. He reached down and pulled his trademark bowie knife from a sheath on his belt.

The knock on the door was as soft as the footsteps.

" 'T's open," Mason slurred around the tape.

James Rankin turned the knob and pushed it open with the confidence that came from twenty years as one of the High Elders of Bar Elohim's inner circle. He walked in with the same blind confidence. Mason imagined that Rankin's long, lean face would register disdain, instead of fear or suspicion, at the plastic curtain on the floor and the table in front of the chair.

But Mason wouldn't be able to confirm that guess. He wouldn't see Rankin's face until after he stepped from the wall and, slipping forward, wrapped one arm around Rankin's neck and jammed the blade against his ribs. He spit the tape on to the floor beside his feet.

"On your knees," Mason said.

"Hardly." The disdain was apparent.

Mason had been hoping for that answer. He shoved the knife point in far enough to draw a gasp, to draw blood.

"Got this knife sideways," Mason said. "It'll slide between your ribs like they're cheese. Tip's about four inches from your heart. Means you'll be on your knees sooner than later. If I must use the knife to force you down, I'll have to drag you onto the shower curtain so your blood won't stain the carpet as you roll around and die."

Rankin lowered himself.

"Good. Now, on your belly. Hands behind your back."

Rankin complied again, with dignity that gave

33

Mason satisfaction, as it'd be all the more fun to strip away. He intended to own the man when they were through.

Mason propped a knee in Rankin's back and set the knife on the floor in easy reach. He taped Rankin's wrists together, pulled another strip from the roll and again clenched the roll in his teeth. Taping wasn't finished yet.

"In the chair." Mason again took hold of his bowie knife, which felt glovelike against his fingers.

"You're aware that doing this to me is essentially like doing it to Bar Elohim." Rankin spoke with no emotion, but it was a deadly threat, enunciated clearly for the benefit of the vidpod that was surely recording this conversation from an inner pocket of Rankin's suit jacket. Mason ignored him, as he, of course, fully knew what was at stake. Danger only made the deliberation of his plans even sweeter.

Mason jabbed the point of his knife into the softness of Rankin's lower back. "Liver's right there. Trust me, it won't take much digging to prove it to you. Now get on the chair."

Rankin rolled over and struggled to his feet. Mason figured Rankin was more concerned about soiling his fine suit jacket than about Mason's intentions. Such was the power of Bar Elohim. But Mason would break that.

Once Rankin was on the chair, Mason knelt behind him and taped Rankin's ankles to the chair legs. He made a couple more long wraps to secure Rankin's upper body and arms to the straight back of the chair.

Rankin was helpless now, facing the table and Mason's specialized hardware.

Mason settled onto the edge of the bed behind Rankin and leaned forward.

He found that whispering was most effective. It didn't disturb folks in other rooms, and the quiet threat coming from the dark behind the victim seemed more lethal than a loud one. Just like Rankin's quiet invocation of Bar Elohim's name less than a minute earlier.

"See on the left of that table in front of you," Mason said. "That's called the Heretic's Fork. I ain't much on history, but I do know folks used it with great effect during the Inquisition. What's the word I'm looking for? Ironic. That's it. You'll find it ironic that the power of the church will be turned against you for a change."

"Five twenty-three a.m.," Rankin said. "The daily meeting with bounty hunter Mason Lee has degenerated into futile threats of torture against me."

Rankin didn't have to explain that he was speaking on the record. Or that the vidpod recording was essentially indestructible and, because of GPS tracking, impossible to hide unless buried ten feet underground.

"See how the Heretic's Fork has prongs on both ends," Mason said. "What I do is prop one end just above the center of your collarbone and the other end under your chin. You'll have to stretch your head as high as it can go just to keep it from pushing through skin. Bring your chin down at all and you'll be skewered. It's tiring enough holding your head like that for even a few minutes, but when I begin with the next gadget, things get interesting, because pain's going to bring your chin into your chest and you won't be able to help it. I've seen it a hundred times. Those prongs are sharp enough, they'll come up through your mouth and pin your tongue. Honest."

"I'm glad you're explaining this." Rankin sounded cold and imperious. "Better your voice than mine when Bar Elohim reviews our conversation."

"Someone in your position knows how to erase conversations. Soon enough, you'll do it for me. You'll do anything for me."

Rankin didn't answer.

Mason smiled at the back of Rankin's head. Power did have privileges, including a way to escape Bar Elohim's ubiquitous presence when necessary. After years of serving them, Mason knew that about the Elders.

"On the table in front of you, to the right of the Heretic's Fork, is something so old-fashioned it's a cliché. You probably don't recognize it, but that tiny vise is a thumbscrew."

Old-fashioned, but highly effective. Two small rods of metal, held together with a long screw in the center. Put a finger or toe on each side of the center screw and then tighten. Mason had seen the simple thumbscrew break a man's spirit in seconds.

"Let's assume you haven't lost your sanity," Rankin

said, his voice huskier. Mason always listened for the huskiness. Fear. Mason lusted for that huskiness even more than the sound of a woman's rising excitement. "You do have a reason for this?"

Mason grinned. "First, let me give you the daily report, *sir.* We captured one of the fugitives, the man, just after dark last evening. Hounds took him down. He's here in Cumberland Gap. The agent is guarding him. A doctor's been called."

What Mason withheld reporting was an unregistered vidpod he found in the man's pocket. That said something in itself. Probably came from the Clan. And on it, the vidpod had enough information to justify threatening, and hopefully torturing, an Elder of Bar Elohim's inner circle.

"The girl?" Rankin asked.

Mason was impressed that in these conditions Rankin was able to focus on his original purpose for this meeting. The daily report. But he believed that his position gave him protection from all dangers.

"I'll find the girl today. I had the valley that holds her sealed. No one escapes me."

"That's all I need to know," Rankin said. "Release me, and I'll erase our conversation."

Mason twitched his knife hand. The man *was* afraid. Or why attempt to negotiate?

"But it's not all that I need to know." Mason leaned in again. "I have a few questions I want answered."

"Good Christians, like good soldiers, don't ask questions."

How many times and in how many sermons had Mason heard that preached to Appalachians, like it was the Almighty Word of God? He didn't intend to be a good soldier for much longer.

"You'll find the bucket interesting," Mason told Rankin. He still whispered, as if having an intimate conversation. Which, in a way, it was. Shared suffering truly brought two people close. "What I'll do, if the Heretic's Fork and the thumbscrew aren't enough, is put you on your back on the plastic sheet, with the bucket overturned on your exposed belly. I'll slip those rats from the sack beneath the bucket and trap them there, tape 'em in. When I heat up the bucket with the blowtorch, those rats will be frantic to escape. They'll chew through your innards and come out your side. Oftentimes, I've noticed, the person's not dead yet and gets the thrill of seeing the animals bursting out. Mostly, I save this for the wives of men too stubborn to answer my questions. I'll make an exception for you though."

Rankin's entire posture shifted into rigidness.

"The other sack holds a copperhead. I notice that suit of yours is tailored—not much room for a copperhead to get out once I slip it down the back of your shirt. Snake like that bites more than once, you know. I'll flip a coin to see if you get the rats or the snake."

Mason was lying. All he'd been able to find today was a garter snake, but it didn't matter. Their own imaginations scared people more than anything else.

"I've heard enough." Rankin's voice shook. He'd

assigned Mason to enough of these situations that he knew Mason enjoyed his work. "What do you want?"

That was the big question, wasn't it?

More than anything, Mason wanted to get Outside. He was tired of Appalachia. The playground was too small. Even with his own special privileges, Mason knew that like Rankin, his power was only granted by the whim of Bar Elohim. From outlawed media materials, the ones confiscated, Mason glimpsed Outside. He hoarded these items in his cabin. Outside, with enough money, Mason could indulge himself without fear or restraint in a much bigger playground. He wanted freedom.

This wasn't the time, however, to tell Rankin to pass on this request to Bar Elohim. That was for later, when Mason had leverage to divulge the information on the fugitive's vidpod.

"Tell me why Bar Elohim needs the girl so badly," Mason said. All these years of following orders, but never once an explanation. He was just hired help to them. *Good Christians, like good soldiers, don't ask questions.*

"Bar Elohim wants the girl because she is a blasphemer."

"I'll confess something. The Heretic's Fork was just a bluff. No sense marking you up. Bar Elohim would have questions then. You can take it as a good sign that I want you leaving the room without much hinting at what happened, but that's only if you tell the truth. And I know you're lying. An agent from Outside wouldn't have any interest in a blasphemer. And Bar Elohim wouldn't let an agent into Appalachia for just a common blasphemer."

Mason eased off the bed, moved around the chair, and knelt in front of Rankin. Maybe Jesus washed feet, but Mason preferred power to servanthood. "And a blasphemer doesn't require a fancy silver canister to hold her innards."

Mason pulled off Rankin's left shoe and left sock. The man's toenails were buffed. Mason put Rankin's two smallest toes into the thumbscrew. He tightened the screw to make a snug fit.

"Bar Elohim has made an agreement with Outside." Rankin's foot trembled and he drew in a breath. "The girl, in exchange for satellite thermal imaging. That's the truth."

Mason stood and, leisurely deliberate, retrieved the roll of duct tape. He ripped off a piece of tape and put it across Rankin's mouth and nose. Rankin's eyeballs bulged immediately as he vainly panicked for air.

Mason watched, smiling, until Rankin passed out. He pulled the tape off and slapped Rankin's face. The man's chest heaved as he gulped air.

"Forgot to mention the tape," Mason said. "Just so you know, I can do it again and again. Usually I hold your wrist and check your pulse. Don't want you dead. You'd be surprised how often a person can suffocate to the point of death and never quite make it to the other side."

"Thermal imaging," Rankin gasped. "It's the truth. I promise. Appalachia doesn't have access to satellites. Outside does, of course. They've monitored the Valley of the Clan for the last two months, tracking people by heat images. There's enough data to pinpoint all their movements. We want that information."

"Still not convinced you're in the mood to tell me the truth." This time Mason only taped Rankin's mouth. Mason tightened the thumbscrew, and Rankin's nostrils flared with an intake of air. Rankin tried to scream against the duct tape, but the noise died in his mouth.

Mason kept tightening the thumbscrew until he heard the bones break. Then he released the thumbscrew and took off Rankin's other shoe and sock. The broken toes on the left foot immediately began to swell with blood.

"If you scream, I'll put the tape back over your nose. And I'll bring out the snake."

Mason slowly pulled the duct tape off Rankin's mouth. The lamp didn't give much light, but enough glowed for Mason to see the glint of tears on Rankin's cheeks. Rankin panted with the effort to hold back sound.

Mason stroked Rankin's undamaged right foot.

"You can beg," Mason said. "That's allowed. As long as you beg quietly, without screaming."

"Please don't hurt me anymore." Although in his fifties and at the top of Appalachia's power structure, Rankin had quickly become a lost, bewildered little boy. He was suddenly aware of an evil that had been invisible to him all his life. "Please, please."

"First, you're going to tell me how to bypass the software on your vidpod. Of course, we need to erase all of this."

Rankin closed his eyes, nodded as if defeated.

Mason patted Rankin's chest and found the vidpod. Rankin talked him through it, step by step.

"Just so you know," Mason said when he was satisfied the previous minutes of conversation were erased. He secured the thumbscrew on the little toes of Rankin's right foot. "If our conversation does get back to Bar Elohim, I'll hunt you down. Understand?"

"Yes, yes," Rankin said.

*It's a cold, harsh world out from under Bar Elohim's wings, isn't it?* Mason thought.

"We're not finished. Confirm this for me. Bar Elohim intends to use the thermal imaging to get rid of the Clan."

"They're like rats. We don't know how many there are. They scurry back into hiding at the slightest sign of danger. Thermal imaging will give Bar Elohim an accurate idea of the count. And where they disappear to. Once they are gone, Appalachians will stop hoping there's a way Outside."

Mason nodded, knowing it made sense. The Valley of the Clan was riddled with ancient coal mines. Only the Clan knew the secret entrances and the labyrinth of passageways between Appalachia and Outside.

"This girl," Mason said, "the fugitive's daughter.

Why is she so important that Outside will stop the Clan?"

All these years, Outside had allowed the Clan to help Appalachians escape. It was almost official Outside policy. Now they were prepared to assist Bar Elohim?

"You've got the canister." A trace of Rankin's former arrogance resurfaced. "And you've been given instructions. Surely you've been able to guess."

Mason blinked, his bad eye stinging. Rankin had essentially called him stupid. A mistake.

Mason put the tape across Rankin's mouth and tightened the thumbscrew until he heard bones break again. He left the thumbscrew in place and walked to the small bathroom. He relieved himself, then enjoyed a glass of water. He refilled his glass and took it back into the room.

On his return to the chair, Mason saw Rankin arched in agony against the duct tape that held him in place. Mason smiled and sipped the water, watching Rankin watch him.

Finally, Mason released the pressure of the thumbscrew. He knew from experience that if he pulled the duct tape now, Rankin would scream, no matter what threats Mason applied. So Mason let Rankin's chest rise and fall until it seemed the man had control over himself.

Mason removed the tape to resume their conversation.

"I have been given a canister," Mason said. It was

43

the size of a quart jar. He'd been told that it had an inner sleeve, and that once it was opened, an ongoing chemical reaction would trigger a refrigeration effect between the outer sleeve and inner sleeve, with such perfect insulation that once the lid was tightened, the contents of the canister would be kept at a constant cold temperature for months. "I know what I'm supposed to do with it. But tell me why. And tell me why it's so important to Outside."

Rankin continuously wept as he explained, and from his answers, Mason began to understand something very profound. That capturing the girl would give him everything he wanted. And that now wasn't the time to reveal what he'd learned on the fugitive's unregistered vidpod.

"We're finished." Mason stood after Rankin's explanation. "You may go. I wouldn't see a doctor about your toes. There's nothing they can do anyway. Tell people you dropped something on them and that will explain why you limp. If I hear that Bar Elohim has any questions about our meeting this morning . . ."

As Mason peeled away the duct tape, Rankin sobbed harder. With gratitude, Mason supposed. As Rankin stood, he briefly draped his arms over Mason's shoulders for support.

Mason felt an unusual swell of affection for the man. After all, Mason owned him.

## THREE

It was just after dawn, and her father's written words echoed in her head, words spoken from the letter.

She was thirsty. Frustrated. Afraid.

She was exhausted too, only able to hobble as she leaned heavily on a walking stick she'd made from a broken branch. The previous night, after leaving the cave, she had stumbled down an embankment and twisted her ankle badly, forcing her to rest every few minutes. She estimated she'd only traveled about a mile over the rugged terrain. Soon enough, she would be found.

She'd have to go down to the stream for water. But not until she found the strength to move ahead. Resting, she leaned one hand against the sun-warmed granite of a large boulder. A tiny brown spider crept onto her wrist, but she didn't brush it away. The spider continued down one of her long fingers before moving back onto the rock and disappearing into a crevice.

*Freak,* she thought. Not that she needed a glance at her fingers to remind her of it. Every furtive step along the path in the shadows of the trees told her that she was a freak. A monster, and hunted because of it.

It was as if the forest around her conspired to prove it to her. A half hour earlier, she'd walked around a fallen log, almost into the jaws of a bear caught in leg traps, dead long enough to be a rotting corpse, swarmed by flies.

She'd never felt more alone. Before, she'd relied on the safety and comfort of her papa. No matter how difficult day-to-day living was, his love and the small, small world the two of them had created had been enough to cushion the apartness she felt.

But now she was without him, and the physical separateness alone she could have endured. Had she been simply lost, it would only have been a matter of finding a way back to him.

No, it wasn't the physical separation that put her into her black loneliness.

Papa had betrayed her. On the mountaintop, he'd slipped a letter inside the microfabric. Its words had burned into her memory.

*"We had agreed—the woman I loved and I—that as soon as you were born, we would perform an act of mercy and decency and wrap you in a towel to drown you in a nearby sink of water . . ."*

She was a freak, and Papa had known it from the beginning. He'd wanted to put her down like an animal because of it. His letter said he'd been overwhelmed by protective love. More like overwhelming pity. Because she'd been born a monster.

There was more than her freakish body that spoke of his betrayal.

In the cave behind the waterfall, she'd found supplies in a backpack as he promised and a note directing her where to go next. Follow the stream downward into the valley that led to the town of Cumberland Gap, and there she was to wait at a certain place until the stroke of midnight.

The letter proved he'd known that he would bring her to a mountaintop and send her away; the equipment left in a hidden place behind the waterfall proved his intentions twofold. Yet Papa had not said a word to her about it. He'd found a way to abandon her. He dropped her into the abyss.

What did her future hold? Nothing a normal human hoped for, she knew. No home. No family. No love.

Maybe if she wandered long enough, her thoughts and loneliness and anger would drive her insane. She'd become what Papa had believed she was from the beginning.

An animal.

## FOUR

Summer heat and humidity gave the small town of Cumberland Gap a drowsy, peaceful feel, with clear blue sky above the thickly leaved branches of the tall oaks. Tall, steep hills towered over the town, covering much of it in shadow.

In a small apartment suite above a store, near the window that overlooked the corner of the town square, Carson Pierce sat in a worn stuffed chair, watching a physician, sitting on a bed in the center of the room, tend to Jordan's wounds.

Pierce wore jeans and a loose black T-shirt that did

a moderate job of hiding how muscular he was. Forty, he could pass for thirty. Any traces of advanced age could be found in his world-weary eyes, a blue so pale they verged on gray. He'd started his career outside the law, so talented that he'd been recruited by the government. Now inside the law, Washington-trained for covert missions, he operated no differently than he had at the top of one of the most ruthless gangs in New York. The only thing that had changed was his objectives.

This was just another assignment to him, and as badly as he wanted to return to the freedom of Outside, he couldn't until it was finished.

Three days of chase, and the objective was in front of him. A fugitive on a makeshift bed, dying. Jordan Brown. Pierce had no sympathy for the injured man, who had slipped into Appalachia years ago to avoid warrants for murder, arson, and intelligence crimes.

The physician leaning over the man clucked an indiscriminate sound of judgment and stood.

"I can't guess how long it might be until this man is conscious again," Dr. Ross said. Ten years younger than Pierce, he looked twenty years older. Pudgy, soft hands. "What exactly happened to him?"

"Fell." Pierce was still furious about that. When they'd finally trapped the man, despite clear orders, Mason Lee had signaled one of the bounty hunters to release his dogs, driving the man backward over the cliff. The fugitive had dropped to a ledge in the dark; it had taken an hour to pull him back up, then hours of night travel back down the mountain to where he'd found the local sheriff and demanded a place to keep the man.

"Hard to believe all this was just from a fall," Dr. Ross said. "He's ripped up, like an animal got hold of him."

The dogs had been savage, and the bounty hunters slow to pull them off. Last night, when Pierce and one of the Appalachian bounty hunters carried Jordan in, he had been conscious, occasionally screaming in pain. If the man was going to die, Pierce wanted information first. Pierce didn't like using torture; he'd hoped pharmaceuticals would do it, but Jordan had fallen unconscious too soon after Pierce had gotten him into the apartment.

"I doubt you're a stupid man," Pierce said to the physician. "Does this really seem like the kind of situation you want to ask questions about?"

"From a medical viewpoint, I need—"

"You need to set his bones, stop the bleeding, and find a way to get him to open his eyes again. Nothing more."

"I will not be intimidated," Dr. Ross said.

It surprised Pierce. The physician looked softer than that.

"Sheriff Carney tells me you have a seven-year-old daughter and a three-year-old son." Pierce walked to the window. "The less you know, the better for them. Your silence buys them a lot of protection."

The threat was a bluff. While other Outside agents

had no compunction about abusing their training and authority, Pierce would not hurt the innocent, especially children. He remembered how his parents had died, futilely trying to protect his sister. He saw his memories in black and white, his parents' spilled blood like dark oil.

Pierce was confident, however, that his bluff would not be called. Because Sheriff Carney had sent Dr. Ross, it would be obvious that Pierce had the sheriff's official support, which meant implicit support from Bar Elohim. Small town like this, the physician would know about the bounty hunters that Pierce had hired and had probably heard one of them was the feared and legendary Mason Lee. Bounty hunters did not travel without that same official endorsement from Bar Elohim.

Dr. Ross closed his eyes for a few seconds. Muscles quivered at the side of his jaws. He opened his eyes again and met Pierce's steady gaze. It was a pleasant surprise for Pierce. He appreciated men with true strength. The physician was not afraid, Pierce could tell, but he wasn't a fool either, so he didn't vocalize his protest.

Dr. Ross knelt beside the dying man and opened the satchel he'd brought into the suite for this house call.

He pulled out a hypodermic needle and syringe filled with clear liquid, tapped it to rid it of air bubbles. With a cotton swab and disinfectant, the doctor prepared Jordan's shoulder for an injection.

Pierce had no interest in how the physician intended

to bring the man back to consciousness, so he looked out the window again, noticing below and across the street the sheriff on a bench beside a huge man with a boyish, innocent face.

Pierce gave the two of them little more thought. His mind was on wrapping up the assignment. Capturing the girl.

They'd found the blouse that Jordan had been using to draw the hounds. Somewhere along the way, she must have made it down the face of the rock. The valley was narrow enough that Mason Lee and the dogs would pick up her scent eventually.

Pierce hoped she would be found alive. She deserved that chance after all that had been done to her.

Yet he knew this would not be possible. She might not have survived the climb down. Or, more likely, she would not survive Mason Lee, armed with his legendary shotgun and an equally legendary lack of discrimination in its use. If Mason found her, he had a dry-ice canister, with very specific harvesting instructions. Pierce would have preferred to handle it himself, but he needed to be here if the man on the bed became conscious again.

All things considered, the assignment should be wrapped up in a day or two. If the fugitive talked, Pierce would learn more about where he sent the girl and why. It might be helpful. At the least, it could lead to more arrests, but that was simply to help the Appalachians. It was part of the agreement that Bar

Elohim had brokered with Pierce's employers to allow Pierce inside.

Pierce didn't really care about the politics. His concern was simply to fulfill his assignment, then return Outside. Back to where it was normal.

Pierce moved away from the window, and his eyes were drawn back to the torn man on the bed. His blood had soaked through the bandages, and in the light of the room, it seemed as black as the blood in Pierce's memories.

## FIVE

Mason Lee roamed the valley, hunting the fugitive's daughter.

No one had ever escaped the bloodhounds before, at least not alive, and Mason Lee was confident the girl would not be the first.

Wearing a buckskin vest, he walked among the trees on the creek bank with the efficiency of a cougar. The top of the grass had already been dried by the sun, but the ground was still wet, soaking his boots and the hem of his denim pants. Mason held his trademark shotgun in his trademark manner, crooked open over his right arm, a double-barrel 12-gauge loaded with shells of deer shot. At close range, the blast could tear through a tree trunk.

Mason was with one of four teams with dogs moving along the creek at the bottom of the valley. Three other teams had dispersed nearby in a grid pattern to pick up her trail, if it existed. Mason had little doubt the girl was dead and the climbers would find her body. But if somehow she had survived the descent of the cliff, Mason would find her.

In two decades of bounty hunting for the Appalachian government, he'd only failed three times—in each case the men had killed themselves before he could capture them. His reputation was such that once fugitives heard that Mason Lee had been hired to track them, as often as not they fled to the sanctuary of the nearest church to seek the protection of an Elder.

This fugitive had avoided hiding among people, keeping to the woods and hills, but Mason still found and trapped the man the night before, after several days of pursuit with the hounds. Although the agent from Outside had made it clear that the fugitive was to be taken unharmed, dusk masked Mason's discreet hand signal directing one of his handlers to release a few dogs. To Mason's satisfaction, the savage attack had nearly killed the man. Nobody, let alone an Outsider, told Mason Lee how to hunt bounty. But there was more at stake for Mason than pride, or his pleasure in seeing and hearing pain. He knew his men were as vicious as the dogs they handled. And just like the dogs, at the slightest sign of personal weakness—such as letting an agent give him orders—they'd turn on him with the same savageness he wielded for his own purposes.

Mason had not been concerned when he found the

man without the girl. The climb down was difficult enough that Mason wouldn't be surprised if she'd jumped, or even if the father had pushed her off as an act of mercy. Mason took pride in the well-known fact that female fugitives suffered worse at his hands.

Either way, Mason didn't expect the final chase to take long. They still had a piece of the girl's clothing, and it was all that the bloodhounds needed to locate their prey.

Even at its widest, here at the open end where it spilled into Cumberland Gap, the valley was narrow. Five miles upstream to the waterfall, the width was only hundreds of yards of deep chasm. Climbers were using ropes there to descend in a careful search for her body. In the meantime, in case she was alive, Mason and his teams would simply crisscross the valley and work upward to the waterfall to flush her out. The girl might slip between the teams as they traversed from side to side, but the hounds wouldn't miss her trail as they crossed it.

Mason rarely considered the reasons behind his assignments. Most of the time, they were straightforward. Fugitives from Bar Elohim, men or women who had transgressed against the Holy Word of God. Thieves, murderers, or worse, anarchists and blasphemers.

This time, however, it was the ultimate hunt. Not because she would be more difficult to find but because of what he'd learned in the hotel room. The reward for her capture was higher than any other in his past. Ending the girl's life meant freedom for him—especially now that he knew what the canister would be worth once he disappeared with it.

Other men might be squeamish about how and what he was supposed to harvest from the body. Not Mason Lee. The canister was designed to preserve human tissue for weeks. Perfect. Much easier to steal and hide a canister than a girl. Much easier to travel with it than an unwilling captive.

The pleasure of harvesting from the girl was an added benefit for Mason. There was something mystical and exciting about watching a life force dissipate. He knew this because he had gutted animals before they were dead.

But never a human.

## SIX

Theo Balder believed that luck had finally turned in his favor. He was hunched behind a log, feeling around in the water for crawfish, when a small man with a backpack knelt to drink about fifty yards upstream.

Theo had become so hungry that he'd begun to wonder if he would die of starvation. Anything but surrender. The backpack, however, could give him life. It might have money inside. Or matches. Or a knife. Or, best of all, maybe food.

In the factory, at night, older kids whispered stories about the people of the Clan who roamed the woods, looking for kids to kill, barbecue, and hang from trees as a warning to stay in the towns.

That's why, at first, when he'd heard someone approaching as he fished, Theo was terrified that his company might be someone from the Clan. He'd crouched behind a fallen log in ankle-deep water, and the man had not noticed him, so he followed when the man left the streambed.

Fortune continued. Theo was farsighted, and anything within thirty yards was blurry, so with the distance between them, he was able to see that the man was limping and could only walk with the aid of a stick.

A small man. Crippled. There weren't many other people that Theo could rob safely. Fate was treating him kindly after dealing him so many blows already.

Theo wouldn't attribute any of this to God. He knew better than to believe in superstition. He saw no logic in believing that if someone had created the entire universe, he would care about a fourteen-year-old scavenging runaway.

Theo needed to be patient, however. With his bad vision, he had no chance of picking his way through leaves and branches to approach quietly enough to have any hope of stealing the man's backpack. He'd have to wait until the man stopped and then decide upon the best plan of attack.

He felt around in the water for a large smooth stone. Big enough to knock the man out.

Theo listened carefully for the man's progress along the path, then began to follow.

Caitlyn held herself to the branches, motionless in the shape of a cross, hanging parallel to the ground from more than ten feet above it. Her face and toes pointed downward.

She'd looked for a place on the path where solid branches would be far enough apart to assist her maneuver. She'd jumped, grabbed the branches, and tilted her body from vertical to horizontal, just as she'd done countless times under Papa's supervision.

Outside, Papa told her, gymnasts called it the Iron Cross, but in Appalachia, there were no gymnasts, so it had no name for most people, and there was no one to be amazed. Papa usually called it, simply, the Cross. The exercise was an unexplained part of her life. Papa would hang two ropes down from a thick tree branch, three feet apart. The ends of each rope were knotted and at least four feet off the ground. The exercise she secretly performed daily would have been astounding to any gymnast. Because her body was so light and thin, she could hold the position almost without effort. From there, her body vertical to the ground, she could tilt forward until her body was parallel to it, arms still outstretched, and remain like that without trembling for half an hour.

Until now, the Cross had seemed purposeless. But she'd finally found use for it, given that it was unlikely her pursuer would look up in the air to find her. Who would expect her to be in this position, and she was well hidden by smaller branches and leaves.

She doubted that her pursuer was much danger anyway.

It was the boy. The annoying skunk boy.

Down at the stream, getting water, she'd smelled skunk and looked around, then saw him hiding in the water behind a log. He'd begun to follow her.

Caitlyn had spent the previous twenty minutes following deer paths up a hill, trying to lose skunk boy as best she could with her twisted ankle, but the boy had stayed with her, keeping a constant distance of twenty or thirty paces behind.

She knew he was behind her, as every few minutes she would hear a grunt as if he had walked into something. Occasionally, the swirling breeze brought her the smell of skunk until she'd decided it was time to end this.

She held herself in the shape of a cross and waited.

## SEVEN

On a bench overlooking the Cumberland Gap town square, Billy Jasper sat beside Sheriff Clarence Carney. Carney was in his midfifties, lean and perpetually serious. Billy was more uncomfortable than usual, because this was the first time that Carney had made a point to spend time with Billy in the two weeks since the town Elders had chosen Billy as deputy.

"What do you see?" Carney asked Billy. Although he was a large man and easily three decades older,

Carney stood a full head shorter than Billy and a hundred pounds lighter. Still, from Carney's tone of voice, there was no doubt the smaller man was in control.

It wasn't just Carney's serious tone and ramrod posture that made people nervous. It was the hard-set face he'd earned through thirty years of enforcing every law, down to the slightest infraction.

"What do you see?"

Billy didn't like questions. This one was worse because there was no obvious answer. And there was a vidpod on the bench between them recording the conversation. Bar Elohim, if he wanted, would be able to hear Billy's answer. He knew, like everyone in Appalachia knew, that Bar Elohim had access to information on all vidpods.

"Talk, boy," Sheriff Carney said, showing, as usual, irritation at Billy's deliberateness.

Billy didn't like this about himself either. As a boy, so large he had often been mistaken at a distance for a man, Billy had been so meek about his size and strength that he'd become a target, unable to find anger when other boys goaded him. Fights weren't fights; he towered above them and would placidly let them pummel him—sometimes two or three at a time—until they were exhausted. Billy was also aware, however, that the people of Cumberland Gap considered him an ox when it came to intelligence. Time and again, he saw others give glib answers that brought smiles or laughter, a skill he envied. Billy wished he could learn to answer without taking time to consider whether it was the best and truest answer possible. Maybe people would stop saying he was slow but nice.

"I see Cumberland Gap," Billy said in answer to Carney's vague question. Was he supposed to mention details, like the empty mockingbird nest in the tree in front of them? Or that the little birds had left the nest two days earlier, and one had fallen from the nest and Billy had barely gotten to it before the courthouse cat pounced?

Was he supposed to point out the apartment above the store across the street, where he knew Carney had a man imprisoned and was keeping it a secret? Was he supposed to mention that Mrs. Andrews on the other side of the street was wearing a shawl across her face, even though the weather was blazing?

"You see men and women walking down the street in peaceful conversation," Carney said. "You see horse-drawn wagons. You see clean sidewalks. Well-built stores. You see harmony."

"Yes sir."

Mr. and Mrs. Andrews had stopped to look through a store window. Both shaped like pears. Mr. Andrews was a dog-kicker. Billy didn't like that. Mrs. Andrews sometimes had a bruise on the side of her face. Probably had one under the shawl right now.

To Billy, that didn't suggest harmony. Nor did the screams that had echoed through town last night, from the apartment above the store. But arguments tightened Billy's stomach, so he found it easier to agree with Sheriff Carney than point out Cumberland Gap wasn't all harmony. Besides, he knew why the Elders had endorsed Billy as deputy. Carney didn't want deputies who thought for themselves. Neither did the Elders. Like an ox, Billy was easy to control, and that didn't bother him. He just wished people would overlook him. But he was too big for that.

"What don't you see?" Carney asked.

By now, Billy realized Carney was going to answer his own question, so he held off replying. That was good. Billy didn't have to think through all the possibilities before answering. He'd been working at the livery before the Elders chose him for a deputy. He'd enjoyed the livery. Not many questions there.

"You don't see fear," Carney said. "You don't see fear because you don't see crime. It's no accident that the Elders don't allow towns to grow to a population of more than three thousand."

Appalachian government policy restricted town size because small towns meant accountability, in sharp contrast to Outside, where the anonymous lifestyles in large cities bred sin.

"Let me repeat. You don't see fear because you don't see crime," Carney said. Carney crossed his legs and leaned back against the bench. "What you see is good, and nothing bad. That's the result of living in a society that follows the literal Word of God."

Billy nodded. Nothing to disagree with there.

"It's why the Elders fought for freedom from Outside," Carney said. "And it's taken two generations to ensure a place where men follow the Word of God. If you want to see all of this destroyed before the Second Coming, all you need to do is invite the snake back into the garden."

"Sir?"

"Adam and Eve had all they needed. But what fruit did the snake tempt them with?" Carney's voice rose. "The snake told Eve that if she ate the fruit from the Tree of Good and Evil, that she would have knowledge like God. The woman wanted God's wisdom. She wanted God's knowledge. She wanted to be like God."

Billy knew this story very well from all the Bible lessons in church. Trouble was, every time it came to the part about the man and woman realizing they were naked, it got him to wondering what a naked woman looked like. Then he'd think some more on what a person might see if women wore dresses made of leaves, like the Good Book described. Especially what a person might see on a windy day, unless the leaves were sewn really securely. None of those thoughts were good, he knew, but they were difficult to push away.

Carney continued, oblivious, of course, to the sinful thoughts that Billy had not invited into his mind. "What you're not often told was that the woman ate of the fruit before giving it to Adam. They didn't each take a bite at the same time. She was corrupted by that first bite. Instead of protecting the man, she wanted him corrupted too and offered some to him, so she wouldn't be alone in her sin."

Carney paused and reached up to put his hand on Billy's shoulder. Man to man.

"There's a woman like that in town right now, son. Mrs. Shelton."

*Mrs. Shelton?* Billy blinked a few times. *Old Mrs. Shelton?*

"I learned a long time ago not to let appearances fool me," Carney said. "She has been corrupted by knowledge, the kind that God sees fit to keep from us, and she wants others corrupted by it too."

Carney gestured at the town square. "If that corruption has a chance to spread, you won't see all this harmony in front of you. That's why it's so important to keep the snake from getting loose anywhere in Appalachia."

"Yes sir." Billy was still trying to comprehend. Why Mrs. Shelton? He'd grown up just down the street from her. She'd made pies for his family when his mother was sick.

"Bar Elohim is the shepherd of Appalachia, just like the men in each town who carry his authority and serve him and report to him. Men of law, like you and me. God has given us shepherds authority over the sheep to keep them from going astray. And you and me . . ."

Another pause. This one was longer. Billy took his eyes off the empty mockingbird nest and looked down at Carney and saw Carney staring at him. Waiting.

So this was a question, Billy realized, although it hadn't been asked like a question. Right after being asked a question that wasn't a question. This was why Billy preferred people to ignore him.

"You and me, we help guard the sheep for the shepherds," Billy answered. Carney had taught him this on the first day. "That's our duty."

"We guard the sheep from Outside." Carney nodded. "Sheep are in danger if they ever leave the flock. It means our duty is to keep sheep where they belong. Inside the safety of the fence. Mrs. Shelton is trying to get people in this town to break down the fence and go Outside. She's a snake on the loose, tempting people to reach for the forbidden tree." Carney's lips tightened. "You know what I mean, don't you?"

"Books, sir."

"Not only that. A Bible."

"A Bible! And she reads . . . " Billy didn't finish verbalizing his thought. Only preachers were allowed access to a Bible, and their copies were only audio versions. Laypeople couldn't be trusted with God's Word because laypeople didn't have the knowledge to truly understand and interpret it. Possessing a Bible meant a life sentence at a factory. Or maybe even execution by stoning. Billy had a difficult time comprehending that the accusations might be true. *Mrs. Shelton?*

"Hold out your vidpod," Carney directed Billy. "I'm going to transfer the arrest warrant."

It was in the shirt pocket of his deputy uniform.

Billy struggled with the button because his fingers were so thick. He finally dug out his vidpod, which was dwarfed in his hand, and turned it toward Carney's vidpod.

The beep of a completed transfer sounded a second later.

"I'm sending you to arrest her, Billy. Handcuff Mrs. Shelton to the chair before you let her listen to the warrant. Don't talk to her. Find the books in the house. Bring her and the books back to the town jail. And the Bible."

*Books.* This was important. Too important.

"How will I know which one is the Bible? I can't read."

"Bring all the books." The sheriff grimaced.

"Sir, are you sure I should be going alone?"

Carney's eyes flicked to the apartment above the store across the street. If Billy had to guess, whatever was happening in there was even more important. Something strange was going on. It had to do with the bounty hunters who had come into Cumberland Gap in the night, and the screams since. There was an undercurrent of whispers in town. As usual, Billy had been excluded.

Carney's eyes returned to Billy. "She's just an old woman, son. You should be able to handle it yourself. If not, maybe the Elders will have to send me a new deputy."

## EIGHT

He's gone," Dr. Ross said to Pierce, in the apartment across the street from Billy. The doctor had just lifted the end of his stethoscope off Jordan's chest.

"Gone."

"Dead," Dr. Ross said.

Pierce closed his eyes briefly. Mason Lee would pay for this.

"I'll need a copy of the death certificate," Pierce said.

"And the body?"

"Do what you need to do," Pierce said. "Then take it away. I'll keep the apartment for myself."

Caitlyn's wait didn't take long. The boy passed below her, the skunk smell wafting to her nose.

She lowered herself from horizontal to vertical, landing on her good foot and wincing as she set the other one down.

The noise of impact was slight, but the boy whirled around at the sound and startled her.

Not nearly as much as the sight of her startled him. That was the effect she'd intended, of course, except she'd wanted to reach forward and surprise him, touch the back of his shoulders to really make him jump.

The boy shrieked and backed away from her.

He was a mess. Greasy dark hair sticking out in all directions. Welts across his arms, red bumps on his face. His right forearm was bound by a blood-crusted strip of cloth, obviously ripped from the bottom of his shirt. He had filthy hands, dirt under his fingernails. And, of course, the smell of skunk.

"Keep going," Caitlyn told him. The boy had a round rock in his hand, and she guessed why. "I can surprise you like this whenever I want. Except next time, I'll be the one with a rock big enough to knock you across the head. You won't even know what hit you."

The boy stopped moving, squinted at her. "How did you do that?"

"I want you to leave me alone," she answered. She reached down and grabbed her walking stick, which she'd placed on the ground at the side of the path earlier.

He squinted again. "What are you?"

She was a freak. That's what he meant. The reminder was like someone pushed a jagged piece of glass through her skin. She blinked at the intensity of the pain. But she wasn't going to show that the insult affected her.

She jabbed him in his chest with the tip of her walking stick. "Whatever I am, I don't stink like you. Now go away."

"No, no, no," he said. "I thought you were a man. But you sound a lot like a girl. Not that I'm trying to insult you."

"You're not listening. If you keep following me, I'll have to ambush you again and whack your head."

He was still squinting. "I wish I had better eyes. Then I could see if you were a girl."

"What difference does that make?"

"I'd be more afraid that a man would whack me. You're not someone from the Clan, right? You're not going to barbecue me and hang me from a tree? The way you appeared out of nowhere . . . that was scary."

"I don't want you following me."

"As long as you're not Clan, I have to. Else I'm going to die of starvation."

She jabbed him again. "Leave me be."

She jabbed his shoulder. It was the most she could force herself to do to harm him physically. She hoped the bluff would work.

"There's a bounty on my head," he said. "I'm a factory runaway."

"Then keep running."

"Ha!" he said. "There's only one reason you wouldn't go to the Elders to collect that bounty. You must be on the run too."

"I just want to be left alone."

"Show me your vidpod," he said. "Got an Elder's verification that you were in church last Sunday?"

"Go away," Caitlyn said.

"See!" Smug triumph. "I knew it. Fugitive. You can't turn me in. Just like I can't turn you in. Hey, where's your backpack? Have anything I can eat?"

Her backpack was hidden a few yards ahead, off the trail. Caitlyn gritted her teeth. "Go. Away. Now."

"Or else what?" Another grin from the smudged face.

She tried to think of an answer that would scare him. In the silence, he cocked his head, but the grin on his face disappeared.

"Trouble," he said. "We're not alone."

She listened. "I don't hear anything."

"Men," he said. "Talking."

He pointed upward, at the branches three-quarters the way up the trees.

Caitlyn looked.

"Skunk boy," she said, "those are leaves."

"Beyond the leaves. I can hear them."

He seemed so convinced that Caitlyn looked more intently. She looked in the angle he pointed and saw the rock of the far wall of the valley. The same sheer rock wall that Caitlyn dropped from when Papa pushed her into the chasm.

She saw movement on the distant rocks. Caitlyn limped past the boy and climbed upward on the deer path.

"I was right, wasn't I," the boy said. He stayed close to her.

She ignored him. She reached a place where the trees thinned. It gave her a better view across the valley.

The boy jumped on a nearby rock and became as tall as Caitlyn.

"Climbers," he said. "I can't see much close up, but I can see far just fine. Those are climbers."

The boy was right. A half dozen men were lowering themselves on ropes and climbing down the sheer face of the rock, high above the waterfall.

"You can hear them?"

"Not what they are saying. But enough to know they are talking. Impressed? You should be. Most people are. I can't see good enough to count my own fingers, but I can hear stuff. It's why I'm afraid at night. Too many things moving in the dark. I hear them all. All the time."

Caitlyn let the boy prattle. In her head, she heard Papa's words. *"You cannot be taken, dead or alive. You must not fall into their hands."*

Who were they? What was it they wanted so badly?

Caitlyn gave the irritating skunk boy her attention again. She'd have to escape him too. But not now. If her pursuers found him, he'd most certainly tell them about her and confirm that she was still alive. She would take him away from here, then abandon him.

"Do you want to go back to the factory?" Caitlyn asked.

"I've been eating worms and crawfish," he said. "I even tried killing a skunk to eat it. That's why I stink. I'm willing to go to the Clan just to get Outside, if I can find my way there. What does that tell you?"

"Stay with me, then," Caitlyn said. She pointed ahead where the valley widened. "We're going to Cumberland Gap. Then Outside. But you have to keep your mouth shut and do everything I tell you."

70

"You can find the Clan? You're not afraid of becoming a floater?"

"Already, you're not listening. You'll need to keep your mouth shut."

"Sorry."

Caitlyn turned back down the path, where the backpack was waiting. Her ankle was feeling a little better. The climbers wouldn't be down for a while, but she'd have to do her best to stay ahead of them.

"My name is Theo," the boy said. "Do you have any food?"

Caitlyn spoke without looking back. "That doesn't sound like silence to me."

"Oh," he said. "Right. Sorry again. It's just been a week all by myself. And I'm hungry."

"Telling me why you're talking, that's talking too."

"Right. Sorry. You know . . . again."

She'd give him some cheese from the backpack. Maybe that would keep him quiet.

"How did you sneak up on me back there?" he said a couple steps later. "No one's ever done that before. My hearing is too good."

She ignored him.

"I can hear great, but I've got extreme hyperopia," he continued. "Means I'm farsighted. I can barely even count my own fingers."

"You said that already," Caitlyn said. "Try to count to yourself. Please."

"Up close, you're a blur to me. At least tell me if you're a girl. Or just a small man with a high voice. If

71

you're going to escape with someone, that's important to know, right?"

"If I feed you," she said, "will you finally give me some peace?"

Then, silence. Blessed silence.

But a second later, he grabbed her arm. With anger, she twisted away. She turned and was about to snap at him, but his head was cocked, and he was holding up a hand to stop her.

His smudged face showed concentration. Then fear.

"Hounds," he said. "Between us and Cumberland Gap."

## NINE

Billy felt miserable while handcuffing Mrs. Shelton's wrists behind the spindle-back cane chair in her kitchen. He squatted behind her, afraid that with the slightest roughness he'd tear through the liver-spotted skin of her frail wrists. He just hoped Mrs. Shelton wouldn't remind him that she'd changed his diapers when he was a baby. Billy had never wanted to be a deputy, but when the Elders gave orders, there was no choice.

Everything about her kitchen was as he remembered. The flowered wallpaper, the lace curtains, the china set out as decoration. She'd put cookies and milk on the table before he could find the courage to tell her why he had knocked on her door.

Billy rose from the floor.

"If it hurts," Billy said, "let me know. Maybe I can put a dishrag or something under the cuffs."

"It's a shame you have to do this." She'd been a widow for two decades, the type of woman who stayed busy in the town, helping out where needed with the energy and mannerisms of a sparrow.

"Ma'am," Billy said. "No offense. Sheriff Carney advised me against any conversation with you."

Billy stood in front of her now, not quite able to meet her eyes. He focused on her forehead instead. A couple of deep blue veins pulsed under the surface of her translucent skin.

"No conversation?" Her smile faltered, adding to Billy's misery.

"He said you were dangerous."

"Sheriff Carney is afraid of a seventy-two-year-old woman?"

"No. He said I should be."

"There's nobody in the county bigger and stronger than you, Billy Jasper. How could I be any danger?"

"You managed to keep me talking," Billy said. "I shouldn't say anything more."

"You can at least tell me why you're doing this," she said.

Billy did have orders to cover that. He pulled a vidpod from the back pocket of his deputy uniform and held the small rectangular screen in front of Mrs. Shelton's face.

"I'm not wearing my glasses," she said. "They are on the counter."

Billy found them folded, beside the sink. He unfolded them and placed the wire frame gently on Mrs. Shelton's nose, tucking the arms onto her ears. A couple wisps of her gray hair had fallen from the bun piled high on her head. He pushed them out of the way.

"You're a kind young man," she said. "I always liked that about you."

*No conversation,* he reminded himself. He'd already slipped.

Billy touched the screen to play the arrest and search warrant for Mrs. Shelton. To authenticate the authority of the warrant, a face on the screen appeared briefly: Bar Elohim. Then Sheriff Carney's image, speaking the words recorded for this occasion.

Carney spoke in monotone. *"By the power vested in me through God and Bar Elohim, this arrest warrant is served on Gloria Shelton on charges of sedition against the state. A simultaneous search warrant of the Shelton residence and grounds has been issued to provide evidence for the arrest charge."*

"Who was it?" Mrs. Shelton said, sighing.

"Ma'am?"

"Who was it that turned me in?"

Billy had been hoping Mrs. Shelton would deny wrongdoing. When he was a boy, she'd always had a pitcher of lemonade ready for children in the neighborhood.

"You know I can't answer that," Billy said. Here he was, somehow engaged in conversation again.

"Can't? Or won't?"

Billy was a new deputy. Carney didn't tell him who his informants were. He saw her vidpod on a desk on the far wall of the kitchen and took the opportunity to avoid her question. "I'll need to transfer this warrant so you have a record of it. Is your infrared activated?"

Mrs. Shelton nodded. Billy beamed the information. It was required as part of any arrest.

"When I was a girl," she said, "we didn't have vidpods. Information was written down to be recorded."

"With vidpods, you don't need to write anything," Billy answered after the small beep told him the transfer was complete. "This is easier and more efficient."

Billy's personal vidpod held everything he needed to know or reference. The filing system had folders with icons. When Bar Elohim needed to speak to all of Appalachia, the message was uploaded automatically on to every vidpod in every household. The vidpod was programmed to beep until the recipient listened to the directive. Billy hated letting the vidpod beep because it sounded to him like a little voice saying that he was sinning against God, so he always listened to his messages right after receiving them.

"Vidpods keep you from needing the ability to read," Mrs. Shelton said.

There it was. In the open. She was almost admitting that she broke the law.

"Ma'am," Billy said, "I have to search your house. For books. And your Bible."

Then he realized he was talking to her again.

"Aren't you curious," she asked, "what it would be like to read books? What you might learn beyond what Bar Elohim permits?"

Carney had been right. She was dangerous. Like the snake, offering fruit from the Tree of Good and Evil.

"Ma'am, I've respected you since I was a boy. I wish I didn't have to do this."

He couldn't stop himself from answering. Remaining silent seemed too cruel to Mrs. Shelton.

"Did the informer give Sheriff Carney a list of everyone?"

Everyone. Now Billy knew it was true. She'd also been secretly teaching people to read.

"No more conversation, Mrs. Shelton. I'm sorry."

"If he doesn't have a list, he's going to make me give him names. You know that, don't you? He's going to hurt me."

Billy didn't want to think about it. But he knew that people shouldn't break the law. "You want to tell me where to find the books? There'll be less of a mess that way."

Mrs. Shelton had always liked her house neat, Billy remembered.

She opened her mouth as if to respond, then leaned toward her middle, groaning. "My stomach!"

"What's wrong?"

"It's my medication," she said. "Every morning about now, it sends me running to the toilet. Please don't make me dirty myself here in my kitchen."

"Of course not," Billy said. "You promise you won't try to run?"

She managed to smile. "From a strong, handsome young man like you?"

Billy blushed.

She grimaced again, bending over. "Hurry!"

Billy unshackled her. He helped her from the chair to her feet. She leaned on his arm as he led her down the hallway, past the photos of her children and her grandchildren and her long-dead husband. She still smelled of peppermint and perfume.

"Thank you, Billy," she said at the door to the bathroom. "You always were a nice young man."

"You won't try to leave through the window?"

"I'm seventy-two."

"Yes ma'am," Billy said. "I'll wait in the kitchen."

The kitchen jutted out from the house. From there, he'd still be able to see the door in the hallway. As well as the neat yard outside. If she actually did try to escape, he'd see that too.

"Don't forget the cookies, then," she said. "Not much sense letting them go to waste."

She closed the door.

Halfway through the second cookie, Billy thought he smelled kerosene. Then smoke.

He frowned, glanced around him.

Black smoke curled from beneath the door down the hallway.

It only took a single punch against the door to force it open. He saw her on the floor. Limp. A small vial had fallen from her hand, and little pills were scattered on the floor. Flames were rising around her, already crackling and devouring a pile of books in the bathtub. The door to the cupboard under the sink was open and empty.

Billy faced a grim choice. Find a way to fight the flames. Or carry Mrs. Shelton away from danger.

He lifted her onto his shoulders and ran back down the hallway.

## TEN

Back and forth," Theo said, his head cocked as he listened intently. "Across the valley. Each pass brings them closer to us. Three sets of hounds. Maybe four."

Caitlyn and Theo had found an overlook that still shielded them from view of the men climbing down the rock face behind them, at the head of the valley.

"What are the dogs' names?" Caitlyn said.

"How in the world could I tell that from what I'm hearing?" Theo said.

"It's a joke, skunk boy. You seem to know so much else about them." The words felt bitter on her tongue. She knew she was being unnecessarily cruel to him, trying to find an outlet for her grief.

"Oh, very funny. Do you find it funny that they are squeezing us in? Unless we figure out a way to fly."

*Unless we figure out a way to fly.* Caitlyn shivered at the thought.

"If we time it right," Theo said, "we can slip past the dogs and end up safely on the other side of them."

"No," Caitlyn answered. "The dogs will cross my scent. They'll know it's fresh. And I have no doubt that I'm the one they want, not you."

"At the factory, everyone said all you have to do is walk through water to lose the dogs."

"Wrong. In pools, the scent stays on top of the water," Caitlyn said. "Where the scent is broken up by fast water, they'll send teams up and down both sides of the creek until they find where we stepped out again."

She knew this because Papa had explained everything about bloodhounds to her. They'd been on the run from Mason Lee for three days, but it wasn't until the final two days that Mason was able to put bloodhounds on the trail. That's when it was over. Papa had used every trick possible, but all it had done was slow the hounds.

"Okay, then. What if you climb a tree and cross over to another tree, branch to branch, and keep going until you are far enough away?"

"Skunk boy, you can't see well enough to count your own fingers. Think you'll make it up the first tree without falling?"

"You do it," he said. "Leave me here. If you can get away, you should. Better that one of us makes it Outside than neither."

He sounded so pathetic yet brave that Caitlyn felt her first twinge of affection for him. "Have something to eat."

She found an energy bar in her backpack and gave it to the boy.

His hands shook so rapidly as he attempted to tear open the wrapping that she sighed, took the bar from him, opened it, and handed it back.

"Besides," Theo continued, barely understandable because he'd crammed so much into his mouth, "you said they were looking for you, not me. I'll hide in the valley and eat more crawfish and worms. That's better than going back to the factory."

His words echoed. *"You said they were looking for you, not me."*

This was true. Papa explained how bloodhounds follow a trail. The bounty hunters give them a piece of clothing that belonged to the fugitive. The hounds follow only that scent. No other scent distracts them.

Theo had given her a way out. *"You said they were looking for you, not me."*

Theo gulped down the rest of the bar and waited for her answer.

Caitlyn thought there might be another way out of the valley. Unfortunately, it meant she would have to trust her life to a nearly blind skunk boy.

## ELEVEN

Sheriff Carney leaned back in his office chair, staring at his computer screen. That's the way his vision was going these days; he couldn't see anything unless he held it at arm's length or more.

He'd already enlarged to maximum size the icons that represented file folders, and that didn't help much either, unless he put on his glasses. But then he'd have to worry about taking them off in a hurry if someone stepped through the door. He wasn't going to betray the slightest hint of weakness in this town.

Now the fugitive was dead, already taken away by the undertaker. But the Outside agent remained in town, and the search was still on for the girl. If Carney could find the girl, things would get back to normal.

Carney tapped an icon on the screen. He was old enough to know that there'd been a time when people used keyboards to command the computer. Now it was icons only, symbols that represented computer actions or files. Keyboards were useful only for those who could read. Multimedia helped curb the need for literacy, making everything simpler. Just tap the right icon, and information was delivered by sight— moving images or still photos—or by sound. Easy and effective. Complete comprehension, without reading.

Input for computers was delivered the same way. Personal vidpods recorded visual and audio information, if needed. It was just a matter of uploading whatever was in the vidpod on to the computer, or vice versa.

Outside, as Bar Elohim always preached, unlimited computer access could lead to all sorts of evils— sedition and pornography at the top of the list. Inside Appalachia, however, all computers were consistently linked to the government mainframe, and personal computers were personal but not private. Bar Elohim and his representatives effectively monitored and managed the hard-drive content throughout Appalachia. Bar Elohim kept people free from temptation and instead made sure they were linked to the right information, the kind they needed. Before Carney's time, people who were caught trying to get past the Internet block to access the Web Outside were sent to the factories. Now, cybersecurity was impossible to break; Appalachia was a locked system.

This morning, Carney had logged in to the town's mainframe, interested in the routine video surveillance that the town's hard drive stored for five years. Cameras were interspersed through town at strategic locations, ensuring very few blind spots. They deterred crime and made it easier to solve, on the rare occasion it took place.

Carney had been searching the video surveillance for the face of the man whom Dr. Ross had declared dead. Now the man could only be found immortalized in electronic bytes, but it was Carney's job to find him there too.

The night before, as local law, Carney had been obliged to provide a place for the fugitive. In the process, he had seen the man's face up close.

Carney's ability to remember a face was strong, and he knew he'd seen the man before, a day or two before the arrival of Mason Lee and the Outside agent, but he couldn't place the when and where.

It didn't matter. In Cumberland Gap, he had the public surveillance cameras to help.

Carney thought through the past week, the places he'd visited. That would winnow down the amount of surveillance video he'd have to review.

Icon by icon, Carney went through different times and locations. He had no sense of impatience. Billy was out of the way, and it would be worth Carney's effort to confirm the fugitive had been in town and whom he had visited.

Carney wondered when Bar Elohim would make it law that everyone in Appalachia have radio-chip implants. The chips were about the size of a grain of rice and held enough computer information to store the person's background and medical information, but most importantly, to track them electronically. The mainframe could keep record of every person's movement over the last year. But Bar Elohim knew, obedient as Appalachians were, that this could spark rebellion, even beyond the actions of the Clan. God's Word, after all, plainly showed that this would be the mark of the Beast. So the radio chips were restricted to convicted criminals and the children of criminals, the factory kids.

Public surveillance cameras were the next best thing. It took Carney only half an hour to find Jordan. There, in front of the bank, just two afternoons earlier.

Yes, that's where he had seen that face.

The video showed Carney stepping out of the bank, just as the man walked down the sidewalk. On the video, Carney watched himself quickly appraise the man and the man ducking his head after noticing Carney's uniform.

*Got you.*

Now it was easy. Carney could backtrack the man to another surveillance camera and pick up that footage. From that surveillance camera to the previous one. And so on.

Carney reviewed the videos until he found the time and place that the man had stepped into town alone. Then he watched as the fugitive approached the house. Mitch Evans's house. The livery owner.

Carney rocked his chair in satisfaction. The Outside agent was looking for a girl, and Carney now had an idea where to set the trap if she slipped past them.

If he was the one to catch her, it would be worth it.

The bigger question was why she'd be worth so much.

## TWELVE

At the head of the valley, Mason Lee stood at the foot of a thin waterfall, which fell from a stream about a hundred feet above. Through the water's veil, Mason could see just well enough to glimpse a small cavern—the only possible refuge for a woman who surely knew she had been trapped. The bloodhounds had tracked her scent to here and blocked all avenues of escape. Mason pictured the girl shivering in fear, making her way down the rock face to the cavern, hoping for safety.

But there was no way to climb back up. Mason was certain: she could only be there, hidden by the water.

He stood just beyond the spray, all the men in his hire behind him. They knew procedure. Mason was always the one to make the final capture.

One of the men had his vidpod in video recording mode and extended it chest high for an unimpeded view of Mason. This was procedure too. The capture would be uploaded for Bar Elohim to distribute to all vidpods in Appalachia, showing everyone that it was useless to defy God and Bar Elohim. Mason liked the publicity, cementing the perception that no one ever escaped him. He'd always wait until the recording was finished to take his private, bloody revenge on the fugitives.

Aware that his next actions would be in full view of Appalachia, Mason Lee held the stock of his shotgun and flipped the front end upward to snap it shut. He aimed the shotgun at the waterfall.

"Come on out," he shouted. "There's no place to go."

This would look good, the girl stepping out from the curtain of water, drenched and pitiful. Where and when he'd gut her he hadn't decided yet, but there would be plenty of time between now and the return to Cumberland Gap to make it look as if she'd tried to escape. Mason knew there was no bounty hunter alive who would be able to find him once he had the canister. He wouldn't mind shooting a couple of his own men to make his escape with the canister even easier.

"Come on out," he shouted again. "Otherwise I'll send the dogs in."

The bloodhounds were anxious, of course. Once they started on a trail, they were obsessive and would never quit. They simply needed the reward of finding the fugitive to settle them down.

The Rottweilers, on the other hand, wanted blood. This suited Mason. He wouldn't even need the excuse of an attempted escape to harvest the girl.

The girl did not leave the waterfall.

Mason looked back over his right shoulder, knowing the vidpod would record this. He didn't turn his head far enough to get both eyes in view. He didn't like having his drifting left eye on every vidpod in Appalachia.

"Send the dogs!" Mason ordered.

The dogs needed no urging. Six of them. Black Rottweilers. Massive shoulders. Bone-snapping jaws. They bolted toward the waterfall, snarling and howling.

Mason felt a tingle of anticipation as he waited for the screams to come.

Instead, the snarls and howling faded. Moments later, the dogs emerged and shook water from their hides before dancing around in confused circles at the base of the waterfall.

*Impossible.* Black anger bubbled within him. *How could the girl have escaped?*

# THIRTEEN

M rs. Shelton is dead and the books are gone."
Carney spoke to Billy in his usual monotone,
staring hard at him.

"She's dead!"

"Dr. Ross did all he could." There was nothing
gentle in Carney's voice. "We needed her to tell us
who she'd been teaching to read. Where she'd gotten
the books. We needed those books to send to Bar
Elohim so he could understand what was getting loose
in Cumberland Gap and tell us how best to protect the
flock."

Billy kept his eyes on the ground. Yes, he'd failed.
When he set the old woman on the ground, she was
already unconscious. Must have been from the pills on
the bathroom floor. And the fire was too big to contain. Everyone in town knew it was his fault. Most
would blame it on how he was raised. Without parents
to properly guide him.

"I've got to send an audio file on this to Bar
Elohim," Carney said. "I'm going to make sure that I
take part of the blame. Had I foreseen that she was evil
enough and unrepentant enough to take her life and
destroy her house, I wouldn't have sent you on your
own. You'll keep your deputy badge."

Billy didn't lift his gaze from the ground. Carney
might see his disappointment that he was to remain
deputy. Billy hated himself that Mrs. Shelton was

dead, and he didn't want to be burdened with any more responsibilities of a deputy. Other things would go bad too.

"Still," Carney said, "I can't pretend you didn't do anything wrong. You're going to be spending nights in the office, watching the livery for me."

"Sir?" Billy said.

"Surveillance camera. Anything happens after curfew, you call me right away. Can you handle that?"

Billy gave it thought. He could tell Carney didn't like that, but Billy didn't want to say he could handle it if there was something about it that would make it difficult for him.

"Will you let me know where I can call you?"

"Of course I'll let you know where I am," Carney snapped. "That goes without saying."

Billy wished, as usual, that he knew what went without saying and what didn't.

"All night?" Billy asked.

"Unless you think there's a particular time that the building doesn't need watching."

That perplexed Billy.

Carney sighed. "Of course, all night."

"By myself?"

"It only takes one person to watch a computer screen."

"Um, sir," Billy paused again in thought. At church, when the sermon was boring or confusing, Billy usually fought off sleep. Not always successfully. He didn't want to promise he could stay up all night if he'd end up breaking his word. "I don't know if I can stay awake that long."

Carney started to form furrows in his forehead, the way he did whenever he broke out of his monotone in anger. Then, strangely, he smiled.

"Sometimes," Carney said, "I guess it pays to think things through. There's a cot in one of the empty jail cells. Get some sleep. All afternoon if you need it."

"That would help a lot, sir."

"All right then." Carney put a hand on Billy's shoulder. "Do this right and we'll forget about your trouble with Mrs. Shelton."

"We've gone far enough," Caitlyn told Theo. "You must be ready to drop."

"No," Theo said. "I'm going to make sure you're safe. Besides, you're not nearly as heavy as I expected."

Caitlyn hadn't heard a peep from Theo over the last mile as he hiked through the streambed and then a hundred yards across an open grassy area. Caitlyn liked the silence. The skunk smell was still hard to get used to though. She guessed that at that point, she probably smelled like skunk too.

She was riding him piggyback, to avoid leaving a scent for the bloodhounds. When the hounds crossed Theo's pungent scent, they'd ignore it.

Although she weighed very little, she was still impressed with Theo's strength and ruggedness. He'd carried her on his back. Theo had gamely splashed through water and across rocks and over logs. Anything so that Caitlyn's body would not brush against anything and leave a scent for the bloodhounds. He had even, at one point, set her down in rapid water and let her hobble forward, because the current would dissipate her scent. Caitlyn could tell he was also thankful for the moment of rest, knowing that he would carry her again. The tricky part came as they had approached the lines of hounds, but they had used Theo's keen sense of hearing to wait until the hounds had traversed away from the stream before hurrying through the gap.

Caitlyn had also depended on Theo's endurance and developed a grudging admiration for him. He hadn't complained, just stuck with his duty like a mule.

"Thank you," Caitlyn said. She said nothing more until they reached the trees at the far edge of the grass. "Here, this big oak is what we need." She relished the relative coolness of the shade. "Stand close."

Chances were extremely remote that the bloodhounds would find this exact tree. Still, to keep her scent from the ground, Caitlyn reached up and pulled herself onto a low limb without letting any of her body brush against the trunk. She straddled the limb and reached downward for Theo's hands, then helped him up.

"You'll need to climb higher," she said. "Up where no one would think of looking."

"I'm afraid," Theo said. "I can't see where I'm going."

"I'll stay below you," Caitlyn answered. She noticed his arm was bleeding through the place where it was wrapped with cloth. Again, her admiration grew. Her legs must have been putting pressure on the wound, but he hadn't once complained.

She helped him climb halfway up the tree.

"Now what?" Theo asked.

"We wait until tonight." She'd already learned to trust Theo's hearing. Because of it, they'd have enough warning to slip down the tree and run if anyone approached. "Sleep as much as we can."

"Sleep? I'll fall!" Her stoic rescuer was suddenly a boy again.

"Not if we are tied in."

She reached for the coil of thin nylon rope in her backpack. She put it through his belt loops and around the tree trunk and made sure he was secure. She did the same for herself with the other half of the rope.

The bark of the tree was warm and felt almost pleasant in the dappled shade of the leaves. She felt comfortable, except for the distant baying of the hounds, an acute reminder of the fate they could expect if they were captured.

"What was that?" Theo's whisper sounded frightened. "I heard something. Not the dogs . . . more like footsteps."

His fear was contagious. Caitlyn craned her head.

"There it is again." He pointed. "Can you see anything over there?"

In the direction of Theo's gesture, shadows were

moving and Caitlyn's heart hammered, her skin prickling with adrenaline. But as she carefully gazed ahead, she realized the shape was a deer, followed by two fawns.

"It's all right," she said. "Deer."

The adrenaline faded. She glumly consoled herself that if anyone had followed them, they would have already arrived at the base of the tree.

"Wish I had something to shoot it with. Ever eaten deer before?"

"Go to sleep."

"I know you don't want me with you," Theo said. "I'm all right with that."

"Sleep."

"No, really. If I were you, I would lie to me too. I'd tell me that you were going to help me Outside, but then find a time to run away from me. People don't like me. I talk too much."

"Sleep." Caitlyn wanted to deny his accusation, but it would have compounded her guilt to blatantly lie. About the need to leave him. And about his ability to irritate.

"I understand," Theo said. "It's because I'm weird. A freak. It's not only because I talk too much. I can't help my weird thoughts either. Like with double numbers."

She couldn't resist. And it was a better direction than the subject of abandoning him when it was necessary. "Double numbers?"

"Like four and nine and sixteen. See, two times two

is four. Three times three is nine. Double twos and double threes and double fours and so on. It helps me go to sleep at night, trying to imagine the highest double number I can. Like 123 times 123. That's how far I got last night. 15,129. And sometimes I figure backwards. Start with a number and see what double number makes it."

"Square roots," Caitlyn said.

"This tree?"

Despite herself, Caitlyn laughed. "No. It's not called a double number. Three is the square root of nine."

"Other people think about this too?" Theo sounded excited.

"Papa taught me." He had spent hours and hours teaching her mathematics. *Papa.* To her, that single word had always meant love. Now, it meant betrayal.

"What about numbers that can't be taken apart by other numbers?" Theo asked. "Like seven. Or seventeen. A number that can only be divided by itself and by one. The biggest that I can figure out so far is 937. That was last night too. It's hard work, but it keeps me from feeling sorry for myself."

"Those are called prime numbers."

"You know this?"

"I learned it."

"So other people *do* think about this stuff! Maybe I'm not so weird. Can you teach me more?"

"Maybe," Caitlyn said.

"It'd be nice if you did. And I'd like to stay with you, but I really don't expect you to help me get Outside."

"How did you hurt your arm?" Caitlyn asked, remembering the fresh blood that gleamed at the edges of the wrap around his arm.

"It feels hot under the bandage," Theo said. "Not like from the sun. I hope it doesn't get worse. But even if it gets worse, I won't regret it. I would rather be dead than live in the factory anymore. Not much difference as they just want you to work to death anyway. And you can't even think there or talk. But I *have* to think. I *have* to talk. I have to talk about what I think."

"I'm beginning to understand that," Caitlyn said, letting out a small laugh despite herself.

"If you leave me, just don't do it when I'm asleep in this tree." Theo's voice sounded drowsy. "I don't know if I can climb down without falling."

Caitlyn didn't answer. She'd have to leave him, sooner than later. But she didn't want to think about it.

He yawned. "Oh, and I didn't explain . . . it's where the radio chip was—"

"Chip?" Caitlyn said. It was hard to follow Theo's train of thought.

"You asked me how I hurt my arm. Factory kids have radio chips embedded in our muscles to keep track of us. I had to dig it out with a knife, otherwise I never would have escaped."

Caitlyn looked up at Theo as if seeing him for the first time. He'd cut through his own skin and muscle? She didn't know what to say.

"You're a girl, right? You're too soft and your voice is beautiful. How old are you? Where were you born?"

Unwanted, haunting words from Papa's letter came back to her. *"But in the motel room that was our home, the woman I loved died while giving birth. You were a tiny bundle of silent and alert vulnerability and all that remained to remind me of the woman."*

A girl? She turned her face away from Theo. She was a freak, with men hunting her for reasons she didn't know. Self-pity and anger threatened to wash over her, but stronger was the image of Theo so determined to escape that he'd cut into his arm with a knife, of Theo falling asleep afraid and doing numbers in his head to keep from feeling sorry for himself.

"I was born Outside," Caitlyn answered. She expected this would lead to a deluge of questions.

But when she looked up to catch his expression, she saw Theo had leaned into the tree trunk and his eyes were closed. Asleep. She watched him stir briefly, and he mumbled one last thing. "Nine hundred and forty-one . . ."

After a moment, she allowed herself a slight smile. The next prime number after 937: 941.


## FOURTEEN

It took until long after dark for Mason to return to Cumberland Gap. He found Pierce in the diner just off the town square, where he pulled up a chair and faced Pierce across the table, arms crossed, making it clear that he had no intention of joining Pierce in a meal.

They were the only customers at the diner. All the others cleared out when Mason walked in.

Mason waited for Pierce to ask what had happened during the day in the valley. He liked making other people speak first.

Pierce kept sipping his coffee. Then he waved at the waitress and asked for his bill.

"It's on Sheriff Carney," she said, standing as far as possible from Mason. Mason leered at her, and she crossed her arms over her chest and made a fidgety move backwards.

Pierce nodded at the waitress, then pushed back his chair. He stood.

"Hang on," Mason said.

Pierce leaned on the table with his palms but didn't sit.

"Don't you want to know about the girl?" Mason asked.

"If you had something to tell me, I should have heard it by now. Table's yours."

"She's not in the valley," Mason said. "Alive or dead."

Pierce raised an eyebrow. Mason didn't like this, the man standing above him, looking down. He was being disrespected. By an Outsider.

"Widen the circle," Pierce said. "This is your territory. I'm not going to tell you how to find her."

"It's not that simple," Mason said, boiling. "You going to sit back down?"

Pierce shrugged and sat. But it was clear that Mason had lost some face by asking.

"We picked up her trail," Mason said, "from the waterfall to about a mile downstream."

"Okay, so she climbed down during the night," Pierce said, "then started walking out until she heard the hounds. Turned back."

"It took awhile with the bloodhounds to figure it out completely," Mason said. "This is what her trail looked like."

Mason pulled a piece of paper from his vest pocket. He'd drawn a crude map with a stream, the waterfall, and the shape of the valley. He'd also drawn a dotted line in the shape of a V, with the bottom of the V at the waterfall.

"From the waterfall," Pierce said, touching the bottom of the V, "she started one way. Retraced her steps, started another way."

"Maybe. But at both these points"—Mason touched each open end of the V—"there's no sign of her. Like an eagle swooped down and picked her up."

"Not a horse," Pierce said.

Mason snapped. "I've been doing this for twenty years, and I'm the best there is. You don't think that's the first thing I'd consider? No horse tracks nearby. No way possible for horses to be that deep in the valley, anyway. Not in that kind of terrain. She didn't leave by horse."

"I believe that's what I just said," Pierce said. "Maybe I need to be clearer about who is boss here."

"Maybe I—"

"You think I didn't see you signal to release the dogs

on Jordan last night?" Pierce said. "That was stupid and unnecessary. Now the man's dead."

"Dead?"

Pierce nodded. "Now there's no way to ask him where the girl might have gone."

Mason scowled and glared at Pierce.

"Which eye?" Pierce said.

"Huh?"

"You're trying to stare me down, but I don't know which eye I should focus on."

Mason pressed his hands on the table, his knuckles going white with tension. "Time you lost some blood."

"If you pull your knife, I'll kill you. In the meantime, you better find that girl."

Mason moved his hands off the table, onto his lap.

"If I pull my knife," Mason said, his hand on the hilt, "you'll be clear on who's boss."

In an instant, the tabletop slammed into Mason's face, spilling him backward in his chair, pinning his arms in place as he crashed on the floor. Just like that, Pierce was kneeling on the table with his full weight, trapping Mason under it like a bug under Pierce's heel.

The waitress disappeared into the kitchen.

"For three days now," Pierce said, "I've put up with your crap."

"You better make sure I'm dead before you lift away this table," Mason said, struggling against the top. "Otherwise, I'll kill you. Whether I have to knife you in the back or strangle you in your sleep, you won't live to Sunday."

"How badly do you want to face Bar Elohim? He knows all the snakes you've been hiding under your pile of rocks. You're a free man only because it suits him. But this is so big, if you don't deliver, Bar Elohim will make sure your face shows up on every vidpod in Appalachia as the most wanted, and even your own men will hunt you. Not a good prospect, given you've spent years showing them the nastiest tricks in the book."

Pierce moved off the table and kicked it away. Mason began to sit, reaching down with his right hand for his knife. Pierce stepped on Mason's wrist, leaned down and grabbed Mason's elbow, yanking it upward so quickly it took Mason a second to comprehend that the horrible snapping sound and the incredible pain in his lower arm were two connected events.

He opened his mouth to gasp for air. Pierce shoved a napkin in it and put his knee on Mason's throat.

"A man like you succeeds because you have no scruples in breaking the rules of civilization, and by the time a normal man realizes this, it's too late for him to fight back." Pierce spoke calmly, his face only inches away from Mason's. "You think I'm a sissy from the city and don't understand what's happening here? What you don't know is that I'm better at this than you. Nod if you understand. Otherwise I'll break your other arm the same way and not think twice about it."

Mason's forehead was cold with sweat. He nodded. Not from fear, but practicality. He wasn't in a position to fight back, and if both his arms were broken, it would be that much more difficult to kill the agent later. Not to mention capture the girl.

"Tomorrow," Pierce said, "we'll go over plans to track the girl down."

Pierce pulled the napkin out of Mason's mouth and walked away from him. Mason focused on his hatred for Pierce to dull the intense pain in his broken arm.

"In the meantime," Pierce continued, "I'll send Dr. Ross to the sheriff's office to set your arm. That's where you're going to spend the night. Watching surveillance video on the public cameras in case the girl tries to sneak into town."

## FIFTEEN

Caitlyn and Theo had waited hours after the dogs quieted, then silently traveled to the edge of town. They looked down at Cumberland Gap from a hill, well hidden by dark and trees. Streetlights illuminated the sidewalks of the city below, but night masked the buildings and alleys. It was past curfew in Cumberland Gap, and the town showed no life.

Even with the blanket of dark, Caitlyn didn't feel safe. Too much ahead. Too many questions.

Her father's letter had instructed her to steal a horse for the next part of her journey.

Although it was just one more crime against Bar

Elohim—and after a certain point, when execution by stoning was inevitable, what did it matter how many more crimes?—the thought still terrified Caitlyn.

Yet what else could she do? Papa's actions had committed her to flee, and without a horse, she'd face certain capture in the next day or two.

*"You can't be taken, dead or alive. You must not fall into their hands."* Words from the letter, to haunt her.

All that remained was forward. For survival and answers, she'd steal a horse.

"I'm afraid you won't come back," Theo said. He shivered slightly.

"You said you were forced into a factory when you were ten," Caitlyn said. She'd already explained that once they were on a horse, the bloodhounds wouldn't be able to track them on it, but she had not explained how she'd get the horse. "So you know and remember enough about the towns to understand how big the liveries are, right?"

"Fifty or sixty horses," Theo said. "Sometimes up to a hundred."

There were paved roads in Appalachia, connecting the towns and suitable for automobile traffic. But the only vehicles on the road were government supply trucks that traveled from town to town. Bar Elohim had outlawed private vehicles and reduced all personal travel to horseback. Because the towns were small and self-contained, people had little reason to travel far anyway, and at the most, it was only an hour or two by horseback or carriage to the next town. The benefits to Appalachia exceeded the simpler, unhurried American life of two centuries earlier; Outside paid a hefty annual fee to Appalachia for carbon emission credits. This, along with the computer chips produced at the factories and the sale of water to Outside, provided a stable economy inside Appalachia.

"The livery man will walk a few blanketed horses out into the feedlot tonight," Caitlyn said. All of it had been on the instructions waiting for her in the cave. From Papa. She didn't even know if he was alive. She swallowed and continued explaining. "He walks them out every night, so it doesn't seem suspicious. Every once in a while, however, one of the horses is already saddled beneath the blanket. He will leave that horse near the gate, out of view of any public surveillance cameras. The timer on the gate is set to be unlocked from 11:55 to 12:05. That's when I step inside the gate and get the horse."

Caitlyn held out a letter, and there was just enough light from the moon for Theo to see it.

"I want you to hold this. There are instructions on where to go once we have the horse."

"You can read?" Theo refused the letter and stepped away nervously, looking at Caitlyn as if she were contagious. "No wonder they want to find you." He shivered again. "Now I'm really afraid you won't come back."

"I'm not going to abandon you here!" Her nostrils had become accustomed to the skunk smell, but the boy still aggravated her. She'd take him farther, just enough for him to get well fed and to be safe. "That's why I told you all that, about the plan, and offered the letter. So you know you can trust me. I can't leave you here, or you could go to the Elders with what you know."

"That's not it," he said. "What I meant is that I'm afraid something will happen to you. The horses have radio chips too. Nobody can steal a horse."

"What if the horse isn't reported stolen?" Caitlyn said.

"Oh." Theo was almost violently shivering. "But I'm still afraid something will go wrong."

"Nothing will go wrong." She wondered if she looked as convincing as she tried to sound. "I promise."

## SIXTEEN

Billy Jasper didn't like the dark presence of Mason Lee, who leaned on his left elbow on the counter that divided the front part of the sheriff's office area. He occasionally lifted his uninjured hand to stroke his waxed mustache.

Mason had walked in five minutes earlier, setting his shotgun on the counter. Billy knew who he was—everyone in Appalachia did—and guessed if Mason could walk the streets with the shotgun, it wasn't against the rules to take it into the sheriff's office.

Mason had yet to speak, but Billy could still hear his hard breathing. Maybe he was waiting for Sheriff

Carney, but there was something odd about how Mason's right arm hung at his side and the constant sweat beading on his forehead. Maybe Mason had been injured while cornering the fugitive. All around town, word spread about how the dogs had torn the man apart and how he'd died already. Billy himself had seen the undertaker and his assistants move a coffin from the apartment on the other side of the town square into a wagon.

With Mason close, Billy had looked over only once and felt guilty even for that brief glance. He had specific instructions to watch the computer screen all night. That one glance, however, had shown the bounty hunter staring at Billy hard, with one milky eye wandering in different directions, adding to Billy's discomfort.

Billy was wondering if he should pick up his two-way radio and call for Sheriff Carney when Dr. Ross pushed open the door to the office.

"Billy," Dr. Ross said pleasantly. "Surprised to see you here at this time of night. You going to be here long?"

Billy thought through Sheriff Carney's instructions. He couldn't find any reason not to answer Dr. Ross.

"Hello, Dr. Ross," Billy said. "Sheriff Carney wants me here all night. Can I help you with something?"

"I'm here to set Mr. Lee's broken arm. Might be easier if he lies on one of the cots."

Dr. Ross referred to the two jail cells which could be reached via the door just left of Billy, where he had slept nearly all of the afternoon. More than once, Dr. Ross had come in to tend to someone who had hurt himself while drunk and disorderly, despite Bar Elohim's strict laws against alcohol.

"Where I'm standing is good," Mason grunted from the counter. "Let's get this done."

Billy moved his eyes back to the screen. He intended to do this assignment without any mistakes. He heard a small *thunk* at the counter and assumed it was the doctor's carrying bag.

"It will take some time for the freezing to set," Dr. Ross told Mason. "You'd be more comfortable on a bed. Or at the least, sitting down."

"No freezing," Mason said. "Just set it and cast it."

"If I don't freeze it," Dr. Ross said, "it's going to—"

"Doc, I've stitched myself up with needle and thread before. Don't need you to freeze it. Just set it and cast it and get out of here."

"Your muscles will be in shock around the bone and spasm. I'm going to pull hard. And if there's any bones grating, it will—"

"You don't hear too good. Just get it done."

Billy was grateful that he had his assignment to hold his focus. He didn't want to watch someone have his arm set, especially without freezing.

He wished there were more interesting images on the computer screen though. Just the front and side view of the livery. He was familiar with it, as he'd spent years of his boyhood working the stables. With no movement on the screen, there was little to distract

Billy from the grunting behind him. He did peek over once and saw that it wasn't Mason making the noise, but Dr. Ross, who had to use all his strength to pull Mason's arm into place.

Mason's face was flat. Except for the beads of sweat, he could have been playing a poker game. Billy found this frightening, along with Mason's calculating stare. It seemed to Billy that Mason was paying special attention to the computer screen, but with that one eye drifting, it was hard to tell.

Mercifully enough, the setting only took about a minute. Dr. Ross went into the back room and found water to mix the plaster for Mason's cast, and afterward, wrapping the arm was finished in another couple of minutes. Dr. Ross bid Billy good night, but pointedly said nothing to Mason before stepping back onto the street.

"Did you like the show, boy?" Mason said as soon as the door shut behind Dr. Ross. "Someday you'll tell your grandchildren how you saw a doctor set Mason Lee's arm. Be sure to tell them how the bones grated."

Billy kept his eyes on the computer screen.

"Switch that screen so it shows all the cameras in town by rotation," Mason said. "I'm going to take over that computer now."

"I can't," Billy said. "Sheriff's orders."

"Then maybe your children and grandchildren *won't* be hearing this story."

Billy watched the screen.

"That was a threat, boy. I meant you may not live

long enough to have children. You aren't too dense to understand that, are you?"

This, Billy decided, was one of those questions that didn't need answering.

Mason said, "What's so important about the livery?"

Billy started giving thought as to whether Sheriff Carney would want Mason to know.

"Are you as stupid as you look?" Mason said. "Answer me."

If he had to answer, the question needed consideration. Billy finally said, "I don't know how stupid I look, so I'm not the one who can tell you."

"Why are you watching the livery?" Mason hissed.

"It's sheriff's business."

"My arm's in a cast," Mason said, "but I could still slit your throat. Don't think because you're big that I couldn't do it."

Billy understood, but he was more afraid of Sheriff Carney. Especially after how bad things had gone wrong at Mrs. Shelton's. He pressed his top teeth hard against his bottom teeth. Couldn't say anything to make Mason Lee kill him if he kept his mouth like that.

"So tell me what you're looking for," Mason snapped.

"Sheriff's business." Billy had to say something. But he didn't take his eyes off the screen. He wondered if he'd be able to turn around in time to stop Mason from slitting his throat.

"You're not afraid of me?" Mason asked.

"I know who you are."

"Then you know well enough to tell me what I want to know."

"Sheriff's business," Billy said.

"All right then," Mason said, grinning like he'd decided to toy with Billy. "Guess I'll just stand here and watch with you."

Billy wished Mason wouldn't, but he didn't have any orders to cover what to do with a bounty hunter who worked directly for Bar Elohim. So Billy said nothing when Mason put the shotgun on his lap, pulled up a chair, and moved it within two feet of Billy, who could feel Mason's glare switching between the screen and his face.

It took a few minutes for Billy to grow accustomed to the smell of drying plaster and Mason's acrid body odor. Even so, the next hour was not comfortable for Billy, with Mason's menacing silence so close. At least Billy didn't get drowsy, wondering if Mason would pull out a knife without warning.

Movement appeared on the screen. Mitch Evans, who managed the livery, led a few horses out the rear door.

Billy knew what to do about that. He reached for the radio to call Sheriff Carney.

"This is what Sheriff Carney was waiting for?" Mason said.

Billy was conflicted. Sheriff Carney wanted to know the minute that Mitch Evans appeared on camera. But did Sheriff Carney want Mason Lee to know what Sheriff Carney wanted to know?

"I'm going to leave you here." Billy pushed away his chair, two-way in hand. He'd call Sheriff Carney from the back room where the jail cells were.

"Don't think so."

Billy was surprised a man could move so fast, especially with one arm in a cast. It seemed before Billy could blink, Mason was standing and pressing the shotgun barrel into Billy's spine.

"You'll talk to him right here," Mason said. "But if you say a word about me, there's going to be a big piece of you spread all across that far wall."

Billy obeyed both sets of orders. He informed Carney about Mitch Evans. He didn't say a word to Sheriff Carney about Mason Lee. The sheriff told Billy to stay put.

"You'll have no problem following those orders," Mason said after Billy put the radio back on the desk. "You ever been in one of your own jail cells before?"

"This afternoon," Billy said. "Getting some sleep. And one other time, last week, I accidentally locked myself in. Sheriff Carney got mad at that."

"Well then," Mason said, pushing Billy away from the counter with the shotgun, "you can handle going back in for a while."

# SEVENTEEN

Sheriff Carney stepped from the shadows beneath the eaves of the livery when Mitch Evans began to slide the livery door shut. The horses nearby did not move.

"Got to say I'm disappointed, Mitch," the sheriff said. "You and me go a long ways back."

Carney had his pistol holstered. The two-way was clipped to his belt, but he'd shut it off. No telling when that simpleton Billy Jasper might call to ask about something, and Carney didn't want any distractions here. Didn't want anyone interfering either. If this could lead to finding the girl, Carney wanted this interaction as off-camera as possible.

"Clarence, you about gave me a heart attack," Mitch said in a relaxed voice. "What brings you out after curfew?"

Mitch was slightly bigger, slightly older. In daylight, his face showed a few more wrinkles, and he was losing hair faster than Carney, but in his usual overalls, he cast an impressive shadow. He could crack walnuts with his bare hands.

"I never thought you were the one. But looking back, it makes sense."

"Clarence?"

The sheriff leaned against the edge of the door. "I've been thinking about it all afternoon, how easy it might be for you, like hiding a needle in a haystack of needles."

"It'd be nice if this conversation started making sense, Clarence." Carney guessed Mitch had repeated his first name to emphasize their longstanding friendship.

"You know how things work in Appalachia," Sheriff Carney said. "Bar Elohim is not intrusive in private affairs. Sure, public moments are recorded, and radio chips track the movements of every horse, every day. And you know the argument about how that protects folks in more ways than one. Gives them privacy. Just like the best place to have a secret conversation is in the middle of a party with fifty other conversations around you. Bar Elohim doesn't have the time and manpower to examine more than half a percent of what gets recorded and saved. On the other hand, everyone knows that all of that information is somewhere on the mainframe, and enforcement can use it to unravel just about any crime against God or Appalachia, right?"

"Sure, Clarence. Just seems like a strange time and place to discuss something we both know."

"I was able to track a recent visitor in town," Carney said. "Don't even know his name, just his face. And the fact that he was a wanted man. I tracked him right to your doorstep. You were the only person in town he had any conversation with."

Mitch leaned against the opposite door frame. "Be glad to help if that's why you're here. Lots of folks come to me for horses."

"Not lots of folks with Mason Lee hard on their trail.

Last thing anyone like that wants is a horse that shows Bar Elohim every movement through a radio chip."

"Can't speak for how others think," Mitch said. "I assume you have a photo or something so I can identify him and tell you what I can about his conversation with me."

"Mitch, I'm thinking there's a saddle under the blanket of one of those horses. That would be strange, wouldn't it?"

Mitch straightened a little.

"See," Carney said, "if the horse isn't reported stolen, then there's no reason to track it by satellite, is there?"

When Mitch remained silent, Carney continued. "Someone shows up at night, leaves with the horse, then sends it back when they get to the next town. Is that how it works? Chances are slight that someone in law enforcement would show up and check your horses to see if all of them are accounted for, especially if you only did this every couple of months. And especially if you were good friends with the sheriff, right, Mitch?"

Mitch took a step away from the livery, toward the horses outside the stable.

"All I want is the girl," Sheriff Carney said. "She's coming for a saddled horse, isn't she? Tell me when you expect her, and then maybe I can go easy on you and your family."

Mitch whirled and dove toward Sheriff Carney. It was fast and unexpected. Carney pulled his pistol to clear it from his holster, but he realized he'd made a mistake, playing this conversation so relaxed.

Mitch's broad shoulder hit the sheriff squarely in the chest, knocking him against the wall. His head slammed back with a thud, dazing him. Before he could breathe, Mitch was on top of him, pinning his arms with his legs, sitting squarely on his chest.

Carney was looking straight up, but Mitch's face was in a shadow, and Carney couldn't read it. He tried squirming, but the man was too big. Mitch pushed the gun away from Carney's reach.

"Don't make this worse, Mitch. Surveillance cameras show me getting here. You kill me and nothing will show me walking away. Any investigation leads right to your door. Let me up right now, and let's talk through a way to keep you from being sent to a factory."

"What's wrong with allowing a few horses to travel unsupervised now and then? What's wrong with a little freedom? I'm tired of all this."

"Tired enough for death by stoning?" Carney was trying to think of a way out of this. "Mitch, I don't want that to happen to you. All you need to do is let me know when someone comes to you for an illegal horse."

Then he heard a whirring sound. A sickening thump. Mitch tilted sideways, fell off Carney's chest.

Carney pushed off his hands into a sitting position. It took him a moment, and the light at the entrance of the livery, to make sense of what he saw.

An outline of a man stood in the light. He held a pitchfork like a baseball bat. Poised to strike again.

Carney was in no position to raise his hands to protect himself from the thunderous blow to his head. The pain lasted only a heartbeat, then all sensation disappeared into a black void.

## EIGHTEEN

Leading the horse by the reins, Caitlyn was halfway through the gate when a monstrous figure rose from a low set of bushes just outside the fence. She took a half step backward and nearly lost her grip on the reins.

"You'll have to turn the horse back into the livery. It's past curfew." The voice speaking to her was male. He sounded young—and apologetic.

She had no idea who he was or of his intent. But anyone out after curfew was disobeying the law. She knew she should feel terrified, but so much had already happened, she felt numb. She had to trust her instincts.

She wasn't an expert rider but had spent enough time in a saddle to ride comfortably. She calculated about ten steps between her and the stranger. She turned the horse slightly to put him between her and the man for protection, then stepped into the stirrup with her good leg, ignoring the pain in her injured foot, and swung up quickly into the saddle.

The man had already lunged toward her. Much

quicker than she expected for someone of his bulk. Before she could urge the horse toward the opening in the brush, he took the reins from her.

"I think the sheriff is looking for you," the voice said. "If not, you're still breaking curfew. And stealing a horse."

Caitlyn thought of jumping down and trying to sprint, even with her sore ankle. Theo was back in the trees. Maybe she could warn him as she fled.

But with his other massive hand, the man reached up and locked one of her wrists in his fingers. "I can squeeze harder," he said, "but I don't want to. I don't like hurting people."

Instinct told her this man, large as he was, was telling the truth. She didn't think he wanted to hurt her. Still, fear finally started pumping past her numbness, and she knew she had to escape arrest.

"Then let go of my wrist. You're holding the horse so I can't go anywhere." She rubbed a foot along the ribs. Maybe she could kick the horse hard enough to bolt.

"I think you can. I don't like being fooled either."

"Please let go of me," Caitlyn said. "I haven't done anything wrong."

"Horse stealing is wrong. There's a criminal code for it, but I haven't learned it yet. Otherwise, I'd officially record this arrest on my vidpod."

"It's not what you think," she said.

"I'm not so good at thinking. That's Sheriff Carney's job."

"My job too," said another voice. "Don't know how you got here, but for someone so stupid, you saved me a lot of trouble."

Caitlyn turned her head. From her elevated perspective on the horse, she saw the man approaching from the livery, maybe twenty paces away. It was too dark to see his features, but she recognized the object cradled in his arm.

A shotgun.

Billy didn't like to hurry decision making because he always seemed to decide wrong. Like now. After leaving the jail, he'd decided not to directly approach the livery, because whatever Mason Lee had planned against Sheriff Carney couldn't be good. If Mason was willing to lock Billy up, it wouldn't be smart to just march into the livery when he knew all about the shotgun and what it felt like to have the barrel pressed into his back.

But when he'd raced around to the gate behind the livery, hoping his escape would make up for what happened with Mrs. Shelton, there'd been this girl, stealing a horse. Billy figured she probably had something to do with why the sheriff wanted him to watch the livery and Mitch in the first place, so she must be important. Even if she wasn't important, she was breaking curfew and stealing a horse.

Now what?

Mason was right there, outlined by the light of the livery in the background, pointing the shotgun. In a way,

Billy felt relieved. Immediate control had been taken away from him. He didn't have to make a decision.

One handed, Mason flipped the shotgun around and offered the butt of it to Billy. "You going to tell me how you got out of that jail cell?"

"You're giving me your gun?" Billy was so surprised at the offer of the shotgun that he kept his grip on the girl's wrist.

"One minute you're smart and the next you're stupid. I'm not aiming at myself. 'Course I'm giving it to you . . . now take it. Watch the girl while I take the reins."

"What about Sheriff Carney?" Billy asked as he accepted the weight of the gun.

"He's in the livery," Mason said. "Now you going to tell me how you got out of jail?"

Mason took the horse's reins.

What had the doctor called the big ox? *Billy.* So how had Billy the simpleton escaped the jail cell?

This bothered Mason more than he would let on, as he prided himself on taking care of details. All of them. After locking Billy in the cell, Mason had gone through the sheriff's office and removed all the firing pins from the weapons. Small as the chance was, with what Mason had in mind, there might come the day that Sheriff Carney had a gun on Mason. It wouldn't hurt knowing the weapon was useless.

Mason would find out how the simpleton escaped the cell, but more important was getting the girl secured, like Carney and Evans. After using the pitch-fork handle to knock the men out, bale twine to tie securely both unconscious men, and Evans's bandanna to gag them, Mason dragged them into a feed room. He came out of the livery to look for the girl, whom he had seen leading the horse out through the gate. He'd intended to follow her first to learn what he could about her escape plans. Instead, Billy had sprung up out of nowhere.

Instead of seeing Billy's arrival as a complication, Mason decided that Billy could be of considerable use once they reached the inside of the livery. So before calling out, he'd emptied the shotgun. It hadn't been easy, cracking it open and dropping the shells into his motionless open hand at the end of the cast. Nor had it been easy keeping the shotgun tucked under his good arm so his other hand could transfer the shells into his pockets—one in each so the shells wouldn't clink as he walked.

But after the men were tied and the gun was emptied, the rest of Mason's plans would be easy. They would end with a fire killing Carney and Evans and framing Billy. Mason would be long gone with the canister before anyone figured out what had happened. Long gone, as in free. Outside.

The girl on the horse was silent as Mason turned them both around. She wouldn't be silent for long, he thought, grinning in the dark. Some pleasures would arrive sooner than others.

With Billy behind him, Mason walked the horse

toward the large, open doors of the livery. As he neared the building, he lifted his face into the security lights, making sure the surveillance camera had a good view. According to his plan, the footage would show the girl on the horse's back and the deputy pointing a shotgun at both of them.

Face toward the camera, Mason clearly mouthed a silent word. *Help.*


## NINETEEN

The livery was built with open rafters, wide beams of wood where rats scurried with impunity, heard but unseen in the deep shadows. The fluorescent lighting that hung from the beams illuminated a corridor of clean concrete running between stalls. Billy felt more at home here than with his adoptive parents and certainly more comfortable than in the sheriff's office. He felt a twinge of sadness at the memory of being plucked away from the livery and forced into the deputy position.

He looked at the clean floor with nostalgia and smelled the hay and straw with approval. The horses were still well cared for.

He glanced at the stalls, and some of the horses looked back with various degrees of curiosity. Billy knew many of the horses better than he knew any people.

Here in the light, Billy finally got a better look at the fugitive. She showed no emotion from her perch on the saddled horse. She stared calmly at Mason Lee's back. She was wearing a cloak, with only her hands visible. And, of course, her face.

Billy blinked, hoping he didn't show how his stomach suddenly felt dizzy. At least that's how he would have explained it if he'd ever risked telling anyone what had happened when her eyes met his. Something about her calmness. Mostly her face, drawing him in so that he could hardly breathe.

He forced himself to look away, searching for Sheriff Carney.

"First tell me how you escaped the jail cell, then I'll tell you where to find the sheriff." Billy didn't understand how Mason could have so easily anticipated Billy's next question.

"I had a key," Billy said.

"You had a key."

"Ever since I locked myself in, I kept a key tied to my shoelace. I didn't want to give Sheriff Carney a reason to yell at me if I locked myself in again."

"Blind pig finding an acorn." Mason shook his head in disgust. Billy couldn't tell if Mason was disgusted with Billy or himself.

"Where's Sheriff Carney?" Billy asked.

"It won't matter to you." Mason reached his good arm behind him and pulled out a pistol he'd tucked into his belt at his lower back. "Might as well drop the shotgun. No shells in it."

Billy felt his mouth drop open. No shells. He wanted to open the gun and look but was afraid that Mason would shoot him or the girl.

120

Mason pointed the pistol at the midsection of the girl on the horse. "Toss the shotgun in the hay. You don't want her to be belly-shot. Trust me."

Billy threw it onto the nearby hay.

"Good boy," Mason said, as if speaking to a dog. "Go down to the far end and open the other set of doors. As you work your way back, open each stall and let the horses out. I want them all out in the yard. Then open the yard gate."

"The horses might run loose," Billy said, recoiling from the instructions. This was the worst thing that could happen. Except for a fire.

"Do it," Mason snapped. "If you don't come back, you'll be leaving the girl to die. Understand?"

Billy thought about it long enough to make sure he understood before nodding his head. He wished Sheriff Carney were nearby.

"Go," Mason said.

Billy returned to Mason in less than five minutes. The horses knew his smell and were accustomed to him moving them out in the yard to clean the stalls. Billy couldn't stand it, thinking that some of the horses might have already escaped through the open gate and were wandering into the hills.

"Now fetch some twine," Mason said.

Billy pulled twine loose from a hay bale, seeing no choice but to obey, and he dropped it in front of Mason.

"Help her down," Mason said, standing well clear of

Billy. Still, Billy could smell the man's sweat, like that of a boar.

"I'm sorry," Billy said to her softly, reaching up. "He's Mason Lee. The bounty hunter. I didn't know things would happen like this."

She surprised him with a small, compassionate smile. She didn't struggle. She was light, bracing on both his arms, and her cloak was soft on his face as he set her on her feet. It seemed to Billy that she didn't weigh anything at all, even accustomed as he was to moving things with little effort.

Mason kept his pistol trained on both of them. "Tie her hands. Behind her back."

As he did, Billy saw that her fingers were long, almost like claws. He didn't find it frightening.

"Tie her ankles," Mason said. "Then set her on her back in that hay."

Billy was as gentle as he could be. "I'm sorry," he whispered again.

When he straightened, he noticed for the first time a strange metal canister near the pile of hay. He'd never seen it in the livery before.

"Sit on the floor, raise your knees, and tie your ankles," Mason directed Billy, now pointing the pistol at his midsection.

Billy lowered himself. He cinched the twine until Mason grunted with approval.

"Roll over."

"You can shoot me this way," Billy said. "I'd just as soon see it coming."

122

Mason walked to him and kicked him in the side of the head. It rocked Billy but didn't turn him over.

"You *are* an ox," Mason said, half in admiration. "That'd put any other man down. Now roll over before I shoot the girl."

Billy turned onto his stomach. Mason pounced on his lower back and sat heavy.

"I've got this pistol tucked under my bad arm," Mason said. "But don't think I'd be slow to pull it on you. Both hands behind your back where I can tie them myself."

Billy thought it would be better to die fighting, but the thought of the girl held him back, as he had no doubt Mason would shoot her. Maybe if Billy obeyed, she'd be okay. He knew now that she was the fugitive and worth bounty money. Billy lifted his hands from the concrete and put them on his back. Mason wrapped his wrists with the remaining twine, then stood.

"Not going to shoot you," Mason said to Billy. "That would spoil my fun."

He knelt beside Billy and showed him the long bowie knife he'd pulled from the sheath on his back. He nicked Billy's cheek. The blood felt like tears.

"You shouldn't have crossed me in the sheriff's office," Mason said. "When I'm finished with her, you're next. Then I burn the place down, and you'll take the blame."

"People here know I don't like hurting anyone," Billy said. He heard a sound, like rats, on the rafters. He wanted to keep Mason talking.

"Not after they see the surveillance camera, with you and the shotgun following us into the livery. A person like you would let the horses out before starting a fire, right? That's on surveillance camera too."

Billy thought about it and realized it was true.

Mason laughed. "If only you could see your face and that frown."

Mason stood again and moved to the girl. He pulled the metal canister close and opened the lid and set it beside the girl. White vapor rose from inside.

Mason held the tip of the knife above the girl's belly. "I'm going to cut you wide open. It's all right if you scream. Please do."

He looked back at Billy. "You watching?"

Billy was watching. What he saw was a big rock that fell on Mason's head.


## TWENTY

I did it! I did it!"

Theo dropped from the rafter above Caitlyn into the hay beside her. Wisps of it clung to his hair.

She was breathing heavily in amazement as she watched him hopping around. She wanted to cry. Anything to release the tension. Before the rock knocked against Mason's skull, he'd already turned the knife sideways and used the tip to pull upward on the fabric of her cloak, toying with her. She'd had no doubt he intended to slice through her skin and stomach muscles, gutting her like a deer as he'd promised. What she didn't understand was why.

"I did it!" Theo said. "I did it! I was so scared, crawling on rafters, and I couldn't see anything. I had to aim for the sound of his voice. And I did it."

Caitlyn couldn't cry. She wouldn't allow it. She forced the numbness to return so she could react without emotion and do what needed to be done.

"Get his knife," Caitlyn said. Mason lay beside her, blood pouring from a gash in the top of his head. What if he opened his eyes? Theo wouldn't have a chance against the man. As much as she wanted to stay numb, terror threatened to seep past her defenses. With it would come paralysis.

"The knife!" Theo said. "He was going to cut you open, wasn't he? I heard everything he said. I had that rock and climbed along the rafters, and I was afraid I might miss him because everything was a blur and—"

"The knife!" she snapped. "Now!"

Theo blinked as if she'd slapped him, but she'd have to apologize later. Didn't the boy have any clue about the urgency of their circumstances? She wanted to shake him.

Theo dropped to his knees and felt around. "Where? Where?"

"To your right," Caitlyn said. Less stridently. "We need to go."

"Yes!" Theo said. "Got it!"

His fingers could barely fit around the handle.

"Hold the blade toward you," Caitlyn held her hands in front of her, lifting them away from her body.

Theo moved the knife in place.

"You hold the knife still," Caitlyn said. "I'll do the sawing."

She pulled her arms toward herself, until the twine between her wrists was tight against the blade. She moved her arms up and down, feeling the strands fall apart.

"How did you know I was here?" she asked.

"I was crouched by the gate," Theo said, speaking in a rush of excitement. "I heard everything when the guy with the shotgun got there. I followed into the yard. Then Billy caught me when he was letting the horses out."

"He caught you!" Caitlyn said.

They both looked at the big man—Theo called him Billy—who was silent. On the floor, on his belly.

"He found a rock for me," Theo said. "He told me about the rafters and how to get up there. He told me what I needed to do."

"True?" Caitlyn asked Billy.

He nodded. "He was wandering around out there like he was blind. I stopped him from walking into a wall. I had to show him where to climb the rafters, but he promised he'd save you."

Caitlyn reached down and cut the twine around her ankles. She had so many questions. But this wasn't the time to think or ask.

"I did great, didn't I?" Theo said. "Up on the rafters,

I was afraid. But I made myself do it. I'm brave, right? If I hadn't—"

"Theo . . . later." Terror tugged her from one direction. Numbness another.

"Right. Later." He grinned, unoffended. "But wasn't it great, dropping the rock?"

Caitlyn spoke to Billy. "The bounty hunter will kill you if he finds you tied up after we're gone. You're a witness."

Billy nodded. "He doesn't like me."

He was like a boy in a man's body, trusting, not begging to be cut loose. She might as well kill him herself if she left him trussed. And she understood the horror that he had spared her by sending Theo into the rafters.

"How do we know you won't arrest us if we cut you loose?" Caitlyn asked.

"Hey!" Theo interrupted, before Billy could answer. "I can't go back to the factory. I just can't!"

"Theo, I can't let him get killed."

"I won't chase you," Billy said.

"What if he's just saying that?" Theo blurted. "Don't trust him."

Caitlyn knelt beside Billy with the knife in her hand.

"Maybe we should hit him on the head with the rock," Theo said. "Just a little. To slow him down."

Caitlyn glanced at Mason Lee, unconscious in the hay. She had to weigh the consequences of leaving Billy helpless against the risk to herself if they cut him loose. Again, she looked at the bounty hunter, and she remembered his knife against her belly. Her mouth tightened with anger, and she cut the twine around Billy's wrists. Then she threw the knife down the corridor. "You can roll down there and get it yourself and cut your ankles loose."

That would give them a head start if Billy couldn't be trusted.

"Thank you." Billy's eyes never left her face.

"On the horse," Caitlyn told Theo. The horse had stamped its feet and quivered during the commotion but hadn't spooked. That suited her as it meant it was docile enough to trust. "We don't have much time."

She helped Theo onto the horse, then lightly swung herself up. With Theo sitting in front of her, she urged the horse out of the livery and into the darkness.

Billy stood at the open doors of the livery, staring out at the night that had just swallowed the fugitives. He held Mason's bowie knife, hardly aware it was in his fingers.

Once again, he had to make a decision in a hurry. Should he worry about finding Sheriff Carney first? Or should he stop the escape? He was bound by duty to give pursuit but also bound by a promise not to follow them. The longer he took in deciding, the farther away they would get.

The dizzy feeling in his stomach returned, as he remembered the intensity in her eyes. He decided to give her and the boy as long as possible to flee. It would give Sheriff Carney a good reason to take away the deputy badge. Billy wouldn't have any more of these kinds of troubles.

He felt good about this decision.

The horses were still in the yard. Nothing had happened to spook them. Billy planned to shut the gate and make sure they came to no harm, but first he should tie up Mason's wrists and ankles.

When Billy turned, he saw that it was too late. His eyes were drawn to flames, already racing through the hay.

Then he saw Mason, who stood a few paces from fire. The side of his head was soaked with blood, and some had spilled over his eyebrows, turning his face into a mask. The pistol was tucked beneath his cast-wrapped arm. In his other hand, he held a lit match above another swatch of hay.

Billy took a step inside.

"Stop there." Mason dropped the match into the hay. He drew the pistol out from his armpit and pointed it at Billy.

Billy stopped. A new set of flames sprang into life and raced away from Mason. Billy held the big knife, but it wouldn't do any good against Mason's pistol.

"You don't know how bad I want to shoot you," Mason said.

A loud crack echoed in the rafters over his head. It took Billy a moment to realize that Mason had fired the pistol.

Mason grinned. He lifted the gun chest high and advanced toward Billy. "Your word against mine.

Want to stick around and see who they believe? Start running, or I just might wing you a little."

Billy turned and ran.

Seconds after he made it outside the gate, the horses began to stream through it too, stampeding away from the fire and the smoke.

Mason hurried to the feed shed as the flames started to crackle.

It had taken all his willpower not to spin a slug through Billy's ribs. Bad as he'd wanted to, however, he wanted to get Outside more. Delayed pleasure. With Billy alive and running, on the surveillance camera fleeing the fire, Carney would be forced to hunt down his deputy, clearing the way for Mason to find the girl.

*Perfect.*

As perfect as the injury on Mason's head. Who wouldn't believe Mason's version of the events now?

But he needed Carney around to believe those events. Another kill he'd have to put off for the greater pleasure of getting Outside. Because what was far from perfect was the fact that the girl was gone.

Mason popped open the clasp of the door to the feed room.

The big man who managed the stable was conscious again, coughing and struggling against the twine that bound him.

"Fire," Mason said.

"Cut me loose," the man said. "I can help you with Carney."

"Can't. The boy that set the fire stole my knife."

Mason had no intention of coming back, but if the man somehow survived, Mason didn't want a witness to put him in an awkward spot. "I'll come back for you."

With his good hand, Mason grabbed Sheriff Carney by the ankle.

Mason dragged him out of the room toward the livery doors. All he needed to do was get Carney to the ground outside, but he wanted to be seen on the surveillance camera, and dragging him the extra fifteen yards took so long that when Mason turned back to the livery, the flames inside were dangerously high.

Good, Mason thought. Now, if it came down to it, nobody could fault him for staying out in the open. In a minute or two, it would be too late for anyone else to rescue the stable man.

Which meant Billy would be wanted for arson. And murder.

## TWENTY-ONE

There was enough moonlight to give Caitlyn a clear view of the road. She wished she could put the horse into a gallop. Even a trot. But she was too keenly aware that she and Theo were fugitives, out after curfew, and afraid that the sound of thudding hooves would draw attention.

"I like the moonlight." Theo sat in front of her on the horse. "In the factory, we never saw the moon or stars."

He was leaning back, and she had wrapped an arm around him because he was shivering so badly, but she held the reins in her right hand.

"Hush," Caitlyn said. Any noise unnerved her, even with the sound of the fire engine sirens echoing through the valley. Her focus was on escape. When they cleared the edge of town, she could risk putting the horse into a trot.

The moon cast shadows, and the paved road ahead looked like a pale ribbon that disappeared at the curve of the hill. If she turned in the saddle, she'd be able to see the glow of a fire behind them. The livery. It wasn't her concern, she told herself, and there was nothing she could have done to prevent it.

Her attention returned to Theo's shivering. She realized she'd been too harsh. Would it really endanger them if they whispered a conversation?

"You were brave in the livery," she said. "You rescued me like a hero."

"I did, didn't I?"

She could almost feel him grinning. Little rascal.

"What number after 941 can only be divided by one and itself?" she asked.

Maybe that would put the boy to sleep. There were hours ahead of them, lonely travel on the road. If Theo slept, maybe his shivering would end.

"You really want to know?" he asked. "Really?"

"Really." Caitlyn smiled in the dark.

"Then I'll figure it out and tell you."

For a moment, it seemed peaceful. Without the past and the future on each side of this moment, it would have been idyllic. But the past and the future were inescapable—and were immediately imposing on the tranquillity.

"What's that?" Theo said, sitting straighter. "I hear something."

Caitlyn pulled the reins. Too late. A man on horseback came out of the trees and blocked the road.

He was armed the way Mason had been armed. Shotgun. He swung it up and pointed it at the horse.

Finally. A decision easy for Billy to make.

He'd been following the girl and the boy, staying back far enough not to be seen, wondering exactly how to ask for help without scaring them.

He needed them as witnesses because Mason was right. The surveillance camera did show Billy to be guilty. But to arrest the girl and the boy would be breaking his word. Maybe there was a way, though, that Sheriff Carney wouldn't arrest them. Carney would take away Billy's badge for letting the fugitives go, and Billy could be relieved of his law enforcement duties, maybe even go back to work in the livery. Except it was burned down now, so he'd have to find other work until it was built again.

Billy felt like it'd been a lot of thinking for him, while walking and half jogging to stay close enough to the horse not to lose the fugitives, but far enough back so they didn't know he was there.

They'd turned around, though. Riding just ahead of another man on horseback, also with a shotgun like Mason Lee's.

Billy had no doubt this was a bounty hunter in Mason Lee's gang. A whole band of them were in town. That meant Mason would soon enough have the young woman captive again. Billy also had no doubt that Mason would kill her, if for no other reason than she was a witness to the events in the livery.

Billy stepped into the shadows behind a tree as they approached. He wasn't armed, but he'd have to stop the bounty hunter.

The woman and the boy on the horse passed the tree. Then came the bounty hunter on his horse, holding the shotgun.

Billy turned sideways. The tree probably wasn't wide enough to hide him completely during the day, but the branches would serve as a shroud. He crouched to push off, and he ran forward on his toes, staying bent, coming up behind the horse. A slight scuffing of his shoes on the ground gave him away. The bounty hunter reacted too slowly as he tried to turn in his saddle, and by then Billy was close enough that the hunter couldn't get the shotgun barrel around and between them in time.

One handed, with a powerful heave, Billy grabbed the man by the back of his collar and yanked hard, pulling him loose from the saddle. For a moment, the man hung there, feet flailing. With his other hand, Billy found the shotgun and yanked it loose from the man's grip.

Without letting go of the man's collar, he let the man fall to his feet. Billy threw the shotgun away, so he had a free hand.

The man twisted but couldn't get loose. He swung at Billy with a wide punch that Billy caught in the center of his palm. The smack of flesh echoed.

Billy held the man's fist.

"Stop," Billy said. "I don't like hurting people."

The bounty hunter tried to kick Billy's knee, but his shifting of balance was enough to alert Billy, and with his iron grip on the man's fist, Billy jerked him sideways.

The man kicked at Billy's crotch. When Billy turned and took the blow on his hip, the hunter threw his other fist, catching Billy's eye socket. It felt like his eyeball had exploded in a flash of white. Something else was white too, the explosion of rage inside Billy.

Time and again he'd been pushed around and beat up and mocked. No more. No more pain. As the next fist came swinging in, Billy blocked it with his bicep. He let go of the man's other fist, and for the first time in his life, he threw a counterpunch, hooking it into the man's ribs.

The audible crack surprised Billy. The man sagged.

But it wasn't enough. Billy hooked another one around, pounding the man's head with the side of his fist. As the man was falling, Billy grabbed with both hands and tossed him like a sack of feed.

There was a horrible thump. The man didn't move.

Billy's rage immediately became remorse. But he turned to the bounty hunter's horse, which had side-stepped away in confusion. Billy grabbed the loose reins and pulled it close.

He discovered he was panting, amazed and per-plexed and sorrowful at what he'd inflicted on the bounty hunter.

"Wow," the boy said, teeth chattering. "Do that again."

Billy didn't have time to answer. The young woman pushed Theo against the mane, goaded the horse, and sent it into a gallop.

No time to think either. Billy pulled himself into the saddle of the bounty hunter's horse and began chasing the two fugitives. It took him a couple of seconds to get into the rhythm of the gallop.

Slowly he closed the gap but only because the woman on the other horse was fighting to keep the boy in the saddle. Then the boy fell.

A moment later, she eased out of the gallop and pulled her horse to a stop.

"Keep it walking," Billy said. "Let it cool down. We'll turn it back to Theo."

She hesitated, as if preferring defiance, then kicked the horse's ribs to nudge it forward and away from him.

"I'm all right!" Theo yelled from behind them. "Really."

"You," the young woman accused. "You made a promise not to chase us."

"I did." Billy thought of the unconscious bounty hunter behind them. Or maybe the man was dead. Even if witnesses cleared him of setting the fire, how could he explain that?

"I just want you to record something on my vidpod," Billy said. The horses were breathing hard. "So Sheriff Carney will know what really happened in the livery. 'Cause the cameras make me look guilty. That's all. And now that I might have killed one of Mason Lee's bounty hunters . . . how will anyone believe me if you don't help?"

Billy looked at the girl, waiting for her answer. He held his breath. If he went back to town without something from her, it'd be worse than losing his deputy badge. He'd probably be sent to a factory.

Theo reached them. "Don't want to do that again!"

Caitlyn ignored Theo and cocked her head. "What's your name?"

"Billy Jasper."

"Billy, you think anyone is going to believe anything I say, on the vidpod or even in person? Someone that Mason Lee is chasing? Think they're going to believe that a near-blind kid climbed the rafters and dropped a rock on his head?"

She was right. And better at thinking than Billy. His hopelessness overwhelmed him. "What do I do?"

"Forcing us to go back won't help you."

For the first time that he could remember, a decision

came to Billy with suddenness and clarity. It almost stunned him. It certainly frightened him—but there was no other way.

"Let me come with you two," Billy said.

"You don't know where we're going."

"I know you can't go back. I can't either."

For several long moments, she studied him. Billy held his breath again.

"Hand me your vidpod."

He was surprised at how much her answer disappointed him. He'd been ready to change his life with that simple decision. Now he'd have to go back and hope her testimony would protect him from the factory.

He unclipped the device from his belt. She held her hand out for it. Instead of speaking into it, with a quick movement of her cloaked arm, she flung it into the trees.

It was far more shocking to Billy than if she'd pulled out a shotgun. He couldn't even react by speaking.

"There it is, Billy Jasper. You can go look for your vidpod. Or you can join us."

# DAY THREE

*Caitlyn, unlike you, I could not entirely endure the solitude inflicted upon us by the deep and rugged valleys of the Appalachians. In the years before we joined the collective, on Sundays, at times, I would lock the door and leave you in the cabin for a few hours and go to church. I first went because it was the safest way to lose myself anonymously in a small crowd; I could listen to others and make small talk when pressed, without placing myself into an intimate conversation or friendship. The music offered distraction. I enjoyed listening to unsophisticated preachers and dissecting their sermons for errors in logic, syntax, science, and omission. That was my weekly entertainment. Yet truth is a diamond; even mishandled, smeared with grease, or buried in mud, it cannot be marred and waits for one with a cloth to polish it clean. That was how God spoke to me again. Through those ignorant preachers. I finally understood, despite their manipulative distortions.*

*As a scientist, I had never found it difficult to acknowledge that there was a Creator behind this universe—the marvels of DNA, the exquisite dance of electron and proton, the boggling forces of gravity and light; all of it forced many of us in science away from agnosticism. Yet to comprehend that this Creator loved us more deeply than I loved you, Caitlyn, gave my life renewed meaning.*

*Deep in the Appalachians, I had found the most important diamond any man can find—God loved me and forgave me, even with you as a daily reminder of how terribly I had sinned . . .*

## TWENTY-TWO

As the fog of morphine faded, Jordan's nerves shrieked with a pain that brought him back to consciousness. His throat was so constricted, it felt like each breath was a red-hot iron into his lungs. His body raged with thirst. His muscles were like heavy granite, and he couldn't even turn his head.

He was on his back. Narrow cracks of light pierced the darkness around him. Trying to make sense of it, he blinked.

He willed himself to lift his right hand. Nothing.

It wasn't only that he was constricted by bindings. His hand simply *would not* move. Nor his fingers. No amount of willpower could force them to wiggle in the slightest. Nor his toes.

He tried to speak into the darkness. But his jaws were slack, his vocal cords mute. He was totally paralyzed.

Yet Jordan's nerves registered enough sensory awareness to feel where the weight of his body pressed on his back and his buttocks and his legs. He realized, too, that even if he could speak, there was a gag around his mouth.

If he was paralyzed, why did he still have sensations? What had happened? He remembered the dogs rushing toward him, remembered bits and pieces of moving through the night as he alternated between consciousness and the welcome relief of a black void without time. He even remembered a bed and a man leaning over him. Then the black timeless void again. Until now.

More blinking as he ignored the screaming pain and tried to make sense of where he was.

His vision became accustomed to the darkness, and he could see peripherally that whatever enclosed him was hardly more than the width of his body.

As if he'd been put in a cheap, unlined coffin.

"I heard people just disappear," Theo said. He was on the horse, now sitting behind Caitlyn, his hands gripping the sides of her cloak. "Or they become floaters. But no one explained that. What's a floater?"

Billy led the horse by the reins, walking. After taking care of the bounty hunter, he'd walked all night, letting Caitlyn and Theo sleep in the saddle.

"There's a dam as part of the divide," Caitlyn said. "One of the rivers that feeds the lake comes from the Clan area. It's how the Clan gets rid of people who enter their valley. Strapped on planks of wood, floating down to the lake on the river. Floaters."

The sky was just beginning to turn from black into the first shades of gray, showing the dark outlines of the tops of the mountains on each side of the narrow valley.

"What about people who disappear?" Theo asked. He still shivered, as if morning could be nudged along by shaking it. "Do they make it out? How do they make it out?"

"I don't have the answers. Billy? What do you know?"

Caitlyn watched Billy's broad back leading their way. She felt warm gratitude at his uncomplaining endurance. She'd been awake for a while in the saddle, holding the unregistered vidpod in her other hand to establish their position.

Billy turned toward her but smiled shyly and ducked his head, unable to meet her eyes. "Don't know. Nobody knows how the Clan does it . . . or if they do, really. Sheriff Carney says it's all just stories. But if someone makes it Outside, we'd never know, right?"

His first words, all night.

He smiled again. She felt compassion and wanted him to relax. "I'm glad you're with us."

"Where are we?" Billy asked, as if unable to accept a compliment.

Without road signs and vidpod GPS, an artificial software voice directing them, Caitlyn knew he couldn't tell. But the GPS signals gave the location to both those traveling—and those watching them.

"I'd rather not tell you," Caitlyn said. "But we're almost ready to go up into the hills."

A half mile ahead, according to her vidpod, maybe twenty more minutes of travel, there would be a fork, with one road leading into an even narrower valley. It wasn't much of a margin. In less than half an hour, nightly curfew would be lifted, and other travelers would be on the road.

"She's like that," Theo mumbled. "She keeps secrets."

143

"I have to," Caitlyn said.

"Why?" Billy asked.

Caitlyn didn't answer. She was doing her best not to think of all the reasons, not to think of Papa, not to think about what they were fleeing or what was ahead. She wanted to stay numb, without allowing the weight of the seriousness to push through and allow the grief to cut at her again.

Theo leaned forward. Although the early morning air was humid and warm, his teeth chattered as he spoke. "All of it's secret. Who she is. Why the bounty hunter wants her. She doesn't really want us with her, but she's afraid if she doesn't keep us near, we'll tell the authorities the last place we saw her."

"Is that true?" Billy asked her. She saw by his wide, honest face that there was no possibility of guile ever hiding his thoughts.

"I don't know why Mason Lee wants me, but as you can see, it's not to be friends." A slight shiver took her as she remembered the knife plucking at the fabric above her belly, the hot breath of the bounty hunter, and the unnatural excitement gleaming in his eyes.

Billy waited a few seconds. "And the rest of it? That you don't want us?"

Caitlyn wished Theo hadn't been so direct. The letter from her father had been very specific. He wanted her to travel in secrecy.

"I won't run away on you, I will tell you that." When the time came, she'd ask them to let her go.

"She can read," Theo said. "Did you know that?"

"Theo!" The boy had a natural ability to exasperate her. Caitlyn's voice was softer as she addressed Billy. "I can't tell you what's ahead. I don't know, and I have to protect whoever will help get us Outside."

"You really think you can get us Outside?" Billy asked. "No one makes it past the divide."

A twenty-five-foot-tall electric fence surrounded the entire perimeter of Appalachia, its top laced with coils of barbwire. There was a quarter mile of cleared land on each side to reach it, mined with motion sensors and heat detectors, monitored by security cameras. All of the technology had been tested and proved for decades along the U.S.-Mexico border.

"Have you seen the divide?" Theo asked Billy. "I've only heard about it."

"Once, when we were kids. The church took us there and explained that the fence was meant to keep Outsiders from getting in. One of the boys got a whipping for saying Outsiders never try to get in. We were all forced to take turns with the whip."

"We can't get too close." Theo shook his head violently. "We might end up floaters. I heard the Clan always gets people who try to make it past them. They trap them, and sometimes they barbecue 'em and hang them from trees."

"We're not going into the Valley of the Clan," Billy said. "Right?"

Both looked at Caitlyn for a response.

"You don't have to come with us," Caitlyn said to

Billy. "I'll understand if you want to turn around now."

"Are you kidding?" Theo blurted. "They think he burned the livery. That's five factory years. He let you throw his vidpod into the trees. When they find it, that's another two factory years. He nearly killed a bounty hunter. Ten more years. If he turns back now, he'll be in a factory until he dies of old age!"

Billy's eyebrows furrowed deeply. "I got nowhere to go. Except with the two of you, so that's where I'm going."

"It's worse than that." Caitlyn tapped the unregistered vidpod. Although it could not be tracked by Bar Elohim, it still accepted the universal broadcast messages. One had been sent across Appalachia a few hours earlier. "There's already a fugitive alert."

She showed them. Billy's photo filled the small screen. He looked earnest and slightly dazed. A reward was offered to anyone who sighted him. Yet another reason they needed to be off the road before curfew lifted.

"A man named Mitch Evans was in the livery," Caitlyn said. "He died in the fire. Billy's wanted for murder."

## TWENTY-THREE

Pierce opened the door of his temporary housing. He held a cup of coffee in his hand. Bad coffee. He missed Outside. This country was so controlled, his cell phone couldn't access Outside, nor could he get an Internet connection. It was an information vacuum here. With bad coffee.

The sheriff stood in the hallway. Clean, pressed uniform. Straight posture. Nothing on Carney's face betrayed any indication of what he was thinking. Nor did it show the least signs of exhaustion.

*Impressive,* Pierce thought. The guy had to be in his fifties. The night before, he'd been knocked out and dragged from a fire. Then he spent an hour at the blaze helping firefighters and another half hour supervising the removal of a charred body from the feed room. Plus another hour reviewing surveillance tapes of the scene. The only thing about Carney that hinted at the previous night's events was the smell of smoke, probably from his hair. Pierce had been there too; showering and shampooing three times hadn't done much to get rid of the smell.

"I've sent an alert out to every town," Carney said. "Right after dawn, each sheriff will be sending people down all the roads. There's a vidpod warrant out on my deputy. A mandatory alert, which every person in Appalachia will see. The reward offered is big enough that he won't be able to move anywhere."

"Where's Lee?" Pierce asked. Pierce gestured for Carney to step inside, but the sheriff stayed where he was in the hallway, hands relaxed at his side.

"Stopped by my office this morning and told me he was done. He gathered his men and dogs and left town an hour ago."

"From what I heard, Mason Lee never quits. Told me himself, more than five times a day." Pierce's coffee was getting cold, but he drank it anyway, then hid his grimace at the taste. Starbucks had been a monopoly as long as anyone could remember. Appalachia wouldn't even let them inside the divide.

"He said his broken arm made it impossible to be part of this."

"Suddenly the pain is too much? Everyone talked about how he had it set without anesthetics."

"Maybe it wasn't the pain. Maybe it was how it got broken." Carney lifted an eyebrow, clearly waiting for how Pierce would respond.

Pierce expected that the waitress at the diner had watched his encounter with Lee from a hidden viewpoint. The noise of the crashing table had only scared her from sight, he imagined.

"A man like him needs to be careful," Pierce answered.

"So does a man like you," Carney said. "A man like him is apt to appear out of nowhere and strike like a snake. Don't like it much that I owe him my life. Nor that I might have to protect yours."

"I'll be fine on my own, Sheriff."

"You won't be on your own." Carney pulled his vidpod out of his shirt pocket and gestured to indicate that it was recording. "You and I will be working together more closely until you leave Appalachia."

Under the scrutiny of Bar Elohim, Pierce understood.

"Make sure to be at my office as soon as you're ready," Carney continued. "I'll expect you there."

Carney gently set the vidpod on the floor, stepped inside Pierce's apartment, and shut the door with a loud click. He walked past the couch where the fugitive had died earlier, moved into the bathroom, turned on the shower, walked back to the doorway of the bath, and waited for Pierce to come closer.

"I'm your baby-sitter." Carney spoke in a low voice. "I don't expect you to like it, but that's the way it is. The sooner I can get you out of Appalachia, the better it will be for the both of us."

"Fine with me." Pierce held his coffee mug tighter. "What have you got on your deputy and the horses? What about that kid with the girl? Any ID? You guys have face recognition software, right? Database of everyone in Appalachia?"

"Not so fast. I'd like to know about the canister. Mason had it when he came into the livery with the girl. Showed up clear on the surveillance footage."

"Doesn't work that way," Pierce said. "I'm not your resource. You're mine. Go ahead and confirm it with Bar Elohim."

"It does work that way." Carney's hands and arms

weren't relaxed any more. His hairline shifted as his face tightened. Slightly. A man had to be watching close to see it. Pierce filed the poker tell away. "We might as well make that clear. I'm not afraid of Bar Elohim. There's more to all of this than meets the eye, and I want to know what's happening. You don't like it, I'll book you on murder charges, and you'll be in the jail cell waiting for me to return from collecting the deputy. You might think you have the juice to get released, and you do. But how many days do think it will take for the international politics to work themselves out?"

"Who'd I kill?" Pierce wasn't sure whether to be amused or irritated by the older man's plan.

"No one. I just lay charges."

"Not much evidence for a murder charge."

"None," Carney said. "But it'll still take time to clear your name after an accusation from the sheriff. Then, too bad, it will appear like I made a big mistake. Nothing I won't survive. And about the time the murder charge gets cleared, I'll put in a couple of heresy indictments, and Appalachian politics will force Bar Elohim to take my side until that's sorted out. You'd spend a week in jail. Maybe two. Understand?"

Pierce nodded. He would have made the same threats himself. "I understand you won't be treated like hired help. Fair enough."

"The canister."

"You want the deputy," Pierce said. "I want the girl.

I'll help you with what you need. But the canister is off the table. And really, you don't want to know."

Carney's hairline dropped fractionally. Pierce took this as a good sign, and he started with a basic question. "Who was the boy with her? His face showed up on the footage clearly too."

"Had him on an electronic warrant. He's a factory runaway. Best guess is she found him somewhere in the woods."

"And your deputy?" Pierce said. "I'd like to know how she convinced him to help."

"Me too," Carney answered. "All I can tell you right now is where he threw his vidpod. About a mile away. Don't expect to find his body with it, but had to send someone to look."

"And the horses from the livery?"

"All except one are accounted for. GPS shows it's stationary, a few miles outside of Cumberland Gap. Want to walk there? Or do you know how to ride a horse?"

"I saw an official vehicle parked by the courthouse. Each town has one, right? We could be there in a few minutes. Mason Lee told me the procedure. You get the engine computer unlocked via satellite."

"Just so you know, if we take the car, it also unlocks the live video and audio monitors inside."

Pierce gulped the last of his coffee. "Horse sounds good."

## TWENTY-FOUR

Factory 22 was set against a postcard-perfect background of forested hills, one mile downstream from Cumberland Gap. Appalachia's economic system had evolved to a perfect symbiosis; each town supported a factory, and each factory provided the town with necessary employment opportunities.

The exterior of 22 was structurally identical to all other factories in Appalachia: a low, one-story brick structure with solar panels, prison-style fencing, and guards at the gate. A lane ran from the gate through a manicured lawn and tasteful landscaping.

Mason Lee was alone, without shotgun, when he approached the guard at the gate, a soft-bellied man in his midforties, whiskers roughly shaven.

"I have authorization." Lee anticipated the guard's question and pulled out his vidpod. "Let's make this fast."

It seemed that the guard became deliberately slow as he unclipped his own vidpod. Mason resisted the impulse to whack the man on the side of the head with his cast.

"Ready," the guard finally said.

Lee beamed his authorization via infrared. The guard peered at his screen, and Mason could hear the words from a vidcast from Bar Elohim.

"Give this man unescorted access anywhere he wants in 22."

*Unescorted access.*

This, coming from the image of the face of Bar Elohim, caused the guard's eyebrows to rise, and to Mason's satisfaction, the insolence disappeared. The guard nearly tripped over himself to open the gates.

Mason Lee was inside.

"Tell me about the dead fugitive," Carney said. "Jordan Brown."

The sun was clearing the mountaintops to the east, and they were only halfway through the five miles to where GPS showed the livery horse was waiting.

"What does it matter?" Pierce said from his saddle. "The man's dead. Well on his way to being buried, I assume."

"I know who he is," Carney continued as if Pierce hadn't dismissed him. "Face recognition software and mandatory registration. I pulled up the information within twenty minutes of snapping his image in the apartment with my vidpod. He arrived at the collective, one of our labor communities, ten or twelve years before that. We can't be sure, because it was before mandatory registration. No record of her birth certificate, so that doesn't help me pinpoint it any better. My guess? He fled here from Outside just after she was born. So tell me why Outside suddenly wants him for a crime committed almost twenty years ago?"

Carney was making simple deductions. Jordan hadn't committed any crimes inside Appalachia, so he must have done it Outside. That would have been before the completion of the perimeter fence, an extensive construction project that divided Appalachia from Outside sixteen years earlier. Unlikely that Jordan would have slipped into Appalachia after that. Even less likely that he'd found a way inside within the last five years, after mandatory face registration had been imposed. A registered population meant a controlled population. Jordan wouldn't have been able to work or find housing without allowing his facial features to be indexed; had he tried, he would have shown up on law-enforcement lists that cross-referenced warrants from Outside.

Jordan clearly slipped in while the fence was being built and found a way to establish himself as a collective worker before face registration.

The girl was from Outside too. Her age dictated it, unless Jordan had adopted her once he was inside. But in Carney's experience, fugitives didn't saddle themselves down. The only explanation was that he'd fled with her.

There was something else. Jordan was dead. Pierce still wanted the girl, but they both knew she hadn't committed any crime.

What did this mean? What was it about the canister that Pierce refused to discuss? Carney wanted to know but reasoned he needed to come at it sideways.

"What was Jordan Brown's crime?" Carney asked again. "And why the interest now? After all those years he'd been gone from Outside, how did you find him?"

"We'd both be better off if I didn't answer that."

"The more I know, the better my chances of helping you find the girl before Mason Lee." Carney wasn't going to push much harder than that. This monitored conversation, after all, could be reviewed at any time, now or in the future, by Bar Elohim.

They rode in silence for about a hundred yards. Jordan had died. Instead of the agent leaving Appalachia at that point, he was still here, enduring a horseback ride. What could the girl have that was so valuable? Carney considered the silver canister, but he couldn't come up with a reasonable answer.

"I'll tell you what I can," Pierce finally offered. "We learned about Jordan because of a surgeon. Dr. Vadis. He comes into Appalachia on a rotating basis."

Carney nodded for Pierce to continue. He didn't need an explanation of visiting surgeons. Appalachia was too small for specialized medical care. Instead, Outsiders came in on visas.

Carney squinted. "If a visiting surgeon passed on information to you, that tells me something troubling."

"Not even close." Pierce shook his head. "We'd like them to help us, but they refuse to break patient confidentiality."

"I don't understand, then."

"Dr. Vadis is a second-generation surgeon. His father, Dr. Vadis Senior, spent nearly a decade as a visiting surgeon before him. Our man showed up expecting to see Dr. Vadis Senior."

"You know this because . . . " Carney waited. Pierce seemed to be struggling with reining his mare but began talking again after she settled.

"Jordan Brown handed a large envelope with x-rays to Dr. Vadis's nurse. He told the nurse that Dr. Vadis would understand, assuming the senior Dr. Vadis, who had taken the x-rays, was the visiting doctor. The son knew nothing about the x-rays, and when he stepped outside his office to ask Jordan about the them, Jordan took them and left without identifying himself."

"X-rays of Jordan?"

"They were the girl's films," Pierce answered.

"Come back after initial surgery how many years earlier?"

"Twelve or thirteen. There's no record of the x-rays or a surgery in the doctor's office."

"So something on the x-rays was significant enough that Jordan expected a surgeon to remember them well over a decade later. Had the surgeon operated on the girl?"

"You asked how we found Jordan. I'm answering. Vadis, the son, made copies of the x-rays before coming out to ask Jordan questions. When Jordan left so abruptly, that raised more questions. The doctor took the copies back Outside with him and started asking around. Which eventually led our agency to the films."

"You won't tell me what was on the them?"

"It took about a month to track Jordan down because

he'd lied about his name at the doctor's office. We found him at a collective. Or rather, we knew he lived at a collective. When I got there to arrest him, he wasn't there, but his registered vidpod was."

"Interesting."

"The short version is that he'd been doing that for years, disappearing for two or three days at a time, unreported by the collective."

"You mean," Carney said, "protected by the collective. Where'd he go?"

"Your guess is as good as mine. Each time he went, he was taking a big risk. Five years in the factory if caught without his vidpod, right?"

"The collective knew this and told you."

Pierce nodded. "Serious trading was done to get this information. We got full disclosure; the collective suffered no penalties."

This was big, Carney thought, if Bar Elohim authorized that kind of immunity. "Why didn't you arrest him when he returned to the collective?"

"First thing I did after the initial interview with the head of the collective was go to the cabin to get the girl, but she was gone. Someone had warned her while I was interviewing. Jordan never returned to the collective. I can only presume he was reached before he headed back home and he had arranged to meet the girl. That's when Mason was brought in to track them down."

"I've got two questions," Carney said. "Why would the collective protect him all those years by letting him go places unregistered and by warning him about you? What was on the x-ray?"

"You'll only get the answer to the first question," Pierce said. "The collective protected him because he wasn't just a laborer. Jordan had been providing everyone in the collective with medical care for years."

Maybe that was significant, Carney thought. But the real significance was in what didn't get answered— what was it about those x-rays that made the girl so important to Outside?

Whatever it was, Carney couldn't help but think it had something to do with the canister.

## TWENTY-FIVE

A man's voice descended into the dark hell that surrounded Jordan. "Heard Mason's dogs ripped this guy apart. Wonder what he looks like."

"You suggesting opening a sealed coffin lid?"

Jordan's heart hammered. Although he'd become accustomed to the confinement and had assumed the worst, confirming his suspicion that he was in a coffin triggered new horror. He was entombed. He tried to yell into the gag filling his mouth, but nothing happened.

Rescue was less than a foot above him. Just a thin layer of wood away. He willed his feet and hands to move, but his body wouldn't obey him. He had to get out. The claustrophobia was overwhelming but still not so strong that Caitlyn was out of his thoughts. Where was she? Did she need his help?

"Wasn't saying we should do it. Just wondering."

Jordan's world tilted. Then he rolled against the side of the box as an outside force lifted it.

"Come on," Jordan heard. "The funeral wagon's waiting. And I'm hungry."

Despite their silence, it wasn't difficult to feel the rhythm of motion and realize that two men were carrying him. The cracks of light grew dimmer and brighter and dimmer again, giving Jordan more clues of movement. Until the light became so bright he could see the rough interior of wood.

The brightness told him that he was outside. Bird sounds confirmed it.

Then he heard a flat smacking sound while the box shuddered with the vibration of impact. The front end of the coffin had been dropped onto the wagon, he imagined.

It slid forward, then Jordan heard departing footsteps, along with the lighter slap of leather. Like reins. He felt a roll into motion.

The funeral wagon was taking him away. To be buried alive.

The factory foreman wore khaki pants and a freshly ironed white shirt. He sat in a cage above the factory floor. The sides of the cage were made of glass for an unimpeded view in all directions, and the floor of the cage was thick Plexiglas. He sat behind a desk in the cage, with a set of controls on the side of the desktop. The cage hung beneath a monorail system that matched the pattern of the assembly line below. By pushing the control buttons, he was able to take the cage anywhere on the factory floor and directly view any of the dozens of children who produced computer chips.

Mason Lee stepped into the cage, knowing the foreman had been alerted for his arrival and his protected status.

"Out," Mason said.

The foreman raised his palms, as if warding off a blow. He moved away from the desk, past Mason, onto the upper deck of the factory.

Mason spent plenty of time in the factories. It was surprising how often one of the imprisoned would give out information, even hurting someone else, if it gave the prisoner some creature comforts. Without hesitation, Mason pushed the start button to move the glass cage along the monorail.

He moved above the dozens of children who worked on the smaller computer parts, their fingers much more dexterous than adults'.

Farther down the line, Mason zeroed in on the one prisoner he needed. He stopped the cage, then put his hands on the levers to control the hydraulics.

The factory was white, sterile, dustless, and nearly noiseless. The fifty children under the age of ten who stood in a long line at the conveyor belt barely made a sound. The workers wore white gowns.

Tasha stood behind her son, fifteenth in the line. He held a tiny Phillips-head screwdriver and was assembling the back cover of a communications device to be shipped Outside.

"That's thirty-one," she whispered. "You need to hurry up. You're five behind for this hour."

He answered without turning his head. "My stomach hurts."

"I'm sorry, baby. Just a couple more hours." She heard a sound that ripped her heart. Her boy was crying. Worse, a monitor had drifted over.

"Silence!" The teenage monitor glared.

Tasha wanted to strike out, but she knew the consequences.

The monitor glanced at a digital readout in front of Tasha. "He's falling behind."

"He's sick. If you'd just call the foreman."

The boy sneered and shook his head. "Not on my shift."

Tasha gritted her teeth, holding back a reflexive reply. She turned away, disgusted with the monitor, then recoiled and brought a knuckle to her lips. The foreman's cage dropped silently to the floor behind her.

And leering at her from inside was the face from her nightmares.

Mason saw the woman's reaction as the cage slowed to a stop. He merely crooked his finger to beckon her inside.

She obeyed, like a zombie. That's the way it was. Once he owned a person, he owned that person forever. Her walk was a broken shuffle. He hoped she'd been walking like that since the day he placed rats beneath a bucket turned upside down on her husband's belly. She'd been too stunned to make any noise above the hiss of the blowtorch, but after the first rat emerged from her husband's side and Mason told her that her son would be next, she agreed to tell Mason about the small network of friends who also owned books.

She opened the glass door to the cage.

"Inside," Mason said. "And shut the door."

He studied her. Since he'd arrested her for teaching her children to read, a year in the factory had dulled her hair, added flesh to her face, turned her complexion to the whiteness and texture of dough. Not much pleasure for the taking now, he thought, although the fear in her expression was a pleasant echo of their last occasion together.

"Walk around to this side of the desk." Mason didn't rise from the chair. "You're going to help me with something."

She began to walk. No protest.

Mason hit the hydraulics and raised the cage. He waited until they were high above the floor again.

"Your fourteen-year-old daughter is at this factory too," Mason said. "You obey me completely, or I might drop the cage on her. I'll see if she sounds anything like her mother when she screams."

162

The woman's head dropped, and he felt a warm tingling in his chest.

Mason stayed in his chair. "There's a vidpod in front of me. It's got writing on it. Read me what it says."

She hesitated. "Reading is illegal."

"So is what I did to you after your husband died. Need a reminder?"

He didn't lift the vidpod toward her. Power meant that he could wait until she reached for it.

Slowly, she did. She frowned as she saw the screen of the vidpod. "There's not much there and it doesn't make sense."

He rabbit-punched her in the belly. As she collapsed forward and brought her face down, he backhanded her across the cheek, straightening her again.

"Good Christians, like good soldiers, don't ask questions," he said. "It wasn't your choice to decide whether it makes sense. Only to answer my question. What does it say?'

"Three p.m. Every day for the next week. Brij will guide you."

The tingle increased for Mason. Not only because of her abject weakness, but because what she read made him nearly certain that his hunch about the unregistered vidpod had been correct. And because of what the knowledge would be worth to him.

He hid this satisfaction. "On your knees and beg that I'll leave your daughter alone."

Immediately, she fell to her knees. Mason locked eyes with her. She didn't even have the willpower to reach up and wipe the blood that trickled from the side of her mouth.

"Please don't hurt her," she said.

"You'll do anything I want?"

She glanced around. "This cage is glass. People will see—"

He lashed again, the smack echoing in the hush of the small cage. "Good Christians, like good soldiers, don't ask questions."

"I'll do anything you want. Just don't hurt her."

"Then look at something else for me," Mason said. He grabbed the vidpod and touched the screen several times until a graphic loaded. This was the image that had first given him an idea of why the fugitive had been carrying the vidpod.

"This." Mason had his thumb and forefinger pinched together on the screen. Leaving them on the screen, he spread them apart, making the image bigger. He held the vidpod screen in front of her so she could see clearly what he meant.

$$\Delta \, \vartheta \, \Sigma \, \Omega$$
$$\varsigma \, \theta \, \lambda \, \varphi$$
$$\phi \, \beta \, \alpha \, \psi$$
$$\Phi \, \notin \, \propto \, \not\subset$$
$$\in \, \Pi \, \pi \, \mu$$

"You've seen symbols like these before, haven't you," Mason said. "You even know what it means—3 p.m., every day for a week."

It seemed like the answer was stuck in her throat. She stared at his chest.

"Think of your daughter. Is this a time you want to lie to me?" He used his voice to caress her.

She lifted her eyes back to his.

"I can't read," Mason said. "But symbols like these were on the sheet of paper that your husband threw into the fire."

When Mason burst into their house, the husband's first move had not been to protect his family, but to race from the kitchen table with a sheet of paper, toward the fire, ignoring the warning blast from Mason's shotgun.

"Yes," she whispered.

"You and your family were going to try to reach the Clan. Who delivered the paper?"

"You tortured my husband for those answers. He was telling you the truth when he said he didn't know. Don't you think he would have told when the . . . the . . ."

She was near hysteria now, certainly remembering the rats.

"You had a GPS location? And a message with it?"

On the fugitive's vidpod in front of him, there'd been a point marked on the map of the Valley of the Clan. Beside it, the message she'd just translated. *Three p.m. Every day for a week. Brij will guide you.*

That's where they'd be waiting for the fugitive Mason killed. No other explanation.

She let out a deep breath. She nodded. "A time and a location."

"And the symbols? Were all the symbols the same?"

"I can't remember. One was underlined too. A different one than on the screen."

"What do the symbols mean? How were they going to help you escape?"

"I don't know."

"But your husband did."

She shook her head. "He would have told you. He was a strong man, but what you did . . ."

Again, she sobbed and couldn't finish.

"Look at me," Mason said.

Her chin trembled, but she stared at his eyes.

"If there's anything you're not telling me, I'm going to find out. And when I do, I'll be back. Not for you. What do the symbols mean?"

"I don't know." She was stronger now. Mason took that, combined with her uncontrollable tears, as a sign that she was telling the truth.

He began to lower the cage and said nothing until it was at the level of the factory floor again. When the door opened, he pointed for her to leave and deliberately waited until she reached the doorway, almost free of him.

"Your daughter's name, Melissa, right?"

It froze her. He spoke to her back.

"I only live but a few miles over the next hill," he finished. "You tell anyone about this conversation, Melissa is mine. Alone. At my cabin. It will only be a day, but she'll come back years older. Nod if you understand."

She didn't turn back toward him, but nodded. She left the cage the same way she'd approached it. With a shuffle as broken as her spirit.

Mason leaned back in his chair. On the way back up in the cage, he gave some thought to returning for the daughter. If he didn't escape Appalachia, he'd sure be in the mood for solace.

## TWENTY-SIX

Caitlyn had been instructed to look for the third post on the downstream side of the railing. A small cross would be scratched into the paint at the base of the post.

She saw it there, even without her vidpod GPS confirming this was the location.

A pile of jagged, fist-sized stones also sat by the post. Nothing in her instructions had mentioned this, but to Caitlyn, as to anyone else in Appalachia, the stones were an ominous reminder of Bar Elohim's power.

"Stop here." Relieved as she'd been to see the small cross scratched at the base of the post, the jagged stones compressed her urgency.

Billy complied. Theo felt warm as he leaned back against her on the horse. He had spoken little since they'd resumed their ride down the road, with Billy still walking and holding the reins.

They stood by a bridge with white railings, some thirty feet over a small river lined with trees on both sides.

"It's here," Caitlyn said. The accuracy of the instructions she could obviously trust, but she'd spent the last few hours of silence wondering if she could still believe the same about her father. He had abandoned her. Yet she still agonized over wondering if he was still alive, and she could hardly deal with the guilt of surviving. And the guilt for doubting him. But the secrets he'd kept hidden haunted her. Why? What was ahead?

Billy, she noticed as she drowned in second thoughts, seemed unburdened by hardly a thought at all. He lifted the sleeping Theo down and set him at the side of the road. Caitlyn began to swing off the saddle, and Billy moved immediately beside the horse, holding up his arm for her to lean against. She made sure that her cloak was covering her arms and the hunch on her back before she accepted his help. Her ankle spasmed in pain, and she transferred most of her weight to the other leg. Yet another reminder that Papa had abandoned her.

"This is what we'll do," Caitlyn said, choosing action to hold the thoughts at bay. "We keep the saddle and send the horse down the road. The next town is over the hill. Someone will find the horse soon, and without the saddle, it'll look like a runaway horse."

Billy began to unbuckle the cinch of the saddle. They'd taken this horse from the bounty hunter. He couldn't report it; they'd left him tied to a tree. "We go through the woods?"

"No," Caitlyn said. "We'll take the river."

"How?" Theo's voice was dull, barely audible.

"Canoe. It will be hidden in a bush below." Caitlyn had instructions for where to find and eventually leave the canoe and look for a trail.

"Where to?" Theo asked.

"The Clan." Just two words. But they felt so heavy.

"I don't want to go," Theo said.

"After everything else you've done to get here?" Caitlyn glanced over. Theo rolled to his side, tucking his hands as a pillow beneath his head.

"I didn't say I wouldn't go." His words had begun to slur. "I just said I don't want to. I'm afraid. But not afraid enough to keep me from trying to get Outside. I'd rather be barbecued than go back."

Billy held the saddle under one arm. "Now?"

"Now," Caitlyn answered. "Let's hide the saddle under the bridge."

With his free hand, Billy smacked the horse solidly on the hindquarters. It bolted forward, and at the other end of the bridge, it settled into a trot.

To Theo, she said, "Wake up. We're ready."

Theo opened his eyes. "Can you hear it? Drums. Coming down the road."

Caitlyn couldn't hear anything, but she had learned to trust Theo's ears.

"We need to hurry. Into the trees."

## TWENTY-SEVEN

The brand on the horse's flank confirmed it was from Mitch Evans's livery. It stood in the shade of an oak, its reins tied in a knot around the branch.

The knot told Carney something. Someone familiar with horses would have made a loop, slid the ends beneath the loop, and pulled it tight. This one, on the other hand, was clumsy and overdone.

He climbed down from his own horse and walked closer.

Pierce, who had ridden in silence, began to dismount. But his lack of expertise with horses was obvious as he struggled out of the saddle, sliding in the stirrup and pulling on the mane. He gave the animal plenty of room as he walked away, as if expecting to be kicked, and Carney had a few seconds alone to study the scene before Pierce made it beside him.

"This explains how the bloodhounds didn't pick up any scent beyond the livery," Pierce said. "They rode it to here. But why park it here? They must have known we would locate it."

Carney grunted. Wasn't worth the effort to tell Pierce that horses weren't parked. He focused on the livery horse's saddle. It was askew—just slightly. As if something heavy had slid off of it.

Carney looked at crushed grass and bent branches just past the horse, in the direction the saddle had shifted.

"Someone rolled off the horse," he said. "Someone bigger than the boy or the girl. Kept rolling too."

Carney pointed to the obvious trail. He followed but didn't have to go far to find footprints at the base of a tree, toes outward. The prints were undefined, as if the feet had shifted back and forth.

He took out his vidpod and snapped some photos. Whoever it was had backed into the tree.

"Busted shoelace." Pierce pointed at the ground. "Strip of cloth."

Carney took another photo and used a twig to pick up the shoelace. He held it out for Pierce to inspect. It was a single piece of bootlace. The ends had been knotted together, and the knot was two-thirds down the length of lace.

Carney watched Pierce look closely at the tree. Waist high. "There," Pierce said. "Like a knife tip had been jammed into the tree."

Carney pretended to take a close look too. While he could see a shoelace clearly enough at arm's length, he'd have to take Pierce's word for the mark on the tree. Not the first time that Carney felt disgust about his failing eyes. "So?"

"You're on a horse, and someone's used that lace to tie your wrists together," Pierce said. "Probably your ankles too, otherwise you would have walked to the tree, not rolled to hit it. Strip of cloth here means you're gagged. They leave you on the horse. You roll off. You've got a knife in your front pocket, and when you get to a tree, you stand. Reach into your pocket for the knife, maybe your hands were tied in front of you, not back. Mistake easily made if whoever tied you hasn't done it much. So you unfold your knife and jam it, blade first, into a tree. Now you have something to cut against. It'll take a few seconds to snap through the lace, and you leave it there, knot in the middle. You ditch the gag and untie the lace around your ankles, but you keep that one, because later you can put it back in your boot. But you're in a hurry now. Any second someone might show up and find the horse."

Not bad, Carney thought.

"Was it your deputy? He big enough to make a hole like that through this brush?" Pierce answered his own question. "Nope. The girl and the boy aren't big enough to lift him on a horse, let alone subdue and tie him. Chances are it was someone else and the deputy did all the hard work."

Carney grunted again.

"Why go to all this work?" Pierce said. "There's three of them. The girl. The factory boy. Your deputy. If this is a fourth person, why kidnap him, tie him up, and leave him with the horse from the livery?

"The one they tied up, whoever it was, and left behind, he must have had a horse when they found him. They took his horse and kept going. Back at your office, the guy is probably waiting to report all this. Once we start tracking his horse, we'll find them."

"Curfew."

"Right." Pierce made a clucking sound. "Anyone

our three met last night was out after curfew. With the horse they took from him. No one will be in your office to incriminate himself."

"Not yet." Carney squinted at the screen of his vidpod and made a few adjustments. "Just logged in the coordinates of this location. We can do a reverse trace. Send in this location and approximate time, and we'll get back a list of all the vidpods that went through this area overnight. That will lead us to the owner."

"Unless the owner threw out his vidpod too."

"Nobody moves anywhere without a vidpod. Penalties are too severe. Besides, people get lost in this territory. These parts are like an overgrown maze, and the vidpod has software to help him find his way around."

"Unless your deputy stole it after dumping his."

"Billy's stupid, but not so stupid he'd ignore a knife while going through the guy's pockets for a vidpod. And if he did steal the vidpod, when we track it, we'll find Billy. He knows that, so he wouldn't steal it. And . . . there's something else," Carney said. "If this played out as we suspect, how could this person have traveled after curfew on horscback without triggering any alarms?"

Pierce shook his head. "Explain."

"Our satellite software is set up to alert the sheriff of the nearest town if any of the horse GPS chips are moving after curfew. So why didn't I know about the other horse last night?"

## TWENTY-EIGHT

Jordan could not guess at how much time had passed. He'd slipped into and out of consciousness as if repeatedly dipping into a cool river.

He was still on the wagon; he could feel the motion. How long until the graveyard?

The light entering the coffin changed shades in an irregular pattern, and he guessed that the wagon drove down a lane arched with trees.

The wheels stopped creaking, but he was too exhausted to try to scream again.

There was a slapping sound. A scraping sound.

Then his coffin shifted. Again, two men were carrying him. He could tell by the rhythm. These men never spoke.

They were carrying him to the gravesite. Jordan pictured it easily. The hole in the ground would be prepared already, then the coffin would be lowered. The first shovelfuls of dirt would thump against the top of the coffin. Too soon, the cracks of light would be filled.

Then there would only be embalming silence. If he were lucky, the dirt would be wet and the weight of it above the coffin would be tightly packed enough to seal him from air. He'd suffocate quickly. If not, it would take him days to die, helpless to move, his thirst amplified by the other agonies of his broken body.

Tears filled his eyes, because the dirt slamming his

coffin lid would also be slamming any hope of seeing Caitlyn again. He continued the prayers that he used to fill his conscious moments, prayers that she would survive the journey to Outside, that he could believe in those he'd entrusted with her life.

The rhythm of steps stopped abruptly. The coffin was lowered and set gently down.

Would there be a preacher at the gravesite to say words over his burial? Or would he be buried as an unknown pauper?

He thought of the years that had brought him there since the fire in the lab. Would he have changed that one act all those years ago?

No, it had to be done.

He was about to close his eyes to pray again when bright light filled his world. He squinted and saw the outlines of two figures against the sky, leaning down, looking at him.

He tried to speak. But he was too exhausted, too stressed.

Jordan felt the black timeless void surrounding his consciousness, and he fell into it yet again.

In the tree, screened by brush, Caitlyn listened to the approaching drums. She wasn't worried that they would be discovered. No one crossing the bridge to their side of the river would think about anything except for what would happen when the march of the procession ended and the drumbeats quickened until the herald's public proclamation.

She was lost in these grim thoughts when Billy nudged her. He pointed at Theo, who sat with his knees drawn to his chin. His face was wet with tears as he stared at the river.

Caitlyn moved closer and sat beside him.

"Theo?"

The procession had reached the bridge.

Theo shook his head, refusing to look at her. "I can't watch. I can't watch. I can't watch."

"You don't have to. We're not part of the crowd."

Theo pushed his head against her shoulder. He pressed his hands against his ears. His body shuddered.

Caitlyn turned her head back to the bridge.

She'd heard about these, recognized what the rock pile meant, but had never seen one.


Bruno was the name Mason had given the black bear. Not original, but Mason never claimed creativity as a talent outside of dealing with prey. The bear paced constantly in the cramped cage, hidden far into the foliage behind Mason's private cabin. The place was in the hills, a quiet perk provided by Bar Elohim.

Mason approached the cage with a dart gun in one hand and a collar dangling from the fingers of his other hand. The air reeked with feces, as cleaning the cage was not high on his priorities. Nor was feeding the bear. He wanted the bear in a constant state of irritable hunger.

The bear stopped pacing and stared suspiciously at Mason, as if sensing this was not another visit to throw half-rotten meat in the cage.

Leaving the collar dangling in his fingers, Mason rested the barrel of the dart gun on a cage bar, resentful that his cast made it necessary to use the bar to steady the gun. Without ceremony, he aimed at the bear's flank and pulled the trigger. With a puff of compressed air, the dart struck the bear solidly. The bear spun in tight circles, trying to identify the source of pain.

Mason leaned the dart gun against the cage and unbuckled the collar as he waited until he saw the first signs of the anesthetic taking effect. Then he opened the cage door, stood in the opening, and taunted the bear.

Groaning in rage and confusion, it staggered out of the enclosure. Once outside, it took a few feeble swipes at Mason before falling on its side. Mason had arranged the whole event with practicality in mind. If he didn't release the bear before it collapsed, he'd be forced to walk into the cage, risk dirtying his polished boots by stepping in bear crap, and have to drag the stinking animal out.

Mason waited another minute, watching the bear's ribs, until a slow rise and fall showed that it was completely unconscious. He knelt beside the bear and attached the collar.

The collar included a small weight to ensure the front remained lodged under the bear's chin—the payload sat on the back of the collar, and Mason didn't want the bear to be able to reach it.

He put the payload in place. Without looking back, Mason hurried into the cabin. When Bruno woke, he would wander the valley, hunting a meal, with Mason's vidpod on his neck. Just in case someone was going to check on Mason's location.

Which now gave Mason about as much freedom as a person could expect in Appalachia.

## TWENTY-NINE

Caitlyn watched through the branches from fifty yards away as townspeople followed a drummer and the local Elders across the bridge. The Elders wore silent grimness like cloaks, their bearded faces straining with the seriousness of their task, but their bold vestments gleamed in the sun. A young woman, not yet thirty, walked in front of the Elders on the far side of the drummer, and it took several minutes for Caitlyn to see her without obstruction. The woman was draped in a brown girdled blanket, her hands bound and hanging in front, and her recently shaven head bowed. The church herald, sweating heavily in a tasseled cassock often worn for these ceremonies, stepped in front of the men and children in the crowd. Caitlyn knew they were all headed for the pile of fist-sized jagged rocks piled like a cairn.

Above the beat of the drum, the herald called out a singsong proclamation of ritual, as if he served an audience of hundreds instead of only the population of a tiny town. Caitlyn strained to hear him, but after he repeated the proclamation, she picked out his words.

"Jaala Branigan, daughter of Michael Branigan, is going to be stoned because she has dishonored him and Bar Elohim through the act of rebellion. If anyone knows anything in favor of her acquittal, let him come and plead it."

The herald stopped and the entire procession followed, with the children straining to peer around the larger bodies of the adults. The herald turned to face the woman with the shaved head.

"Make your confession," he commanded her. Caitlyn knew a formal confession was required by Appalachian law, a practice the preachers said was based on Old Testament law.

She could see that the woman raised her head and looked at the herald. She had folded her bound hands together. From what Caitlyn could tell, she had the build of a laborer. Caitlyn imagined that any beauty Jaala had was in her eyes and wondered what lights glowed there now in the face of such terror.

"Make your confession," the herald demanded again. While Caitlyn had never witnessed this type of execution, her father had taught her all about Bar Elohim's rules and punishment. The woman was supposed to say, "May my death be an atonement for all my sins."

Caitlyn watched as Jaala silently shook her shaved head.

Wanting guidance, the herald looked to the town Elders, who stood away from the crowd to his left.

"Let her die without peace then!" An Elder declared this to the crowd. He was the largest of the trio, with the face above his untrimmed beard flushed red.

He waved the townsmen to move forward and push the woman toward the pile of stones. They grabbed the woman's arms and forced her forward. She shook them off and walked alone to her place of execution.

Caitlyn silently moved a branch to see Jaala. Now that the woman was close enough, she saw the tears trail from her eyes and her large hands clench and strain at the bounds of rope.

The Elders still had not taken any rocks from the nearby pile. Instead, two of them marched toward the woman. Wordlessly, they stripped the brown tunic from her body and left it at her feet. Because of the watching children, they allowed her undergarments to remain in place. The renewed humiliation appeared to lower her head once more.

The two Elders returned to the group. The first spoke loudly, facing another man in the crowd. "This is your daughter, Michael. You are bound to throw the first stone."

This man, same square face as the woman, stood as if paralyzed.

The large spokesman Elder began reciting. "If a man have a stubborn and rebellious son, which will not obey the voice of his father or the voice of his mother

. . . then shall his father and his mother lay hold on him, and bring him out unto the elders of his city . . . and all the men of his city shall stone him with stones, that he die."

"She will obey!" the anguished father said. "I promise! Give her another chance."

Caitlyn thought she saw the Elder smile, as if waiting for this response from Michael. He turned to the young woman. "Jaala Branigan, will you give up your defiance? Will you stop serving the evil of the Clan?"

"Don't call the Clan evil."

"So you admit again that you are part of the Clan?"

"I have never denied it." The unexpected sound of joy replaced the remnants of fear in her voice.

"Will you tell the authorities who led you to the Clan?"

She didn't answer.

"Please, Jaala. Save your life." The woman's father sobbed now.

"And lose my soul?"

The large Elder was the first man to step to the pile of rocks. The other men followed and armed themselves.

At that moment, wind came up from the valley and kicked a cloud of dust over the bridge. Caitlyn thought she heard a branch crack and thought Billy might be shifting in his tree. Somewhere in the crowd, a voice wailed.

The group waited for Michael Branigan, her father. Caitlyn knew the stoning could not begin until he threw first, but he remained stone-still in place. Men returned to drag him forward. The spokesman Elder forced a rock into Branigan's hand.

He dropped it at his feet, weeping.

"As required by law, the first stone has been cast." The Elder hefted his own rock, only a few paces away from the young woman.

"No!" she cried. "Allow me to speak."

The men hesitated.

With both bound hands, she raised her arms above her head. "Since childhood, like you, I was told to serve the church. But I learned that God is different than the church."

The Elder spoke. "You had your chance. You have no say."

She ignored him and yelled to the crowd. "The church is a prison!"

"Enough!" The Elder hurled his rock, and it struck her upper arm, gashing a streak of bright red.

Caitlyn saw the woman's father fall to his knees and bury his head beneath his arms.

"We must be free to believe." Jaala continued her shouting as the stones were hurled. "God's love is not a prison."

"You blaspheme, woman! God has commanded us to purge this evil from the people," the Elder shouted. He lifted another rock and threw it. The woman chose not to duck; she stood very still, and Caitlyn thought her lips were moving as the stone hit her cheekbone, knocking her to her knees.

As all the other men threw rocks, Caitlyn turned away.

On the road, the body was still beneath a pile of stones.

The crowd was gone, and Caitlyn put an arm around Theo's narrow shoulders. She felt how he shook with sobs, fighting to keep them silent.

"Don't . . . " He could hardly speak.

"What?"

"No . . . matter . . . what . . ."

"What are you trying to say, Theo?"

"Don't . . . take . . . me . . . to . . . a . . . doctor." His shaking was rapidly becoming more than silent sobs.

"Theo?"

"The stoning. That's how my parents died. I had to throw the first rock. I'd . . . rather . . . be . . . dead . . . than . . . go . . . back."

He fell against her shoulder. She saw his eyes roll back into his head.

Caitlyn gently took his chin in her hand. "Theo! Wake up!"

No response.

## THIRTY

Pierce had rolled up an office chair to watch the computer screen in Carney's office.

The keyboard didn't have any lettering but icons that matched the icons on the screen. Carney was fast, using the keyboard to open various files by punching the keyboard icons or directing the programs with the computer mouse. Occasionally, the computer requested input, which Carney did orally, speaking in a slow measured voice that the software obviously had been trained to recognize, for there were very few mistakes. Information was delivered in a soothing female voice from the computer speakers. Pierce marveled that all of it could be accomplished without any reading or writing.

"I've been in Appalachia for long enough," Pierce said. "All I see are contradictions. It's like living in Mayberry."

Carney's frown showed he didn't understand.

"A fictional town, part of a popular television series from the last century," Pierce corrected himself. "But, Sheriff, Mayberry had cars. You've gone even farther back in time, to horses and wagons. Yet you have as much tech as Outside."

Carney clicked on another icon. Pierce wasn't familiar with it. He realized that Appalachians did have an alphabet of sorts, like Egyptian hieroglyphics or Chinese characters.

"So why mix horses with high tech? Mayberry meets Star Trek?"

Carney sighed. He pulled out his vidpod. Pierce understood the sheriff was making it obvious again that the conversation was on official record.

"I don't know what Star Trek is. I do know that Outsiders are slaves to technology, whereas Appalachians pick and choose. We're a small country; we don't need highways. And Greenhouse credits from the Outside make up a third of our exports."

"Along with slave labor churning out computer chips."

"I'm supposed to comment on that?"

"Probably not." Pierce glanced at the vidpod. "Fine. I'll shut up."

Carney clicked at the keyboard again, then turned suddenly toward Pierce. "That's why secession has worked. Outside minds its own business. We mind ours. We prefer not to murder unborn children. Or genetically manipulate embryos."

"I said I'll shut up already."

Carney swung back to his computer screen. He clicked another icon on the keyboard. "Got it. The personal identification number on the vidpod that was moving around near the horse's location last night near the stable. Movement matches where we found the abandoned livery horse too."

The female computer voice gave Carney a name. Paul Gentry.

"It's one of Mason's men. They don't have to

answer to local enforcement. Now we know who was out after curfew."

"Mason helped your girl and the deputy escape?"

"Don't think so." Carney pointed at the computer screen. "Mason's vidpod shows he went to a nearby factory, then to his cabin in the hills. He's probably up there poaching deer."

"You're not curious about the side trip to the factory he took before that?"

"Nope," Carney said, but Pierce watched him nod while he pointed at his vidpod. Carney was curious. But didn't want that on record.

"I am," Pierce said. "So take me there."

"Well, it's your call. Let me take care of sending a message."

The sheriff held his vidpod at arm's length and spoke into it. "Steve, I need some help here. I've been tracking the vidpod movements of Paul Gentry, one of Mason Lee's men. Looks like he's at home now. But his horse went somewhere without him. Stop by, will you? Get him to tell you what happened last night, then send the interview to my vidpod. Sooner is better than later; you know I'm good for returning the favor."

Carney stopped speaking. He ran his fingers across the vidpod screen. "Done and sent. I guess we can go."

Pierce stood and rolled the chair back away from Carney's desk. "Let's go by car this time. I didn't like the horse much."

In truth, he could take or leave the horse. But he, unlike Carney, knew that Mason Lee wasn't really poaching in the woods, and having efficient transportation if quick pursuit became necessary wasn't a choice.

## THIRTY-ONE

When Caitlyn limped back to Billy and Theo, she was carrying an armful of long, cone-headed purple flowers. They'd found the canoe, as instructed, waiting under the bridge, then traveled a mile downstream and pulled ashore to hide the canoe.

"I wanted to do this sooner for Theo, but there was never time for me to collect the flowers. I'd hoped things wouldn't get this bad so quickly."

Theo lay on the grass unconscious, his head propped by a pillow made from his coat, his face flushed with fever. His arm and shoulder were exposed, and the purple swelling was ominous, with pus oozing from where he'd cut himself open to remove the chip. Caitlyn set the flowers down beside Theo, whose eyes were closed, fluttering behind the eyelids.

Billy sat cross-legged beside the flowers, and with quick, dexterous movements—unnaturally so, considering his massive hands—he began to strip the flowers and stems.

"You've done this before." Caitlyn kept her hands hidden. If he was going to do this, she wouldn't have to let him see her fingers.

"My grandmother showed me, before she passed on and I was adopted. I didn't know what you meant when you said needed to find etcha . . . echo . . . echy—"

"Echinacea," she said. Her cloak was hot and she knew it was growing damp with sweat, but she needed to keep it loosely around her to hide her deformed back from Billy.

"Grams called it purple coneflower." He kept his head down, focused on stripping the flowers.

"I hope it works. He needs a doctor."

"You don't need to look farther than his arm to know a doctor's not an option. He cut the chip out himself— that tells you how bad he hates the factory. He was starving to death in the woods, and yet he still wouldn't turn back. If you brought him to a doctor, you wouldn't be saving him at all. I think he would rather be dead."

"Thanks." Caitlyn's voice was hardly a whisper. It surprised her how much she wanted Theo to survive and how much of a comfort the big, quiet man in front of her was turning out to be during each new hour of stress.

Billy focused on the flowers. "We need to cut farther into Theo's arm to clean it. I can do that if you don't want to. I helped the vet with horses. I've seen this before. On horses, I mean."

Again she found comfort in his steadiness. "Do you need me to hold him for you?"

Billy shook his head. "He's tiny."

She watched as he gently doctored the wound. Theo turned and groaned but did not come to full consciousness. Billy took the poultice and pressed it against Theo's arm. Then he removed his outer shirt, cut strips for bandages, and tied the poultice in place.

"We're ready," he said. "I'll lift him back into the canoe."

His trust at her leadership amazed her. He hadn't asked what was ahead. Theo would have rattled through a hundred rapid-fire questions already.

They'd known each other only a few hours, but she felt comfortable around him. She had never experienced that comfort with anyone before, except Papa. Yet whenever Billy gave her a shy, sideways glance, something in her heart surged.

"Billy . . ."

There it was again. The shy look. It eased her loneliness.

"I'm afraid," she said. "Not too afraid to do what needs to be done, but still afraid. It's good to have you here."

"You make me feel strong. I don't know why they are chasing you, but I don't care."

"Do you know that Mason Lee had been hunting me with the hounds?"

He nodded, but as he spoke, he looked at the ground. "You disappeared from a mountaintop, is what I heard."

"Yes, I scaled down the rock face." She had escaped the hounds and the hunters, but she knew her father paid the price. The question was, how much of a price? No matter how numb she'd tried to make herself, that question haunted her still.

"I'm afraid for my father too." She half hoped Billy would put his arms around her and let her lean her head against his chest. Just a couple of moments of comfort.

Billy didn't look up. Something about his shoulders changed, and it wasn't shyness that kept him from looking at her. Before he answered, she knew—but his words broke her anyway.

"I'm sorry." Billy lifted his head and looked at her without flinching. "He's dead."

## THIRTY-TWO

Dr. Ross's patient was set on a table, deep within the forest. He had found a clearing wide enough to support the table but small enough to keep himself and his supposedly dead patient hidden. He noted that Jordan's wounds were clotting well, and it appeared that all the stitches were holding in the jagged lines where dogs' jaws had ripped through skin.

"Sensation has returned to your fingers and toes?" Dr. Ross asked. He wore a surgeon's mask to protect his identity. Better safe than sorry. Always.

Jordan slightly nodded. Dr. Ross laid a pillow beneath Jordan's head. His face was extensively bruised; the black splotches would begin to turn yellow in a few days. While the doctor had removed the man's gag, his wrists and ankles were still bound. The gagging and binding had to be done to keep Jordan from making noise in the coffin.

"It's a side effect," Dr. Ross said. "While you were in custody, I injected you with a slight paralyzing agent. To anyone but a medical doctor, you appeared dead. It was necessary to facilitate your escape."

"I don't remember the injection." Jordan spoke as if his throat were constricted. Dr. Ross had given him water, but it would be days before the man's body was fully hydrated.

"You were unconscious."

"I remember the dogs. I remember being taken down the mountain. Mason Lee—"

"It's no longer a concern," Dr. Ross said. "To Appalachia, you're dead and buried. The wagon carrying you continued to the graveyard once the casket was switched. You don't have to worry about the hunters anymore."

"Thank you, Doctor. But I don't care about myself anymore. There's a girl. I need to know that she's safe. I made arrangements. She—"

"No more. I don't want to hear anything about arrangements."

Every six or eight months, it would happen. Dr. Ross would be riding down a trail to make a house call, and he'd be stopped by masked men. They'd tell him who he was required to sedate and pronounce dead. The payment was more than fair, but Ross didn't do it for the money. He had his suspicions where the patients would go after the caskets were filled with sandbags and placed into the ground and buried. He never saw the undead again, but those suspicions were enough to give him satisfaction. Someday he'd do the same for his daughter and his son, spacing their deaths far enough apart to keep Bar Elohim from guessing. It broke his heart to think he'd never see them again; it broke his heart more to imagine them spending their lives in Appalachia.

On this occasion, however, he'd been required to make sure the patient was healthy enough to survive what was ahead. But the exam, of course, could not take place in a hospital. He had to make his best judgment here.

"Listen," Dr. Ross said, "you have some broken ribs. A mild concussion. And stitches all over your body. You need to take these antibiotics—one pill three times a day until all the pills are gone. Understand? And make sure to have the bandages replaced frequently. As long as the pus remains clear, you will be all right."

"Yes, but—"

"The yellow pills are painkillers. You'll know when to take those."

"The girl. Please. What happened?"

"I don't have an answer." Dr. Ross showed a syringe to his patient. "I need to sedate you. It's for your protection. The journey might be rough, and you're better off not feeling it. More importantly, you won't know where you are and how you got there. That's what will save your life. If they wanted you dead, they wouldn't go to the effort of ensuring this."

"They?"

Dr. Ross merely shook his head to the negative. "You're getting a drug called flunitrazepam. It's going to mess with your short-term memory. To protect them."

He jabbed the syringe into the man's shoulder and pressed the plunger. Moments later, Jordan's eyes closed.

It would be a dreamless sleep. But at least it was sleep, Dr. Ross thought, not death. Or worse. Back in the hands of Mason Lee.

## THIRTY-THREE

It was a standard transportation truck, parked at the side of the road, with its driver changing a flat tire at the front passenger side. The trailer was standard white, giving no indication of what it contained. To anyone riding by on a horse, it might have held crates of potatoes or stacks of milk cartons. To that same person on horseback, there was no way of seeing the roof of the trailer—smoked glass that allowed ample sunlight to the interior.

The inside of the trailer was partitioned. The front half was command central, filled with computers and electronics that allowed Bar Elohim the same access to Appalachia's network as if he were in the center of his compound. The back half was a luxury compartment for the ease of his travel.

A limousine with escorts traveled Appalachia's highways on a daily basis. While it gave the appearance that Bar Elohim was constantly moving among the people, he rarely rode in the limousine. It was literally a smoke-and-mirrors trick to fool Appalachians—smoke from the exhaust, mirrored windows that made it impossible for anyone to see inside and know Bar Elohim was not there.

This transportation truck worked much better for him. He could travel where he wanted, anonymously.

The flat tire was not an accident but a diversion to wait in a prearranged spot.

Mason Lee had an appointment with Bar Elohim.

Carney drove at a sedate pace along the curving road through the valley, a set of earbuds hooked into his vidpod.

"We've got one mystery solved." Carney pulled the earbuds loose. "The second horse. Gentry's. They used it to get away. Tells me the girl must be smart, because my deputy wouldn't be able to think that way. I'll beam you the interview."

Pierce glanced at Carney. Traveling in the town's official car, Pierce was acutely aware that the entire journey was audio and video recorded.

Pierce fiddled with the touch controls on his vidpod screen, taking longer than he wanted to put it into reception mode. A beep signaled his success.

Carney grunted acknowledgment and pushed the screen of his device. Another beep told Pierce the download was complete. Pierce focused on the transmission, allowing the bounty hunter's voice to fill the silence of their ride.

"That deputy came out of the dark like a train," the face on the screen said. The bounty hunter was squinting and slightly cross-eyed. Drunk, Pierce guessed. He'd been speaking into a vidpod, and the shot was wide angle. "I didn't have a chance against the big one."

"You had the girl in custody?" The off-screen voice belonged to the sheriff doing Carney's work.

"The girl and some boy. Mason put us all around the edges of town and told us to watch for them. Then the deputy, that was him, right? A big guy? The deputy charged in and knocked me out, I'm guessing. For a few minutes, I wasn't seeing or hearing anything. When I woke, I was on the girl's horse, almost on top of the girl in the saddle. My feet and ankles were tied with my own laces. That deputy and the boy rode my horse. I guess to keep the hounds from tracking them."

Pierce followed the rest of the story easily. It matched the evidence that he and Carney had found near the livery horse.

When the deputy and the girl had reached the next intersection, a few miles down from Cumberland Gap, the girl had transferred to the bounty hunter's horse without touching the ground. The boy—the hunter described him as scrawny—had led the livery horse

195

and the bounty hunter south, then off the road and down a trail. The boy walked away, leaving the bounty hunter on the livery horse, tied to a branch. Pierce presumed the boy had rejoined the girl and the deputy on the horse stolen from the bounty hunter.

"Smart," Pierce agreed. "They knew it would be a few hours before we realized they'd switched horses. Still, if all horses have radio chips, it shouldn't be too hard to find the second horse."

"Wasn't hard at all," Carney said. "It's already showed up in the next town. No saddle."

"That reduces the search area. Somewhere between where we found the livery horse and that town where they let the horse loose and started traveling on foot."

"Ten miles of road, with ten miles on each side of the road. That's a ten-by-twenty-mile area. Two hundred square miles of rugged valley and hills. Won't be easy."

Carney had a point, but Pierce stared out the window of the car, distracted, thinking it wouldn't do much good to discuss Mason Lee in a government car.

## THIRTY-FOUR

Mason felt claustrophobic in the rear half of the trailer. Almost helpless. The door had no handle on the inside, and when he'd entered, he'd heard the click of the lock, activated by remote control.

The drill was familiar. Enter the booth in the trailer when the rear compartment was empty; Bar Elohim was secure in the front half, protected by solid walls and a bulletproof door. It didn't matter whether Mason was armed. Once the door shut and the lock was activated, he couldn't harm Bar Elohim. The booth's walls and doors were armament- and light-proof. Mason sat in total darkness. If Bar Elohim decided not to open the door, Mason was trapped until he died of thirst. Not a comforting thought. Mason hoped he wouldn't have too long to wait, but soon enough, Bar Elohim's voice came from speakers above him.

"This better be worth my while."

The high-pitched voice was familiar to Mason, identifiable to everyone in Appalachia over the age of ten. His transmissions always showed Bar Elohim looking straight out of the vidpod, a head-and-shoulders shot of a middle-aged bland face, with a full head of middle-aged, graying hair. There was nothing threatening about his persona, only his position.

"What I have to tell you is not something I could trust anyone else to pass on to you," Mason said.

"You meet with Elders from the inner circle. That's how information reaches me."

"I've discovered a way to help you trap the Clan. I figure I should only trust one person with that knowledge."

Silence in the darkness. Mason knew that there'd been at least a half dozen full-scale attempts to wipe out the Clan and that they were all unsuccessful. The Clan had anticipated each attack.

"What do you have?"

This would be delicate. Mason needed to show enough to put himself in a good bargaining position, but not so much he'd no longer be necessary in the hunt.

"The girl's father had an unregistered vidpod." Mason explained how he matched the GPS location in the Valley of the Clan with the message the factory woman, Tasha, had read to him. But he held back information about the strange symbols. "If Jordan Brown had those instructions, so did his daughter. A time and place to meet the Clan. I can get there before her."

"You captured him two nights ago. Why wait this long to pass it on?"

A chill laced that question. The truth was that he'd hoped to capture the girl and run with the canister, never having a meeting in this tiny booth. But the truth, like any other wrong kind of answer, would get him sent to a factory.

"I don't trust anyone else but you with something so important. And yesterday, I was trying to catch the girl."

"If what you're saying is correct, you could have dropped the chase and gone straight to the point where she was going to meet the Clan."

"Thought she was holed earlier, in Cumberland Gap. I wanted to play it safe. Fill the canister for you, get what we need, then send in another girl, like a decoy."

Again, Bar Elohim was silent. In the hushed dark-

198

ness, Mason felt unnerved. He hated lots of things and really hated the dark. He always made sure there was some kind of light burning when he slept inside or a small fire going through the night when he was outside. In the dark, he saw too many faces.

Mason started speaking again. Too fast and too soon, but with the dark squeezing on him, he was doing all he could not to bang on the walls.

"If only you and me know this, you can get enough men ready just outside the valley. Have them ready this afternoon at three. Send them in choppers."

"The Clan will just hide in the mines."

"Not this time. I'll follow the girl underground. I'll leave markings on the walls for soldiers to follow. Like stringing out a ball of twine. Wherever they take the girl, that's where they are hiding out."

Mason's skin felt like worms were rippling beneath. He had to escape the darkness, but not until he got what he wanted.

"What are the GPS coordinates?"

"I'll bring some flares in with me. I'll light them just before going in after the girl. People inside the mountain won't know soldiers are on the way."

"What are the GPS coordinates? I want them now."

"And I want the Outside agent dead," Mason said. "It's personal."

"You're negotiating with me?"

"He's with the sheriff. They'll hear I went to the factory, and they'll go too, to find out why. They might learn what I did. Is that what you want? Better that I go into the valley alone, with nobody knowing but you and me."

"The sheriff has already put a trace request on your vidpod movements," Bar Elohim said. "If I block the request, that will raise questions too."

"I already solved it."

"How?"

"No," Mason said. He knew now that he was in a position of strength and preferred to keep his secrets. He might need them again. "That's my business."

"There's no business in Appalachia beyond my knowledge."

"Do I get the Outside agent?"

Bar Elohim was silent for another moment. "The sheriff will get orders to arrest him. Deliver what I need."

"One other thing," Mason said, still fighting the sensation of rippling worms under his skin. "Think of it as a good trade for you."

"You've already asked for too much."

"No, not if I can deliver the Clan"—Mason paused, knowing he'd saved the biggest bait for last: the leader of the Clan—"and Brij."

"What?" The man's sharp intake of air caused the speakers to crackle.

"You want him locked in the factory? I can deliver him."

"That's not me offering a trade. That's a directive."

Mason had never failed to follow orders before. "It's a trade or nothing."

"Then you'll be placed in a factory."

"You won't get Brij. How many years have you had a bounty on him?"

"What do you want?" Bar Elohim finally asked.

"Outside." Mason allowed himself to breathe. "Send me Outside with enough money, and I'll start hunting down every person that's ever escaped your leadership and Appalachia."

Carney stopped the car at the guarded gate of Factory 22. He shut off the ignition. "Outsiders aren't allowed inside a factory. My source tells me that Mason spent time with a woman in there. I'll vidpod my interview with her and let you review it when I get back."

Pierce stared out the passenger window. "Sure."

Carney's vidpod vibrated. The pattern told him it was an incoming message from Bar Elohim, so he slipped his earbuds back in. He touched the screen of his vidpod and listened.

It was a short message. *Turn around now. Deliver the agent to me at the church grounds. Make an immediate arrest. No detours. No stops.*

Carney got out. He stretched, then tied his shoe, stalling for a moment to think about the transmission.

Carney was driving a government car, wired with audio and video. Bar Elohim knew where they were. Was it a coincidence that the message had been delivered before he could get inside the factory and discover why Mason had visited?

One way to find out. Carney didn't look back as he walked to the gate.

The guard gave him a nod of recognition. Factory 22 was Cumberland Gap's factory, and all the guards knew Carney. Instead of a casual smile, however, the guard remained tight lipped. His eyes met Carney's only for a second before looking down.

Carney didn't have to ask. When Carney had called ahead to arrange the visit, there'd been no problem. Not any longer. The guard's body language told Carney that the guard had received orders not to let him in. It answered Carney's question. It wasn't coincidence that the message from Bar Elohim had come in when it did.

"I don't need access to the factory," Carney said. "Just need to use the phone. Get Larry on the line."

The guard's relief was noticeable and his smile returned. It was all the confirmation that Carney needed. It also meant that putting the factory foreman on the line wasn't breaking any orders from Bar Elohim.

Carney didn't have a long time to speak and, as soon as the foreman was on the phone, launched into it. "Larry, it's Carney. Do what it takes to find out what Mason Lee wanted from the woman you told me he interviewed. Mason probably made threats to shut her up. You make bigger threats to get her to talk. Record the interview and send it to my vidpod. Get it done in the next five minutes, and I'll owe you."

Carney ended the call. Except for a one-minute

delay, he had not disobeyed any orders from Bar Elohim. It was time to get moving. Under direct monitoring all the way, Carney wouldn't be allowed detours.

Whatever happened, Carney would no longer be part of the investigation. Still, it wouldn't hurt to find a way to discuss it with the Outside agent.

He opened the front passenger door. Pierce's raised eyebrows were enough of a question.

"I'll need to put you in the backseat," Carney told him. "You're under arrest."

## THIRTY-FIVE

Billy paddled from the back, using hard, steady strokes that seemed effortless but sent the canoe ahead in surges. The river moved slowly, pooled and deep. Caitlyn sat in the center, sideways with her back leaned against the ribs of the canoe. Her back was no longer just hot, it stung in pain. It felt to Caitlyn like it was splitting apart.

Caitlyn's sideways position also allowed Billy to see ahead for possible logs or boulders in shallow water. And with a turn of her head in either direction, she could scan ahead for trouble or behind for possible pursuers.

They had propped Theo in the front, and he seemed to be sleeping peacefully.

Now that they were far enough downstream from the bridge, Caitlyn took out her vidpod and checked the screen to confirm their progress. She had difficulty seeing the screen. Her vision was blurred by steady tears.

Papa was dead. Memory after memory bubbled up. Their quiet picnic times. The sense of security she always felt around him. The unconditional love. The pain on his face whenever they were hiding from locals who might discover that Caitlyn was a freak. She just wanted to see Papa's face again—when it was happy.

She realized the canoe had stopped the steady surges forward, that the river was silent of splashing. She glanced at Billy. His paddle was paused midair. Water dripped from the end of the paddle into the river.

Caitlyn leaned her head into her shoulder and wiped away her tears. She saw that he was staring, a look of fear forming on his face.

Billy's steady paddling had taken them to where the banks of the river narrowed and the water moved faster. Mature trees grew straight up out of the bank, with branches hanging low over the water.

Dozens of human skeletons hung on the tree limbs, wisps of clothing attached to the bones.

They'd reached the outlaw perimeter to the Valley of the Clan.

*Under arrest.*

Pierce wondered what could possibly have happened as he leaned his head against the backseat and closed his eyes, feeling the hum of the car tires.

He doubted his arrest was Carney's idea. Why drive to the factory, stop at the gate, and turn around? He noticed Carney slip on the earbuds and listen to his vidpod for a few seconds when they arrived . . . that must have something to do with this.

Carney drove past the road into Cumberland Gap and continued to follow the curves of the highway. He didn't seem to be driving so sedately anymore. Just slowing down whenever there was someone on horseback to pass. He'd plugged his earbuds back in and was obviously listening to a long message on his vidpod.

Pierce waited until Carney pulled out the earbuds again. "How long till we stop?"

"Half hour." Carney spoke through the wire mesh that separated them.

Half an hour. That answered one question. More than likely Carney was taking Pierce to the Church, his first stop in Appalachia.

The Church was more than a worship building. It was the name given to a papal compound that overlooked a mountain lake. It was command central for Bar Elohim.

Pierce wondered if he was being deported, sent back Outside. If so, why had Carney made a point of telling him he was under arrest? Carney knew the car was monitored. Carney wouldn't lie to Pierce if he knew that what he was saying would reach the ears of Bar Elohim. So Carney was telling the truth.

Pierce knew he had done nothing to deserve arrest.

He was supposed to be protected inside Appalachia during his hunt for the girl, but clearly, the politics had shifted.

The fact that Carney announced to Pierce that he'd been arrested told him something else. Carney could just as easily have remained silent and simply driven Pierce to the Church.

Whatever needed discussion, though, wasn't going to happen inside the monitored car. He'd have to get them both out.

"Don't you feel that wobble?" Pierce said. "I think your tire's flat."

"Nope." He paused, then Pierce saw the sheriff's eyes open wide in conspiracy. "Hang on . . . you're right."

Carney slowed the vehicle. At the side of the road, Carney put the car in park. He lowered the rear window on Pierce's side a few inches. "I don't want you in here rocking the car while it's on a jack. Get out. I'll step around and drop some cuffs through the window. Ankles and wrists. Give me a good look at them when you're ready."

Carney spoke loudly. For the sake of the audio monitor, Pierce assumed.

Carney walked around the vehicle. Before handing Pierce the cuffs, though, he knelt down to examine the tire. Immediately after, Pierce heard the click of an opening jackknife blade, then hissing air.

"Definitely going flat." Carney dropped two sets of cuffs into the back. Pierce did as directed. He showed the sheriff his wrists and ankles, and Carney opened the door.

Outside, Pierce tried shuffling. The handcuffs around his ankles didn't have enough slack. He hopped to the shoulder of the road, far enough from the car to avoid audio monitoring.

Carney moved beside him.

"Where's your vidpod?" Pierce asked.

"Left it on the front seat. Didn't want it to get in the way of changing a tire."

"We're clear for a private conversation then?" Pierce looked straight ahead at the deep green of the heavy forest.

"A short one. I need to start on changing the tire." Carney spoke in a low voice. "Bar Elohim is supporting Mason and not the local law on whatever this chase has become. And since I've been pulled out of the loop, it means Mason must be making progress. Don't know if that does you much good. As you can see, Outside isn't holding much weight now either."

"You still able to track Mason's vidpod movements from your own vidpod?"

"First thing I checked. If it had been blocked, that would have told me something."

"Where does it show him?" Pierce asked.

"You've got about twenty seconds before you need to get back in the car. Otherwise this is going to look like a conversation."

"Where does it show him?"

"He's still in the hills behind his cabin."

"Wrong."

"You got a way to prove that?"

"Radio chip. Didn't want him to ambush me. Paid the doctor to mix a radio chip into the plaster of Mason's cast. I've been tracking Mason ever since."

Carney didn't waste any time on surprise. "Where is he now?"

"If I'm right about your geography, deep in Clan territory. That mean anything to you?"

## THIRTY-SIX

A single snapped twig gave Mason warning that he was being watched. Then he heard a giggle.

He spun, the skin on his neck covered with goose bumps.

Through the rugged valleys, Mason had traveled in two hours what would have taken anybody else six. Silent and efficient as a deer. But as good as he was, outlaws guarded the perimeter of the valley with many of the same skills. Bar Elohim tolerated, even encouraged, their predatory actions as an obstacle to Appalachians seeking a way Outside.

Still, he'd expected nobody would get near him unless he allowed it.

To see someone a stone's throw away, stepping around a tree behind him, was startling enough. To see that it was an attractive girl, barely marrying age, was an even bigger surprise. He trusted she'd been waiting there when he passed her. He didn't want to think she'd managed to follow him without his knowing it.

She giggled again. She had dark hair, tied in pony-tails. Wide, shining eyes set atop a body equally alluring in tight pants and a partially unbuttoned shirt.

"A stranger," she said, showing no fear. "Here in the middle of nowhere. What's your name, stranger? You are plenty handsome. You lost? I've got lots of time."

Mason Lee rubbed his face. "Maybe you can help me."

The girl was good-looking all right.

Her smile widened. "Be happy to."

"I need to find someone named Brij," Lee said. "He's supposed to live somewhere up here."

"You're looking for the Clan?"

Mason nodded.

"You're not in a hurry, are you?" She leaned against the tree. "It gets boring around here. A stranger is an exciting thing for someone like me."

Mason's cast was heavy, and the arm inside it throbbed. He smoothed his mustache with his other hand as studied her. In her face, he saw flashes of a little girl he remembered. "I think you'd enjoy watching a couple of your brothers take the boots to me. Maybe after that, you'd help them strap me to a log."

Her eyes narrowed and her face grew hard.

"So . . . you going to give me directions to find a man named Brij, or am I on my own again?"

As a reply, she lifted her hands to her mouth and used her fingers to whistle shrilly.

Seconds later, two men appeared on the path in front of Mason. Both carried polished clubs.

"What kind of a welcome is this?" Mason grinned. "You're all treating me like a stranger."

"Mason Lee," the thin man said, shaking his head. "Got time to come down to the river? We're getting ready for another floater. He's been there a couple of days and about to expire anyway."

"I've always got time for some family-style entertainment."

"This is Mason Lee?" The girl shrank back toward a tree trunk.

"None other. Took me a few minutes to recognize you, little girl," Mason said. "A man's got to come home once in a while."

Jordan sat on the front porch of a cabin, somewhere deep in the valley. He swayed in a rocker, staring at the horizon, letting his muscles relax. He had a glass of lemonade beside him and sipped from it occasionally, moving his arm slowly to do so, afraid to crack stitches.

He saw movement in the trees just down the hill. An older man entered the clearing, wearing khakis and a brown shirt. Dark sunglasses with small round lenses. Short gray hair, short gray goatee. A deliberate soft and slow walk.

Jordan knew him by only one name—Brij. He tried to stand as Brij stepped onto the porch, but the effort hurt too much. Jordan leaned back in the rocker.

"Welcome home." Like his movements, Brij's voice was slow.

"It's good to see you, Brij," Jordan said. "I expected to be in a factory. Or dead, but never here again."

"After all you've done for us . . . " Brij sat on a rocker beside Jordan. "We couldn't tell you ahead of time. Or even warn you about the coffin. It's hard to hold back information if they give you pharmaceuticals."

"Caitlyn . . . " Jordan lost his voice to the emotion he could barely contain.

"Her vidpod location shows us that she's made it into the valley," Brij said. "I put the word out among the outlaws. As long as she doesn't offend them, I expect she'll be at the GPS coordinates today. Three o'clock. I promise I'll be there waiting for her."

At the river, Mason saw a small, naked man, arms wrapped and tied around the circumference of a floater log set upright.

The base of the log rested on the ground and was short enough for the man's chin to rest on it, with his chest firmly pressed into the bark of the log by the pressure of the bindings that held him to it. His mouth was gagged.

"He didn't have much to take," the girl said. "But he sure was in a hurry to give me something."

She walked over and slapped the man's butt, obviously showing off for Mason. "Next time, you don't try stuff like that on a girl you find in the woods." She giggled. "Oops, never mind, there won't be a next time."

She pushed the log, and it toppled the man over. A muffled cry of pain escaped the gag.

"Anyone going to help me?" she asked her two brothers and Mason.

"You're doing fine, Sis." The red-headed brother didn't look up when he spoke, picking at dead skin on his hand with a penknife.

"Jessie Cutter, you are all grown up from when I last saw you, but still barely bigger than a twig." Mason helped her roll the log toward the river, with the log thumping the man every revolution. He knew what would happen next. Once the man was in the river, his own weight would roll him under the log, under the surface of the water. Well before the log had floated a hundred yards downstream, he would be drowned. His body would eventually be found at the dam, still tied to the log.

Just another floater.

## THIRTY-SEVEN

You buckled up?" Carney's voice was loud and urgent. They were about fifteen miles beyond where they had stopped the car. The road had entered a steep descent with hairpin curves and sheer drops into a deep ravine. The ride since fixing the flat had been silent, and Carney's voice came as a surprise to Pierce.

"What?"

"Buckle up. Fast. Car's lost the brakes. Knew I should have had it checked out."

"You're kidding, right?"

"Does this look like I'm kidding?" Carney angled into a set of guardrails. The car body shrieked, and sparks flew in a cascade past Pierce's window. "Got to grind this thing to the slowest speed possible!"

The car kept shuddering against the rails, and it seemed to be working. Carney rammed the car into a lower gear, the car jerked, and the engine roared as the lower gear slowed the car more.

Then the railing ran out, and Carney was forced to swerve back to center to avoid plunging down the ravine.

"Hang on! Next corner looks worse!"

To Pierce, it seemed like the car tilted on just two wheels as it went through the corner. But making the turn wasn't much consolation. Another corner loomed ahead.

"Don't know if we can—!" Carney shouted again.

The car shot through the turn. Small trees and bushes filled the windshield, then horrible popping sounds of impact. Branches shredded against the grill and the sides of the car as it plunged forward, bouncing violently.

Time altered for Pierce, slowing in a weird way, like he was prisoner in a dream. The car bounced, throwing him side to side. He expected it to plunge straight down any moment; he'd seen the drop-offs at some of the curves.

Then, with a suddenness that seemed equally violent, total silence engulfed them. No motion, no sound.

Pierce drew in a breath and said nothing. Let it out.

"Pretty good ride, huh," Carney said. "Almost like I knew what I was doing."

Pierce slowly refocused. Carney had turned and grinned at him.

Pierce still didn't say anything.

"You can talk now." Carney lifted a hand, showed a set of wires with loose ends. "We're clear."

"Clear?"

"Just yanked out video and audio. We're clear, but the footage of the crash that went in should be spectacular."

"Glad to be part of the show."

"You don't know half of it." Carney kicked open his door. He opened the back door for Pierce, threw Pierce keys to the handcuffs, then went to the trunk.

First he came out with a shotgun he'd loaded there before leaving for the factory, and handed it to Pierce. By the time Pierce unshackled himself and crawled out of the car with the shotgun, wobbling on shaky legs, Carney had opened a small can of gasoline and held a lighter.

"Here's where we die," Carney said. He splashed gasoline all over the interior of the trunk. "You might want to stand back."

Carney lit the gasoline. Small flames sprang upward.

"Run!"

Carney threw the gasoline container in the trunk and shut the lid. He jumped backwards and sprinted down the hill. Pierce followed him through the trees and down to the river, trying to be cautious with the shotgun. This explained why the car hadn't dropped hundreds of feet. The final corner had been almost to the valley bottom.

"Explosion should do a good job of slowing Bar Elohim's people down," Carney said, looking back toward the crash site.

"Cars don't explode when they burn," Pierce panted. "That's just a myth."

Carney grinned and plugged his ears. Within a second, a massive *whomp* came from the car, and a moment later, pieces of steel spiraled upward.

Carney waited a few seconds. "Helps when there's dynamite hidden in the trunk."

Pierce nodded, starting to understand. "Some accident."

Carney didn't answer but motioned for his shotgun. "Like I said. Almost like I knew what I was doing."

Brij had walked off into the woods again, leaving Jordan alone on the porch. An elderly woman stepped up the path, holding flowers. She was the one who had woken him by placing a wet cloth on his face. She had white hair and a deeply wrinkled face but moved with surprising vitality.

"Hello, Jordan. I'm Gloria Shelton and I lived in

Cumberland Gap. They only told me your name and to be with you when you woke. Is the Clan helping you too? Or are you one of their own?"

"You could say that." He wasn't in a mood to talk but didn't want to be unfriendly.

She moved to the other rocker, farther down on the porch from Jordan. In the shade of the overhang it was pleasant, especially with a breeze. If it weren't for the anxiety about Caitlyn gnawing at him, Jordan would have been content to lose himself in the moment. Although Brij would try to protect her, so much could still go wrong.

Jordan stared at the edge of the far mountains for a few more minutes. The mysterious blue haze always enchanted him.

Jordan had spent years slipping into Clan territory to give medical help. It was how he had earned Caitlyn's passage Outside. He wished he and Caitlyn could have lived among the Clan from the beginning. But her only chance to be normal was surgery, and he had needed to be registered at the collective to get that kind of specialized medical help. Nor was it an option to take her back Outside before the surgery.

He realized this after leaving the surgeon's office the day after Caitlyn's sixth birthday, that there would be a short window of opportunity once she was old enough for the operation. He'd needed to make sure he could help her get Outside, almost as soon as she was recovered. He'd been planning the escape from that day forward. She couldn't remain inside

Appalachia after the surgery; the oppression was almost as much of a prison as the abnormality of her body.

"I looked carefully. I didn't see barbecued bodies anywhere." She smiled at him. "You know, like all those stories we hear."

"Most of the stuff that the outlaws do gets blamed on the Clan. Bar Elohim likes encouraging those myths. The Clan doesn't discourage them either. Keeps people from making casual decisions about trying to escape. For the most part, the outlaws only do anything to people who fail their tests."

"I thought so," the woman said. "That man, Brij, told me he was going to talk with me about whether I wanted to join the Clan. Does it only help believers?"

Jordan was startled enough to pull himself away from his thoughts. "No . . . then they'd be no different than the rest of Appalachia."

"I was worried about that." Gloria plucked at a few flower petals. "I'm a believer, but I've always thought it was wrong for one person to impose morals on another. Not even Jesus did that. He gave people a choice, didn't he?"

She appeared to slip into a contented silence, assisted by the beauty of the valley.

Jordan thought about Caitlyn. How badly he wanted her to have a chance at living where she wouldn't be judged. On her unique differences or by moral guardians. Like Bar Elohim and the Elders.

Outside, most people knew that decades ago, the

religious fundamentalists lost the ability to transform society when they became a political movement. Their boycotts and protests were so commonplace, any outcry against anything beyond the narrow range of what they saw as biblically acceptable was dismissed as a knee-jerk reaction. Once Appalachia was established, there was no one Outside who opposed liberalism and humanism.

*Caitlyn,* he thought again. *If only there had been a check in place to stop experiments on humans.*

When the river widened again, the canoe floated into a shallow pool, separated from the bank by a narrow and long island. A young woman with dark hair sat on the edge of the bank, startled by Caitlyn and Billy. She wore a ragged blue dress, and she'd pulled it up to her knees, soaking her feet in the water.

Two boys, close to Theo's age, splashed in front of her, wearing only shorts. The woman jumped up immediately and called to the boys. "Let's go!"

One of them hesitated, pointing to a small pile of clothing on the narrow island. "But our money!"

"No. Now! Let's go!"

The boy still hesitated.

The woman shouted. "Leave your money. Let's go."

The boys ran through the shallow water and followed her into the trees, gone before Caitlyn could reassure them that she and Billy meant no harm.

The canoe slid past the small island. A couple of shirts lay in the pile. Worn shoes. And two wallets.

"Should we try to find them?" Billy raised the paddle and water ran from its edges. "They'll want their money."

"I'm sure they've stopped where they can watch us," Caitlyn said. "They'll see us go by and see that the wallets are still there. They'll come back out when they feel it's safe."

Billy nodded. He began digging the paddle into the water again, leaving the island behind as they approached another bend.

Once they rounded the bend, four men on horses trotted into the water. All of them were armed with rifles, pointing their weapons directly at Billy and Caitlyn.

The lead man, wearing a ball cap that kept his face in shadow, jumped down from his horse. He walked through knee-deep water, grabbed the front of the canoe, and steadied it. He looked wiry, a good ten years older than Billy. He was close enough that Caitlyn smelled a combination of grease and smoke on the man's denim pants and jacket.

"This is judgment day." His accent was peculiar, one that Caitlyn had heard only occasionally, the result of generations of isolation in these hills. "Keep your mouths shut until I tell you otherwise."

He began to pull the canoe to shore.

Caitlyn saw Billy's shoulders tense, so she shook her head, warning him not to move.

Before the man in the ball cap had made it to the moss-lined bank, the woman in a ragged blue dress stepped out of the woods, hands on her hips.

"They touch the wallets?" the man in the cap asked her.

"No sir."

The man in the cap grinned at Caitlyn. "You passed the test. That means you live. At least long enough to tell us what you're doing on your way into Clan territory."

Billy groaned. She glanced over.

Billy had his arms clutched around his stomach.

"Billy!"

He remained doubled over. "It's bad. Real bad. I never felt it this bad before."

Pierce watched Carney prop the shotgun up against a tree. The sheriff pulled off his shirt, then his undershirt. Not much fat, Pierce noticed. In their hours together, he had learned Carney didn't do things without reason.

"Get us a couple pieces of deadwood." Carney put his top shirt back on.

Pierce didn't have to go farther than the nearest underbrush. He looked back at Carney before picking up the wood.

"Not logs, but good-sized branches, understand?" With the jackknife he'd used on the car tire, Carney had begun to cut long strips from the undershirt.

Again Pierce followed directions without asking questions. He was interested in seeing where this went, as long as they weren't headed to the Church and closer to Mason Lee.

"If Mason's in this valley," Carney said, "then he found a way to move his registered vidpod so that anyone tracking him believes he's miles away." The sheriff lifted one of the pieces of deadwood and used a strip of cloth to strap his vidpod to it. "We're going to do the same."

When Carney seemed satisfied that he'd tied it tightly enough, he tossed the branch into the stream. "Dang things are indestructible. Hopefully, it will look like we're walking downstream for help. After surviving the explosion."

"We?"

"Toss me your vidpod. You don't want to go back to Cumberland Gap. And you don't want to wait around until someone investigates the wreck." Carney began wrapping Pierce's vidpod to the other stick. "But you do want to find Mason because he's after the girl. You've still got a way to track him with that device you planted in his cast, right?"

"Yes."

"Okay, then. After a couple of miles on the river, we'll go up into the hills . . . the hard way. Outlaws mainly watch the river farther down and the easy paths along it, so we'll avoid thcm."

"How do you know this?"

"I know it. That should be enough for you."

Pierce made a point to watch the current as it bumped the sticks with the vidpods until they rounded the next bend. He deliberately surveyed the steep walls of the valley on each side, then turned back to

Carney. "I don't understand you, Carney. Wrecked car. No vidpod. You get home and you're in a factory. Automatic."

"It should be obvious by now that you won't be allowed to take the girl Outside through official channels," Carney said. "You'd be stupid to let Bar Elohim put you in custody, which is his plan. He and Mason Lee will get the girl, and Lee will probably torture and kill you. Bar Elohim doesn't see any value in you, so you need to get out of Appalachia. I assume you'll want help."

"One way or another."

"Exactly." Carney grabbed the shotgun and started walking. "It's the same thing I want. Escape, then asylum. We can help each other."

## THIRTY-EIGHT

Caitlyn checked her vidpod for the time every few minutes.

The group felt like it was collectively crawling; it had taken nearly an hour to travel only a couple of miles. She walked slowly because of her limp. Billy was unable to carry Theo because of his stomach cramps. Another one of the men carried Theo, and one of them walked well ahead, occasionally talking on his vidpod.

She didn't think they would make it to the rendezvous in time. The GPS location pinpointed on her vidpod was less than an hour away. If she missed it, she'd have to wait another twenty-four hours. Every hour seemed to bring new dangers, and she didn't want to spend a night in the woods again.

But she couldn't abandon Billy or Theo. The boy was unconscious, and Billy's effort at hiding pain showed in a sweat that made his face shine.

Caitlyn realized they were walking through a clearing and that the men with shotguns were steering them toward a grove of trees. She thought she saw a cabin, sitting in the shade of a tall pine. When they'd cleared the field, the two men told Caitlyn and Billy to wait, and they took Theo with them inside. Billy collapsed into a rocking chair on the porch, and Caitlyn stood near him, wondering how long they'd be delayed. She consoled herself by thinking about Theo getting the medical attention he needed.

Ten minutes later, an older man with a goatee walked up the path to the cabin. He wore dark sunglasses, and his face was expressionless.

When he arrived, he spoke. "I'm Brij. You've been looking for me."

"My father, Jordan, sent me. How did you find me? We aren't at the rendezvous spot." Caitlyn searched his face for answers, but Brij remained blank. Could she finally relax? Was she safe? Would he answer all her questions?

"I was halfway to the rendezvous and was called back here."

Caitlyn took a step toward Billy. Was this an accusation? Had they made a mistake trusting these men?

"I couldn't leave either of my friends." Caitlyn addressed Brij earnestly. "There's a boy in the cabin. His name is Theo and he's a factory runaway. He cut a chip out of his own arm. Can you make sure he gets help?"

"No one gets turned away." Brij was gentle. "Inside, someone is already looking after him."

Brij turned his face toward Billy. "You know her, son. Gloria Shelton from Cumberland Gap."

"Mrs. Shelton!" Billy straightened briefly in surprise but doubled again as the next stomach cramp seized him.

"It's Saturday. This happens to you every Saturday, doesn't it? Maybe not always this bad, but regularly." Brij put his hand on Billy's shoulder.

"Yes, how did you—" Billy convulsed again.

"You attend church every Sunday, right, son? Partake of communion?"

Billy managed to nod.

"Ever take more than one communion wafer?"

"No sir," he grunted. "That would be stealing."

The old man nodded; a slight tightening pulled the corners of his mouth.

"You need a couple of communion wafers. Someone as big as you won't get enough dosage with just one."

"Dosage?" Caitlyn echoed.

Brij turned his attention back to her. "Caitlyn, during the Eucharist, did your father allow you to eat the wafers?"

"He always told me to slip them to him when no one was looking."

"Jordan knows what I know." Brij walked to the edge of the porch and seemed to look toward the clearing. He stood with his hands behind his back, as if expecting someone. "At least when it comes to Bar Elohim's worship services."

In churches, Caitlyn knew that every Sunday the sermon was delivered via video screen by Bar Elohim.

Before Caitlyn could comment, Brij asked Billy another question.

"Felt good, didn't it, being in the presence of the Lord?"

"Communion on Sundays?" Billy's face showed a brief spasm of pain. "Yes."

"Describe it to me."

Billy took awhile to respond as he appeared to give it thought. "Like a happy feeling. If I closed my eyes, it was like I could move through the sky . . . but not flying. More like I wasn't heavy and the clouds were reaching toward me."

"How about you?" the old man asked Caitlyn. "Did your soul feel like it was soaring with the Lord during your communion time? Were you feeling happy?"

Caitlyn was worried about Theo and frustrated that Billy wasn't getting any relief, but there was something about how the old man asked questions that interested her. Especially these questions. Billy was so big and so deliberate, she couldn't imagine how prayer and communion did that to him, especially when the church experience always nagged at her. She seemed to be the only one bored and distracted, when everyone else seemed deep in joyful contemplation of Bar Elohim's words.

She shook her head. "No happy feelings."

"Your father's doing," the old man told her. "He didn't want you addicted. The wafers are laced with a form of opium which keeps everybody as happy as possible. Ensures their need to be in church."

Caitlyn tried to register the information, but movement below distracted her. At first, she glanced quickly at it. Then it riveted her.

Another man walked up the path, hobbling on a cane. His face was bruised and swollen, but she recognized him instantly.

*Papa!*


Mason had enjoyed grade school. He had fond memories of his domination of other children his age and the sense of hunting prey during the playtimes.

He had not struggled during instructions either and was able to remember numbers and calculations with the same cold logic he used as a predator.

He'd climbed partway up a thick pine tree and had a good view of the coordinates that he was easily able to recall: 36:34:14 N, 83:40:22 W. Without those coordinates, and without the unregistered vidpod locator to bring him here, he would have been convinced his wait would be futile.

His tree overlooked a sheer rock face, with the sunshine directly upon the cracks and fissures, but nothing indicated an entrance into the mountain. Didn't matter. He'd find out, sooner or later.

He settled against the tree with the same strange mixture of contentment and excitement that he'd felt while sitting in a deer stand. In the morning heat, the smell of pine sap was pleasant. His senses were focused. He imagined he could hear the scuttling of a beetle as it climbed the bark of the tree near his face.

He slipped into a state of timelessness. The ultimate hunter. Not even the constant pain of his broken arm intruded into his concentration.

It might have been a minute later or an hour later when a sound broke into his concentration. The slap of a branch.

His nostrils flared. His mouth opened slightly.

A ten-point buck, majestic in the power it exuded, stepped along the path below him. Mason could have dropped on the buck, straddling it and ripping a knife across its throat. He'd done that once before, thinking shooting it would have been too easy. Riding a buck as its lifeblood drained, yelling victoriously until he was hoarse in the sheer exhilaration of unleashed savageness.

The buck's ears twitched and turned.

Seconds later it sprang forward and disappeared down the path.

Mason knew that his patience was about to be rewarded. Footsteps, light on the carpet of pine needles.

A middle-aged man passed below him, pathetically unaware of the buck that passed earlier, and equally unaware of Mason's watching eyes, unaware that the circle of thinning hair at the top of his skull was under observation.

With no hesitation, the man turned toward the rock face. Mason wasn't surprised, as he'd been expecting the entrance to be hidden there. He now saw how he'd been fooled.

The man squatted and felt with his fingers. Mason was close enough to see the man's fingers disappear under a flat rock. He lifted with his legs and raised a door that had been laid horizontally into the ground.

It surfaced fluidly, powered by hydraulic hinges.

The door stayed open for a few seconds, long enough for the man to climb down. Then the door automatically shut upon him, seamlessly fitting back into the ground, still covered with a mat of pine needles.

Mason waited five minutes, then lowered himself from the tree. That he could do it without sound was a remarkable achievement given that he was climbing one-handed, holding his cast away from the trunk.

On the ground, from the backpack that he'd hidden in brush, he found a large can filled with powder. He held it in the hand at the end of his cast. Keeping his shotgun in his other hand, he stepped into the clearing.

He set the shotgun down beside him and moved to where the man had squatted. Without disturbing the man's footprints, he knelt, sunlight on his neck, and began to sprinkle the powder that immediately became invisible in the sunlight.

He heard another snap of deadwood. He dropped the can and whirled, his free hand grabbing for the stock of his shotgun.

"Too late," a voice said.

Mason recognized the voice immediately. *Pierce.*

## THIRTY-NINE

"Most everyone who makes it this far is offered a choice," Brij told Gloria Shelton, safe inside the cabin. She was sitting beside the bed where Theo was under sheets, muttering as he rolled from side to side.

Gloria kept wiping Theo's forehead with a damp cloth but turned her head toward Brij. Jordan had looked at the boy before leaving with Caitlyn. Penicillin was all Theo needed. "Most everyone?"

"If you had children, you wouldn't be offered a chance to remain among the Clan. Living among the Clan is dangerous enough. Having a child among us would restrict our mobility. Worse, we would make decisions to protect the child that would put us in more harm. And lastly, it's unfair to the child, who has no choice. Anyone in the Clan must be here by choice and must make the choice fully aware of the cost. Families are always sent Outside, where there would be a home waiting and support until you found work."

"I have the choice, then. To stay among you?"

"What do you know about us?" he asked in return. "The Clan."

Gloria chuckled. "Only the boogeyman legends. That the Clan shows up at night. Disappears at will. People only remember bits and pieces of a visit." She spread her arms. "Like this. I'm here. But my last memory is Cumberland Gap. When I try to remember in between, it feels dark. Frightening. So I understand the boogeyman legends."

"It wasn't a pleasant journey," Brij said. "I'm not at liberty to tell you more about it, except that there's a drug involved. During the journey, the drug doesn't allow you to move your short-term memories into long term. It protects us and keeps Bar Elohim from searching for refugees like you." More softly, he added, "To Cumberland Gap, you're dead. Your funeral is today. I'm told you will be well grieved."

"That's as much as one could hope for from this life."

"Freedom," Brij said. "One can hope for that. It's why the Clan exists."

As Gloria nodded, her eyes bright in her wrinkled face, Brij continued. "In the garden, God allowed Adam and Eve to choose. When the rich young man walked away from Christ after learning what he needed to do to reach heaven, Christ didn't chase him to persuade him to change his mind. Any other way is the kingdom of the sword."

"The sword?"

"Imposing beliefs by using earthly power. Like the

Crusades, the Inquisition, and, in the last century, the political banding of Christians that finally resulted in Appalachia."

Brij shook his head. "Christ's followers begged him to overthrow Rome. Instead, he chose the kingdom of the cross. Power through powerlessness. Love and sacrifice. That's what you'll accept if you join us. We will not fight for Christ. But we will die for him."

In the silence, Gloria Shelton continued to soothe Theo's fever. She turned her hand over and gently touched her old fingers across his forehead.

"No," she finally said. "I don't want to join the Clan."

Brij raised his eyebrows. "Nearly always, I know the answer before I hear it. You've surprised me. You already risked your life by teaching from a Bible. I expected you would stay."

"Billy's told me what this boy has gone through to get Outside. He watched his parents die in an execution by stoning. When he's ready to leave, I'd like to go with him. Outside. To help him as long as I can."

"I thought you were dead." Caitlyn hugged Jordan. They stood several yards away from the cabin.

Feeling her arms around his back made him again conscious of how her body had changed so rapidly in the last days. He closed his eyes, washed in guilt. And relief. Mostly though, overwhelming love.

"I thought I'd be dead too," Jordan said.

"You mean when you sent me over the cliff?" She

pushed back and stared at him. He hoped her expression simply reflected a reaction to how he must have looked with the deep bruising, but he knew better.

He nodded.

"Why?"

"If we didn't separate, the bounty hunter would have gotten us both. It wasn't a difficult decision." Especially, he thought, because of his guilt. And his love.

"No. I meant, why this plan? The letter. The horse. Instructions to come here. Why didn't you tell me?"

"That was part of the conditions of help. Secrecy. It protects the Clan. In return, you will have a chance to save the Clan."

"Save the Clan?" Each word was measured with disbelief.

"Brij will tell you."

Caitlyn's expression hardened. "I had a right to know. Before you abandoned me on the cliff."

"It was to save you." Jordan kept his eyes on hers, but it took effort.

"I'm here, safe, and even now you won't tell me why." She backed away from him. He was losing her again.

It was a chasm. His love for her on one side. His duty and honor to the Clan on the other. And a horrible darkness lay between.

"Everything I've done since you were little was to find a way for you to live normally, to get Outside. Where you will be free to make your own choices. Of faith or love. Tomorrow, you will be Outside. I've made arrangements, and there will be money waiting for you. A doctor. Surgery. A new identity."

"Are you going Outside too?" For a moment, she was a faltering child again, terrified of losing her Papa.

He wished he could rush forward, pull her close and protect her. Tell her that he wouldn't leave her this time.

"I can't." He struggled for a way to say it that wouldn't endanger her further. "They want what I know too badly. If we are together, we will always be hunted."

"What do they want?" Her face had instantly transformed, from lost child to resolute adult.

Jordan still could not find the strength to tell her.

"Mason was going to cut me open. He has a silver canister. What does he want?"

She raised her voice. "What does he want?"

Jordan shook his head, barely able to look her in the eyes.

She took a half step back. "What does Mason want from me?"

Jordan knew he was losing her but still could not answer. Because if he did, he'd lose her anyway.

She waited. As the silence lengthened, he knew their chasm was becoming unbridgeable.

Brij appeared on the porch of the cabin, and Jordan knew he'd lost. There was no time left and nothing he could say.

Caitlyn walked away.

Carney stood next to Pierce, maybe twenty feet away from Mason, but far enough that the dispersion pattern of shot would make it impossible to miss his target. He was close enough that the pellets would tear holes through Mason's body.

Mason slowly stood, blinking against the sunlight. "We've got them, Carney. This is the entrance to the mines. The powder here shows up in ultraviolet light. We wait for someone else to go in, then follow the tracks. I've got the ultraviolet light in my backpack. And paint with the same kind of chemical for marking the turns in the mine. We won't get lost."

"No." Shotgun held motionless, Carney used his head to motion for Pierce to get Mason's backpack. "Duct tape. He's always got a roll or two on him."

Carney stared at Mason while Pierce pulled out the contents. Flashlight. The silver canister. A small spray can. Flares. And a roll of duct tape.

"Don't do this," Mason said. "We're on the same side. If not, Bar Elohim will have you in a factory by tonight."

Carney ignored Lee again. "We'll need to tape his hands behind his back. I'd rather he walked, but if he doesn't, tape his ankles and we'll carry him."

"Where to?"

Carney saw no point in answering Mason. His plan was to move the bounty hunter at least a mile away, then he and Pierce would come back. Go inside the mines and alert the Clan that this entrance had been found. As in all other times of discovery, the Clan would use explosives to obliterate it and make it impossible to find a way inside. The mountain was honeycombed with entrances. The Clan would shift to a new one.

"Where's the girl?" Carney asked. "Inside already?"

"Doesn't matter to you." Mason knelt and reached for his shotgun.

"You touch that . . . I'll let Pierce finish his job on you. No bluff."

Mason ignored him, wrapping his fingers around the stock of his shotgun.

"Guess it'll be me then." Carney pulled the trigger without hesitation. Instead of a roar and recoil, he heard a futile click. Mason rose from his knees, swinging the barrel of his own shotgun toward Carney.

Carney pulled frantically, again and again. Nothing but ineffective clicking.

"What a shame," Mason said. "Almost like someone got into your office and filed away the firing pins."

Mason stepped closer. "Now that you have that duct tape out, Agent, go ahead and follow the sheriff's plan. His hands, behind his back, like hc said. Then lie on the ground so I can do the same to you. Unfortunately, you're worth more to me alive than dead right now, but shooting you is easier than fighting you. Not nearly as good as cutting you up like you deserve."

## FORTY

"Jordan believes you are ready?" Brij asked gently. The two of them followed a path up the hills, away from the cabin, where they'd left all the others behind.

"Soon." Caitlyn didn't want to elaborate. Her joy in seeing Papa alive had not dissipated, but she was overwhelmed by their conversation. And what he'd asked her to do.

"Papa has been one of the Clan for years, hasn't he?" She felt there was so much she hadn't known about him.

"He's been serving us and those around him since he first fled to Appalachia."

"With me."

"With you." Brij must have understood some of her bitterness. "Don't be harsh on him. He had no choice. Coming here with you was the only way he could protect you. And now, it seems, you are the only way to protect us. He did explain, didn't he?"

Caitlyn nodded.

"It wasn't his idea. It was mine."

They pushed upward, with Caitlyn leaning on her cane every step. Papa had wrapped her ankle, but it still throbbed.

"Since you were a little girl, he's wanted you to have the surgery. It was impossible when you were young, at least here in Appalachia."

Caitlyn remembered that day in the doctor's office, the day after her sixth birthday. Wearing the red shoes. Hearing her father and the doctor talk about wings. And believing they had meant the crippled bird.

"He did tell you that there is a surgeon waiting for you Outside?"

Caitlyn barely fought back quiet tears. She managed to nod.

"I was the one to ask Jordan to find a way for officials Outside to learn of your presence in Appalachia," Brij said. "To assure they'd send someone in to get the two of you."

"Why?"

"Instead of telling you," Brij said, "let me show you."

He pointed up the mountain.

Pierce knew when he heard the sound of the choppers that it would be the roar of defeat. Mason had forced Carney and him downhill far enough that when the girl approached, she'd be unaware that the men were there—especially Mason, the watchful hunter who'd be hiding in a tree.

He and Carney would be in the hands of Bar Elohim by nightfall, the girl would probably be dead, and Pierce's mission to capture Caitlyn a failure. He was unaccustomed to experiencing defeat, but this bizarre country kept him confused and off balance. No one was who they claimed to be.

The entire way downhill, Mason gloated to the bound men.

"After the girl goes into the mountain, I light the heat flares, which will bring in Bar Elohim's men, the soldiers. I'm going to tell them where to find you. Then, I get the girl and destroy the Clan."

Mason told them to stop, and after a warning shot that nearly grazed Carney's head, he forced the sheriff to wrap Pierce to a tree with duct tape, then his own legs and waist. Mason finished the rest, and with final flourishes, he pasted tape over their mouths. "Hope you've enjoyed Appalachia, Agent. I think you'll get to see some more *elite* attractions soon. You might never want to leave."

Mason left to watch for the girl, and Pierce continued to wait for the choppers.

From his hidden viewpoint in the tree, Mason sat motionless near the hidden entrance. In the heat, he was slick with his own sweat, but he didn't mind. He knew his body was working hard to keep his temperature regulated.

The sweat led to a deep thirst that was worsened because he had deliberately avoided drinking water earlier, anticipating the effect it would have on his bladder. He couldn't afford to move to relieve himself and had no intention of wetting his pants like an infant or a debilitated old man.

He was fine with the thirst. His reward would be well worth it.

Time continued to pass easily for him as he waited for the girl. He enjoyed visualizing the moment when his knife would cut through flesh and muscle and imagining all the different ways that Caitlyn would react in horror.

This pleasure gave him a feeling like serenity, and he was almost disappointed when he caught his first glimpse of her, walking up the path with an old man leaning on a walking stick and showing a distinct limp.

They moved to the entrance without even looking around to see if it was safe. The old man lifted the door, and they disappeared down the steps.

Mason decided to give them a five-minute head start.


## FORTY-ONE

As she followed Brij down the steps into the mountain, Caitlyn still marveled at the door that had been set into the ground. Even from three feet away, she'd been unable to see it, camouflaged by a mat of pine needles and flat rocks that looked like part of the ground.

Her amazement continued when the door silently slid shut on its hydraulic hinges, for it did not enclose them in darkness.

The tunnel was square, easily two feet higher than her head, wide enough for a car to drive through, shored up with beams of lumber. She was able to take all of it in because of string lighting—the small white bulbs used on Christmas trees. It stretched as far as she could see down the length of the tunnel, and the gentle slope of the passageway was obvious as it continued into the heart of the mountain.

"The tunnels are part of a mine that existed a hundred years ago," Brij said. "We've expanded the system, of course. The lights and ventilation fans are powered by a water turbine deep inside the mountain."

Although the tunnel continued straight ahead, they had reached another tunnel that bisected this one. It too had a string of lights stretching downward on a long, gentle slope. A breeze touched Caitlyn's face, and she was grateful for the cool air.

Her silence was a trait belonging to her curiosity. She remembered reading a forbidden book with Papa in her childhood, *Alice's Adventures in Wonderland*, and how she always wondered if Alice was very afraid, falling into that strange place. As she stopped to examine a flat-screen monitor on the wall, she thought how she never imagined Wonderland to be a world of mine shafts.

The monitor showed red symbols against a black background:

$$\Delta \; \vartheta \; \Sigma \; \Omega$$
$$\varsigma \; \theta \; \lambda \; \varphi$$
$$\phi \; \beta \; \alpha \; \psi$$
$$\Phi \; \notin \; \propto \; \not\subset$$
$$\in \; \Pi \; \pi \; \mu$$

"It's how we navigate," Brij explained. "There are over a hundred miles of tunnels. At every intersection, you'll find a monitor with battery backup. Each monitor has twenty of twenty-six symbols."

He pointed at the markings to their side and hovered his finger above the ∉ symbol.

"Look at the wall of the other tunnel where it reaches this one. You won't see the same symbol there."

Caitlyn studied it. By comparing both sets of symbols, she saw that the ∉ had been replaced with a ɘ.

"Which tunnel do we take?" Brij tapped the monitor.

Because of the symbols on her vidpod, Caitlyn had no difficulty answering. She pointed at the ∉. "This one. Underlined on my vidpod."

"Essentially, that's our system. Once you know the symbol or combination of symbols that marks your passage, you simply check each intersection for it."

"Combination?"

"Twenty symbols, but hundreds of tunnels. Sometimes it's a combination of two symbols, sometimes three. The screens are networked to a mainframe computer. When we want to change the patterns, it's done instantly."

"Easy to get confused," Caitlyn said. "A lot of the symbols look the same."

Brij nodded. "By design. It takes years and years to learn the tunnel mazes. Even then, not all of the Clan know every tunnel. Nor will they. We've accumulated a lot of resources. Medical, technical, even wealth. It's dispersed and hidden throughout the mountain. Our headquarters too. Even if Bar Elohim's soldiers penetrated the mountain, it's unlikely they'd know where to go. And all the tunnels are rigged with explosives at certain points to collapse them. We can seal off any area we need to and retreat elsewhere."

"What about the legends?" Caitlyn followed Brij down the tunnel. "The stories we were told as children to scare us. That the Clan let people wander for days and days until they die of thirst. Sometimes worse."

"Just legend," Brij said simply. "We don't fight. We don't allow people to die. I can tell you how the legends get started, though. The outlaw perimeter. Or drug-induced anterograde amnesia."

Caitlyn stopped short. "You force someone to take drugs?"

"Never forced. It's voluntary. Unless it's someone like the woman attending to Theo, who needed to be rescued quickly. Usually, when we find someone, it's a condition of the rescue. The drug flunitrazepam is dissolved in water, and for the next ten hours, the short-term memory can't transfer events to long-term memory. Anything beyond their immediate attention span disappears when it's replaced by the next event. That protects us when we let them go, keeps our operational secrets intact and successful. But I'm sure the occasional nightmares that follow get embellished."

"Did you give me the drug?"

"Can you recall our conversation as we walked from the cabin?"

"Yes."

"That's your answer. You haven't lost the ability to access short-term memories."

"I guess you trust me."

Brij put a light hand on her shoulder. "Caitlyn, we are trusting you with everything, including our future."

When he reached the entrance, Mason unscrewed the cigar-sized tube he'd been carrying in his back pocket. He looked around for a place to prop it and found a small crack in a sheet of rock.

*Perfect.*

The crack was clear of any natural debris that might catch fire, which was important. If a fire spread into the valley, it would be an obstacle to dropping choppers into the valley and would threaten the entire operation.

Mason set the small tube into place. He took his canteen from his belt and poured water into the tube.

Instantly, the magnesium powder inside burst into a white flame, burning at over a thousand degrees Fahrenheit.

Mason lifted the door to the entrance and took a few steps down inside. He jammed a rock into the hinges so that it wouldn't close. The soldiers would find it easily.

Then he climbed down into the tunnel.

Jordan approached Billy, who was sitting on the steps of the cabin, head hanging down, as if recovering from a horrible hangover.

"I need you," Jordan said.

Billy raised his head and blinked. He looked confused, like Jordan had spoken to him in an alien language.

"Help me up the path." Jordan felt like he could barely move. The beating he'd taken from Mason and the dogs would take weeks of recovery. "Two men are still up on the mountain. The bounty hunter bound and left them. We need to get them down before the choppers arrive."

Billy stood. "I can do it."

Jordan was glad the boy didn't ask how Jordan knew that choppers would be coming. Or how he knew about the men and what Mason Lee had done with them.

Jordan didn't have time to explain.

Or to fabricate a lie.

## FORTY-TWO

The choppers hovered in place above the entrance into the mountain. Although Pierce faced downhill, he was able to turn his head and clearly see soldier after soldier dropping down by rope from the choppers.

He found himself surprised that it was so well organized. Appalachia obviously knew how to successfully pull off military domination. Even if the Clan believed in combating military force with force, they didn't have a chance.

How long would it take before the soldiers arrived to take Carney and him away? Would they be heading to a factory or something more fatal? Pierce knew that Bar Elohim would provide falsified evidence to his superiors Outside, showing how he disappeared into the Appalachian wilderness. While they considered him a top operative, they wouldn't be surprised. It had happened before, and investigating his disappearance would risk unnecessary relationship tensions between the two U.S. countries.

Pierce didn't have to wonder about his fate for too long. He spotted movement farther down the path. A big man pushed his way through the bush.

He'd seen him before, but it took him a second to remember the kid's name. Big kid. The deputy.

*Billy. That's it. Billy.*

The kid got closer, bug-eyed as he saw them strapped to the tree. "Sheriff Carney?"

Carney reacted by frantically pulling against the duct tape. Making noise from behind the tape on his mouth.

Billy took hesitant steps closer like he was scared that somehow Carney had the power to do something to him.

Carney yelled more from behind the tape.

Billy reached for it and tugged slowly. The ripping tape elongated the flesh on Carney's face, and he scowled.

Billy gave it a good yank, and the tape ripped loose. "Sheriff Carney?"

Carney panted, nodding. Billy started cutting the tape from his arms.

"I mean, how did you get here? They told me to come up here and help a couple of men. I didn't know it would be you."

"Who told you to help us?" Carney began unwrapping his legs.

To get attention, Pierce grunted from behind his own tape. They could talk about this somewhere else. Who knew how long they had before soldiers came looking for them as Mason had threatened.

Billy looked at Carney for permission to help Pierce. Another nod.

Pierce braced himself for the sharp pull. He was glad he'd shaved. Smooth skin hurt less. He, too, gasped for air after Billy pulled the tape loose.

"Let's go, kid," he said. "You two can compare notes later."

"You going to arrest me?" Billy asked Carney. "You came here looking for me, right?"

"He can't go back to town either," Pierce snapped, nodding toward the sheriff. "He's one of them."

"One of them what?" Billy looked from Pierce to Carney, then back to Pierce.

"One of the Clan," Pierce said. "He's been helping people escape Cumberland Gap for years. Aren't I right, Sheriff?"

# FORTY-THREE

I'm not drinking it." Pierce set the glass of water on a table.

He stood in the center of the cabin facing Jordan. An old lady sat with a boy in one corner, the big deputy and Carney in another.

The *thump-thump* of the idling helicopters on the mountainside, hundreds of yards above the cabin, underscored the urgency of the situation.

"We can't take you through the tunnels any other way," Jordan said. "The flunitrazepam is safe and—"

"It's a roofie," Pierce interjected. "Trust me. I know how to use pharmaceuticals. I'm just not going to drink it."

"You want escape, and this is the only option." Jordan's face was distorted by bruises and obvious pain. Pierce still couldn't believe that the man was alive and telling *him* what to do. Should have him on the floor, in cuffs by now.

"I want you, Dr. Brown, to think back a couple of decades. Arson. Destruction of hundreds of millions of dollars of government property. There's no statute of limitations for your crimes."

"We don't make it through the caves without him, Pierce," Carney said. "None of us. This area is too hot with Bar Elohim's men. The way Mason Lee is acting, I don't think they are too inclined to leave you alive."

"You're thinking we owe him?" Pierce said. "You forget I have a duty to follow."

"Without him, we're dead. It's pretty simple."

"With him in custody, Bar Elohim gives us a pass Outside. All of us in this cabin. You have any idea how badly my agency wants him? What his knowledge is worth? To get Jordan, my government will do whatever it takes to negotiate our freedom."

Carney took a step toward Pierce. "My apologies, but this is going to get ugly."

"You're going to fight me?"

"Unless you stand down and drink the stuff."

"I'm not going to pull something cheap here, Carney. All of us escape, but we do it my way."

"Strangely enough, I believe you really think you can do this. I just don't like your way."

Carney threw a punch, low and hard.

Pierce deflected it with his forearm. Then he came under Carney's next punch, used Carney's momentum against him, swung the man around and kicked his feet out from under him. Carney fell on his belly, his face rebounded against the floor.

Pierce knelt beside him. "I don't have any choice, Carney. I found the man, and now I have to take him in."

Pierce watched Carney closely for the slightest resistance. He didn't want to hurt the Sheriff, but he wasn't going to take chances. He was so focused that by the time he felt Billy's arms wrapped around his chest, it was too late.

Billy lifted him like he was a pillow, and Pierce found himself dangling. The kid's arms were as powerful as hydraulics, pinning Pierce's own arms to his chest.

"Mr. Jordan." Billy spoke without any hint of exertion. "Is all that true? About the stealing and destruction?"

Pierce kicked futilely, but it felt ridiculous and undignified.

"You should put him down," Jordan said.

"Is it true?" Billy kept his crushing hold on Pierce.

"It's true."

"Why did you do it?" Billy asked.

"Bad people were doing bad things," Jordan answered. "Someone had to stop it."

"I believe you." Billy backed away with Pierce. "You all go. Maybe Sheriff Carney can help Mrs. Shelton and Theo. I'll just hold him like this for a while."

Jordan stepped up to Billy. "Really, Billy, put him down. If he's going to make sure all of us get Outside, I won't fight it."

Carney was back off the floor by then. "Hold him good, Billy."

Carney took the glass of water that Pierce had set down. "If I hadn't seen it and felt it, I would never have believed a man could move as fast as you. But it's not doing you much good now. More to Billy than meets the eye."

"Jordan is a criminal," Pierce said. "You want to set him free?"

"You can drink this nice," Carney said. "Or I'll plug your nose and pour it down. Which way do you want it?"

Pierce tried shaking himself loose. He felt like he was squeezed between two mountains.

Carney plugged Pierce's nose. When Pierce opened his mouth for air, Carney began to pour.

Brij handed Caitlyn a headlamp, like the type she and Papa would take when they went caving. They stood at the entrance to one of six tunnels radiating out from the central headquarters.

"This is for when the power goes off. Please put it on."

Not *if,* Caitlyn noted, but *when.*

Caitlyn didn't ask about this. She was trying to stay in the moment, but everything was happening so quickly. They'd reached the open area at the end of the entrance tunnel, where two dozen Clan members sat in front of computer screens and monitors. Brij hadn't stopped to introduce her to any of them or explain the area but escorted her through it to a tunnel on the far side of the room.

"Jordan explained what to expect once you reach the waterfall, right?" Brij asked. "You'll see the turbine there."

"And a rope bridge across and a series of ladders down." Caitlyn felt a stab of pain in her back but ignored it.

Brij pointed at the set of symbols on the tunnel wall.

$$\in \notin \propto \Omega$$
$$\varsigma \psi \lambda \varphi$$
$$\phi \beta \alpha \theta$$
$$\Phi \vartheta \Sigma \not\subset$$
$$\Delta \Pi \pi \mu$$

"From this point on, here's what to look for to get there." He touched the ψ symbol. "There will only be three intersections. Got it?"

"Yes."

"Good. Then go, Caitlyn. Godspeed."

"Soldiers," Theo croaked. He'd been in and out of his delirium since leaving the cabin. "They're behind us."

The group formed a ragged procession, walking a narrow path with a steep wall of rocks on one side and a long drop on the other, skirting the side of the mountain, staying well out of sight of the choppers.

Theo leaned on Gloria as they walked, and Billy held Jordan up. Carney had a firm grip on the rope that they'd used to tie Pierce's hands behind his back.

Carney half-turned, frowning. "I don't hear anything."

"Sheriff Carney," Billy said, "if Theo says he hears something, believe him."

Unlike Theo and Gloria, Billy did not drink the water with flunitrazepam. Carney and Jordan had decided it would be better to wait until just before an entrance into the cave system. They wanted Billy's help with Pierce along the way, in case he shook off the drug and gave them trouble.

"We'll pick up the pace," Carney whispered. "How far we got?"

"Too far." Jordan leaned against the rock face. "If they're on this path, we won't get there before they catch us."

Carney gauged the wall behind Jordan. "I'll stay back."

"It's suicide." Jordan shook his head.

"Should be able to climb up some, work on that loose scrabble up there. How much time you need anyway?"

"You don't have a weapon."

"A bunch of falling rocks will distract them." Carney shrugged. "If I get high enough where they can't see me, I can turn this path into an obstacle and shell a few of them when they slow to scale it."

"But that leaves you—"

"Look," Carney said, "here's my secret. All I really expected Outside was six months, maybe eight. Long enough to enjoy some freedom. I'm sick."

Jordan bowed his head.

"Sick? What?" Billy asked.

"Cancer. Don't feel sorry for me, Billy. You go ahead. I'm proud of what you've done to get us here."

Billy blinked a few times. "You really were a part of the Clan all along."

Carney nodded. "I was."

"But all the things you told me on the town square, about being a shepherd and all that."

"Official talk. I knew it was being recorded."

Billy cocked his head, clearly processing, then he finally spoke. "All the prisoners who died while you've been in charge—they escaped, didn't they? Like Mrs. Shelton. And you sent me to arrest her because you knew I'd mess up."

"Don't let anyone ever tell you that you're stupid, Billy. You remember that and take care of these people. They need you."

The end of the tunnel brightened for Mason. He'd been armed with the $\notin$ symbol from the vidpod he'd taken from Jordan. Still, as agreed with Bar Elohim during their roadside meeting, it might not be enough to navigate the warren of tunnels.

So he'd been using his ultraviolet light to follow the footprints of the old man and the girl in the tunnel. He was certain he had not lost them. To guide the soldiers, he'd used the spray paint on the tunnel wall every few feet, as also instructed by Bar Elohim. If this was their chance to stomp out the Clan, they would take every precaution.

Near the end of the tunnel, he heard the buzz of conversation.

Mason held his shotgun loosely in the crook of his good arm. The Clan were pacifists, and they'd run before attacking him. But they couldn't outrun shotgun pellets.

Mason didn't bother sneaking to the end of the tunnel. He walked boldly toward it, keeping to the center. He broke into the open, discovering the source of the brightness.

It looked like a command center, a circular area the size of a small house, with other tunnels radiating from it in five directions. About twenty men and women stood or sat in front of computers. He took it all in. Some froze as they spotted him, and the conversations stopped.

Mason lifted his shotgun. He leveled it at the closest person. A woman with dark hair, about his age.

"Anybody moves," Mason said, "she dies first. I'll get about five more of you before you manage to scatter."

Again, silence, except for the slight hissing of circulated air.

"Guess nobody likes those odds. I'm kind of disappointed, to tell you the truth."

He surveyed the faces in the group. Not many showed fear. More like shock and surprise.

"All right then," Mason said. "Every one of you, get on your belly. You'll wait until the soldiers arrive."

He did another count of everyone, as ordered. He'd been wrong. There were twenty-five Clan here. And this was the obvious base for their operations. He'd just broken the back of the group, and that warranted a big reward.

But not big enough.

He looked for the girl. She was the real prize.

None of the women on the floor looked the age of the fugitive's daughter or were wrapped in that dark cloak she wore. He saw the old man instead. Watching carefully that no one swung an arm to trip him, he walked among the prone bodies toward the old man. Brij.

Already, he could hear the distant thumping of the boots of the approaching soldiers.

"Where'd she go?"

The old man didn't answer.

"Where'd she go?" Mason kicked the man in the kidneys. He arched as if struck by electricity, then fell and stayed motionless.

What Mason wanted to do was go back and grab that first woman by the hair with his casted hand and hold a knife to her throat with his other. No. He wanted to run the knife against her throat, feel the give of cartilage and let her bleed all over his arm. Warm blood. That would show the rest he was serious.

But to do it, he'd have to set down the shotgun. Pacifists or not, he doubted they'd meekly let him control them without a shotgun. He'd have to wait. The soldiers were almost upon them anyway.

"There are only five minutes left," one of the men called out, his voice traveling over the hard floor.

"Five minutes?" Mason said.

"On my computer. I set the timer. This area is rigged for destruction just like our entrances. We have to protect the rest of our tunnels."

"Five minutes?" Mason felt a chill spread through his chest. "Five minutes."

It would serve all of them right if he made them stay. But there's no way they'd obey his orders unless he monitored them with his shotgun, which meant the mountain would crash in on him too.

"All of you—on your feet!"

They all obeyed. Even the old man attempted to get to his knees, groaning. A woman near him stooped to help.

"Leave him," Mason barked.

"No." Her defiance showed no fear. Mason hated it when people didn't fear him. His finger twitched on the shotgun. He really wanted to kill someone. Right now, the woman defying him. But he was all too aware that the shotgun blast might set off the detonation. No sense committing suicide when he could torture her later.

The soldiers arrived, and Mason rushed forward, waving his cast. "Take them out, and keep them in close custody! This is the headquarters. Set to destruct in minutes!"

In seconds, the soldiers had surrounded the men and women and were hurrying them back out of the tunnel.

Mason turned on his ultraviolet light and began scanning the floor.

He saw it almost instantly. The same small footprints he'd been following down the tunnel. The same small circles where the tip of her walking stick touched the tunnel floor.

It was easy to see where the footprints led into another tunnel, going deeper into the mountain.

*They were protecting her,* Mason thought. *She was given directions to find her way out by a different route.*

If he followed her, he'd have a way out too.

Without a second's hesitation, Mason ran down the same tunnel. He wanted to get as far away from the explosion as possible before it happened.

## FORTY-FOUR

Billy was lost, of course, as he pushed Jordan in a wheelchair through the tunnel, thinking about the shots they'd heard just before going into the mountain. Occasionally, Jordan directed him to turn down another tunnel at an intersection. Then another. Billy had no sense of direction in the maze of tunnels that had once formed a coal mine.

Pierce walked silently with them but didn't seem to mind that they were lost. Jordan was taking them to safety.

Trouble was, Billy knew he wasn't lost enough.

Jordan had made Billy promise that he wouldn't remember which path they had used to reach a hidden entrance into the mountain. Jordan had promised that Billy wouldn't even remember that a wheelchair had been waiting.

So it bothered Billy that he could still vaguely remember those promises. Wasn't he supposed to forget them too? Or was he so big that they hadn't given him enough dosage, like with the communion wafers?

His memories were like shifting sheets of fog. Occasionally, they would lift, and he'd see it clearly. The path that took them away from where the choppers had dropped soldiers. One of the Clan waiting inside the tunnel with a wheelchair for Jordan, because Jordan was having too much difficulty walking.

And he'd remember, too, that Caitlyn had left the cabin, and that there had been an undercurrent of tension, like she was going into some kind of danger that no one discussed, no matter how many times he asked. He would remember, certainly, that he missed her.

Then the fog would return, and Billy would be happy. He only remembered that he and Pierce and Theo and Gloria were going to be sent Outside. He didn't know how or where. That was the entire reason that all three had agreed to drink the water with a drug to erase their short-term memories.

But he wasn't even supposed to remember that!

Maybe he should have had more of the water to drink. After all, if his body was so big that a regular dose of communion wafers didn't do to him what it did to others, maybe that was the same for the drugged water.

He felt guilty over this.

He leaned forward to tell Jordan that maybe he shouldn't be allowed to escape because he knew too much, but the fog descended, and Billy found himself opening his mouth but forgetting what he was going to say.

He kept pushing the wheelchair. When Jordan gave him directions again at another intersection of tunnels, Billy remembered Caitlyn again.

He began to worry once more. Until, mercifully, another patch of fog shifted his thoughts away.

A hundred yards into the tunnel beyond the headquarters, Mason reached the end, where the tunnel formed a T.

*Left or right?*

His ultraviolet light picked up the small giveaway circle of the tip of Caitlyn's cane going down the left tunnel. The circle was fading; he needed to catch her soon.

He stepped left.

A split second later, the tunnel lights went black. A brief orange flare threw illumination ripples down the dirt walls, and then the sound of the explosion thundered behind him. Delayed by a heartbeat, the whoosh of air blew past Mason, taking with it a cloud of dust that continued down the tunnel.

It dropped him to his knees. He choked on the dust.

When he stood, he searched with his ultraviolet light for the glowing white circles of the girl's cane tracks.

Nothing.

He switched on his flashlight and cursed.

The tunnel behind him was blocked. The soldiers of Bar Elohim couldn't chase him and take away his trophy, leaving him as the sole hunter. But the fine dust was settling on the floor of the tunnel, wiping out the ultraviolet tracks.

If she reached another turn, how would he track her? And now there was more at stake than just catching her. She wouldn't have fled if she didn't know a way out of the mountain.

Mason needed to follow her just to save his own life.

At that thought, the tunnel walls seemed to squeeze the life from him. He couldn't endure the thought of being lost in the depths of the mountain, wandering around until first his batteries ran out, then his own energy, then his life, until time dried him out like a mummy.

The image made him lick his lips. All he tasted was dust.

He cursed again, looking down. The floor of the tunnel had a uniform layer of dust. Each step he took left a smudged print.

So would she.

All he had to do was continue until he found her tracks. At maximum, she had only a five-minute head start.

And she was walking with an injured foot. At this thought, he shed his claustrophobia and fear of darkness. He was a hunter. Doing what he did best.

## FORTY-FIVE

Caitlyn's ankle ached, and it seemed to her that with each step, she needed to put more and more weight on her walking stick, jabbing it into the floor of the tunnel.

She needed to move faster.

Twice she'd seen a flash of light in the depths of darkness behind her. Both times had happened when she'd reached the end of a long straight stretch, flashes of light so brief she'd hoped they were her imagination.

She knew otherwise, though, and was convinced it could be none other than Mason Lee. He was like the devil, supernatural in his ability to hunt.

She pushed on. The coal miner's flashlight on her head seemed to be growing dimmer each minute, and that added to her sense of urgency. She had made two turns. Brij had promised her that the third would take her to the waterfall. She didn't need much extra time to finally lose Mason.

She reached a fork in the tunnels, then searched the monitor for the symbol among the nineteen others. She saw it on the right-hand turn.

$$\psi$$

As she entered the new tunnel, a cool breeze pushed into her face.

It gave her renewed energy. Somewhere ahead was the bridge. She could hear the muted rush of water.

The waterfall Papa had described! All she had to do was cross the bridge and—

It felt like a giant knife plunging into her back. The pain drove her to her knees. Without the walking cane, she would have fallen.

Then, just as quickly and just as mysteriously, it disappeared, leaving her panting.

Four steps later, another bolt of pain speared her, like lightning appearing from nowhere. This time she was unable to keep her balance. She fell, rolling over her injured ankle.

On her stomach, she clenched her teeth to keep from screaming. It felt like the skin of her back was rippling and had come to life, like an alien creature was struggling to escape from her body.

She couldn't do anything but fight it. It had taken over her body, and she shook as if in a violent seizure.

Something was pulling her apart.

Pulling, pulling, pulling.

A final, intense rip contracted, and Caitlyn beat a fist against the floor, fighting the pain.

Then nothing. The pain was gone, like the aftermath of a thunderstorm.

She pushed to her knees. With her upper body vertical, a warm fluid seeped onto her hips.

Was she bleeding? Was she dying?

Then she became aware of another sensation on her back, and her mind explored it with wonder.

Was it . . . ?

Another flash of light. Not behind closed eyelids, the bursting of white from jaw-clenching pain, but a flashlight, bouncing off the tunnel walls.

Her pursuer was closing in. No time to wonder.

She hobbled forward in a half run.

If she could cross the bridge in time, she'd lose him. Brij had promised the bridge was safety.

Here the cool wind was stronger. Her beam of light showed a web of ropes. The bridge. And at her feet, the floor of the tunnel ended abruptly. A drop-off.

She turned her light downward, but the darkness extended far beyond its beam. She turned it to the sound of water and saw cascading falls, dozens of feet wide. Spray came from a turbine centered in the heavy stream of water.

She sensed a feeling of height and trembled.

It was the same trembling of joy she'd always experienced as a child when Papa took her on mountain climbs, especially on the edge of a cliff. The feeling that all she had to do was step out into the air and she would be home.

Here, however, the feeling was so overwhelming that she threw her walking stick out into the void. Watched it with the beam of her flashlight until it disappeared.

*Jump,* her instincts commanded. *Jump!*

She clutched at the rope beside her, as if she were holding herself back against a force trying to suck her into the void. It was the guide rope to the bridge.

Behind her, another flash of light. Her pursuer. This time, the light did not disappear.

Whoever it was had made it into the final stretch of tunnel.

Caitlyn had no choice but to step onto the bridge. With her injured ankle, it was agony. But the rope bridge was constructed with a waist-high guide rope on each side. She held on to the ropes and shuffled forward. Her back was warm and wet, as if a thick fluid seeped across her skin.

Progress was slow. Too slow.

She was only halfway across when her pursuer reached the end of the tunnel.

She tried to make herself shrink as the beam of light seemed to pin her in place.

## FORTY-SIX

Where the tunnel ended in a void, Mason discovered the source of the roar.

A waterfall a dozen steps from the end of the tunnel. He played his flashlight across it and noticed a turbine. This must be what powered the Clan's energy needs. The water was a thin, wide curtain, flowing hard and fast, disappearing into the darkness at the end of his flashlight beam. He flicked the light to his right. The rock was smooth and vertical.

Mason gave little thought to the incredible natural phenomenon of an underground river that, over millennia, had carved sheer tubes through soft limestone over a waterfall deep inside the mountain. He was a hunter. Hunting, surveying his surroundings, and evaluating.

Ahead of him, the chasm was black, but there was a heavy iron hook embedded into each side of the tunnel, with a loop of thick rope on each.

He flicked his beam along the rope to his left. It was a guide rope, matching the one on the other side. Wooden slats hung from shorter pieces of rope, forming the bottom of a bridge. The slats were tied together with short loops, a couple of inches between each. Mason shivered at the thought of stepping into the chasm trusting only those slats. He could slip through the side of the bridge and fall. The darkness pressed against him even in his thrill at being so close to his goal.

With his light, he illuminated the bridge and froze Caitlyn in place, throwing a giant shadow onto the sheer rock wall on the other side of the chasm. She was turned sideways, and Mason imagined for a moment that she was a humpbacked monster. It only lasted for that moment, because Caitlyn immediately used the light to help her find better footing on the rope bridge and began to scramble away, sending the bridge swaying. She was limping badly, and Mason smiled.

Mason flicked the beam past Caitlyn, trying to anticipate her escape route. It was easy to see.

The chasm was maybe fifty feet across. The tunnel that Mason had been following did not continue on the other side. Instead, there was a narrow ledge, with that sheer rock face behind it.

His flashlight beam found a ladder beside the bridge, also made of rope, hanging down the rock face, leading to another ledge about a hundred feet down. And from that second ledge, another rope ladder led to a third ledge. His beam was not powerful enough to reach completely into the depths, but Mason guessed there was a series of rope ladders all the way to the bottom. Why else would she be here but to escape from the mines?

To confirm his guess, a steady breeze blew upward from the depths. The air flow would not be this strong unless there was a way out at the bottom, maybe another tunnel.

Mason assessed his chances of crossing the rope bridge. On his side the ends of the bridge could simply be lifted from the iron hooks holding them in place. If he unhooked the rope, Caitlyn would be flung against the wall and tumble hundreds of feet into the darkness. But because of the deal he'd made with Bar Elohim, he wanted her captured, not dead. Worse, without the bridge to cross the chasm, he'd be stranded on this side, with the one way to safety destroyed by the explosion and an impossible labyrinth of tunnels as his only hope for escape.

With another flick of the beam across the chasm, he confirmed that the bridge was also looped on similar iron hooks at Caitlyn's end.

If she had arrived minutes earlier, after crossing she

could have lifted those loops and let the bridge fall, uselessly secured only on Mason's end. He would have had no way across.

As it was, he briefly wondered if she had the capacity to release the rope with him on it. He told himself she didn't. He would walk the bridge, and she wouldn't remove the loops. Unless she had a knife. He had to trust his instincts that if she did, she'd have it out. What choice did he have? There was victory ahead.

He snarled at his fear and took a step onto the bridge. The air seemed colder, and spray from the waterfall splashed his face. His backpack thumped loosely against his ribs. It was comforting in a way, reminding him that once he filled the canister, he'd have what he wanted. That thought helped him drive past his fear.

On the other side, he'd be able to do what Caitlyn couldn't. He'd drop the bridge and ensure his own escape, just in case the soldiers tracked him via another tunnel. They'd never be able to cross the chasm, and he could take his time moving down the series of ladders to the bottom.

The problem was, as he quickly discovered, he'd miscalculated.

The footing was trickier than he'd expected, because the bottom of the bridge was made of webbed rope and wooden slats. Waist high on each side, rope as thick as his wrist gave him the same guides that it gave Caitlyn, only he was at a disadvantage. He had only one hand to clutch the rope because he held the flashlight in the hand at the end of his cast.

The bridge swayed and twisted sideways, and Mason gasped. Without the strangled grip of his good hand, he would have plunged over. As it was, panic forced him to drop the flashlight and clutch for the other guide rope with his injured arm. He flailed, ignoring the pain, and managed to find the other rope.

Eerily, the flashlight tumbled in silence, the light shrinking until it disappeared. Not because the flashlight smashed as it hit bottom, but because the depth of the chasm simply swallowed it.

That sent him into another bout of panic and paralysis. Mason panted with horror and almost wept as he waited for the bridge to stop the pendulum swing from side to side.

If he waited too long, she'd be across. And if she decided to lift the bridge off the hooks, the bridge would simply become a ladder with him hanging on, thousands of feet from the bottom of an abyss, until he lost his strength and let go. That thought galvanized him, and he staggered forward, biting the inside of his cheek to keep from whimpering. If he were far enough across, she wouldn't be able to lift his weight.

Step by step, palms sweating, he advanced, grateful that he couldn't see below him, trying to keep his imagination at bay.

Then light again.

Caitlyn's.

She'd crossed and now pointed her headlamp

toward him. She shined it on Mason, and the light pierced his eyes. He directed his snarl at her.

The beam moved away and illuminated the end of the rope bridge, secured by heavy iron hooks, on her side. She began to struggle to pull it loose. Her figure was a blurred outline of shadow and light.

As he guessed, she didn't have the physical strength to unhook the bridge with his weight on it.

He moved forward another couple of steps but with less urgency than before. Now she was down to two options. Wait for him on the ledge or begin climbing down the rope ladder beside the bridge, slowed by her injured leg. Even with one arm in a cast, he'd be able to follow, and then, because of her injured ankle, it was only a matter of time until he caught up with her.

Her beam turned to the edge of the ledge, and Mason saw Caitlyn squat and examine the top of the rope ladder. The beam marked her downward progress. Something looked strange about her back. It didn't matter, though, as he'd kill her first and examine her later.

The light would also help him find the ladder.

Ten steps left, he guessed.

Down to five.

Then he was on the ledge.

Because of the contrast of the darkness against Caitlyn's light, Mason had no difficulty seeing the loops of the thick rope that held the bridge in place on the iron hooks.

He lifted them and let go.

With a swish, the bridge fell away. Seconds later, he heard it slap against the far side of the chasm.

Now the tunnels behind him were no longer an issue. Nor the soldiers, if they found a way around the destroyed headquarters. No way for them to cross should they make it this far. No way for them to reattach the bridge on this side.

With a grim smile, Mason echoed Caitlyn's actions only a minute earlier.

He squatted and found the top of the rope ladder, held in place by iron hooks similar to those that had held the rope bridge in place. With his good hand, Mason held tight and felt his way down.

In seconds, he was vertical and able to also use the hand of his casted arm to hold himself secure. Unlike the bridge, this ladder didn't sway. He began the descent.

The beam below him brightened.

He looked down but saw only a circle of light. Caitlyn had pointed the headlamp upward, catching him in the beam as he had caught her earlier, and now she would see that he was close.

Nothing would stop him now.

## FORTY-SEVEN

Because of her injured ankle's restricted movement, Caitlyn knew that Mason could travel faster down the ladders than she could. Climbing one ladder wouldn't matter much, but a series of ladders were ahead.

Jordan had explained to Caitlyn what remained of her journey. The ladders descended hundreds of feet. Then a bridge would take her across the river at the bottom, back to the side that she'd started from.

But she knew that eventually, at this pace, Mason would catch her on one of the ledges. Even if she somehow managed to stay ahead of him, even if she managed to get across the bridge at the bottom of the chasm, she faced the same problem she hadn't been able to overcome on the first rope bridge. While the plan had been for her to cross the top of the chasm and then drop the bridge to seal off any pursuers, with Mason's weight, it had been impossible. She didn't see it happening any differently below.

If she didn't stop Mason somehow, he'd cross the river again at the bottom and discover what so many people had already made such a sacrifice to hide.

And she could hear Papa's words. *"You can't be taken, dead or alive. You must not fall into their hands."*

No, even if it meant her own life, she had no choice.

When she reached the second ledge at the bottom of the first ladder, she didn't begin scrambling down the next ladder.

Instead, she removed her cloak, set it down, and waited for Mason.

Mason lightly stepped onto the second ledge and slowly turned. He expected to move slowly, even crawl, as he searched for the hooks that held the next rope ladder.

He didn't expect a beam directly in his face. Caitlyn was still on this ledge.

"I heard you release the bridge up there," she told him, her volume raised above the water cascading past the ledge.

Mason snorted, then spoke, raising his voice too. "I want you for myself. All alone."

He reached down with his good hand and unsheathed his knife. Mason didn't move forward. He could at any time, of course. But it was too much pleasure to savor this. Nor did he want to risk any sudden moves. Not until he knew where the edge of the ledge was.

"Stop," she said. "Without that bridge for you to get back, your life is going to depend on what I explain to you."

"I'm sure I'll find my way out." Mason scraped his thumb against the knife blade to test the sharpness. "Without your help."

"The only way out is down," she answered from behind the light. "More ladders. Like the one above you. I'm holding the ladder from this ledge right now. I unhooked it while I was waiting for you. If I drop it, you'll be stuck here."

Mason snorted again. "I don't believe you."

"Think about it," she said. "If I know you're going to kill me, what difference does it make how I die? Move toward me, and I throw the ladder away as I jump. Dying that way is quicker and less painful than facing your knife."

Mason knew she was telling the truth. His mouth tasted like it had filled with ashes. His knife hand shook.

"So get rid of the knife and climb back to the top and wait," she said. "All I want is a head start. Let me get to the bottom. If you start chasing me again, I'll do this again at the next ledge. Whether you're trapped here or one or two ledges below, it doesn't matter. You'll still be trapped."

"You expect me to let you escape."

"We both live," she said, "or we both die. Your choice."

The light shifted away from his face. It lowered, showing the dark shadow of her lower body on the rock floor of the ledge. He focused on the thick iron hooks, where the loops of the rope ladder should have been.

*Nothing. She hadn't lied. The ladder is gone.*

The light shifted to her feet. She'd placed the loops around her left ankle, the leg closest to the ledge, and her heel was off the ground. If she moved slightly, the weight of the rope would slide down her foot. The ladder would be gone. Mason croaked, like the low croak of a raven that had wrapped its talons around his throat. In that instant, he fully understood the horror of it. Trapped. No food. No water. If she jumped, he would not even have light. The worms of terror began crawling under his skin.

"If you were on the other side," she said, "this wouldn't have happened. But the others can't be found."

"Others?" Mason wanted the conversation to continue, because he'd just noticed something. She'd made a mistake. The drop-off was to her left, but straight behind her was a sheer rock face. She was only ten feet away. If she fell backward, he'd have her.

*Keep her talking.* He shifted the knife slightly.

"Bar Elohim did not win," she said.

"The soldiers captured everyone," he answered. *Keep her talking.* "You saw that."

"The Clan has not been destroyed."

He wanted her. Dead. He wasn't going to retreat. He shifted the knife slightly. What he was going to do was fire it into her chest. She'd fall backward. Forward, the rope ladder would slide off her ankle. Backward, it would go up her leg. He'd be on top of her before she could move.

"You can't do it." He moved a step toward her, intending to distract her by talk and by movement. "You don't have the steel to jump. You're just a girl. You want to live so bad, you won't drop that ladder."

"You're wrong," she said.

With the snakelike quickness that had always given him so much pride, he snapped his wrist, firing the knife through the air, expecting to track her fall by the way the light moved.

There was a barely discernible thud above the noise of the water. She cried out in pain.

Mason leaped forward, but the light didn't move backward. It moved sideways. Out into the chasm! Plummeting into the darkness.

*She jumped.*

Then Mason blinked in disbelief as the light defied gravity, as if it had landed on an invisible hand, and then it began to turn in a slow circle.

## FORTY-EIGHT

Pierce cinched a life jacket on Billy. "This should do it."

Because of Billy's size, it had been a struggle to adjust the straps. He held another life jacket in his arms, in case the first one didn't provide enough buoyancy.

Theo, Gloria, and Pierce already wore theirs. The group had reached a long, low cavern with a river flowing strongly through the center.

Jordan had to raise his voice from his wheelchair. "I need to repeat this, in case you've forgotten already. The river runs through about a half mile of rock until it reaches Outside. Most of the way, there's enough room to keep your head above water. In places, though, the water level reaches the ceiling of the rock. You're going to have to hold your breath and trust that there's only ten or twenty seconds until you have clearance again. When you reach open air, you'll be Outside. People there always watch the river for refugees. You'll be taken care of. I promise."

Pierce laughed too. Billy thought laughter seemed out of place for Pierce anywhere, but particularly in an underground cavern. Particularly now.

"Hey," Pierce said, "the man sending me down this river is the man I was sent to arrest. But I guess I won't even remember that he saved my life." Billy watched Pierce look at Jordan. "You're still a wanted man. If you ever get Outside, I'll have to hunt you. If I'm allowed to keep my job, that's my duty. You know that."

Then Pierce stepped away from them and fell backward into the river.

Billy helped lower Gloria into the river. Then Theo.

Jordan trained a flashlight on Gloria and Theo, showing them in life jackets as they bobbed down the subterranean river. Within seconds, the current took both of them into a passageway that had only about a foot of clearance above the surface.

"Your turn," Jordan said to Billy.

"Okay," Billy said. He pointed upstream, where it appeared that the river simply came from a wall at the far end of the cavern. "Where does this water start?"

"On that side, the passageway is completely underwater for about a hundred yards."

Billy nodded as if it mattered. It turned out that it did.


Jordan cared a great deal about the river's flow. They'd come in through a tunnel that bypassed the waterfall. But on the other side of the cavern, a hundred yards upstream, was where the giant subterranean waterfall fed this river.

Where Caitlyn would be making her escape.

Jordan had a sense of unease. He'd half expected she would already be here.

"You ready?" he asked Billy.

"Yes sir."

Jordan turned the flashlight toward the river to guide Billy's steps. That's when he saw it.

A snake riding the current.

No, not a snake, but thick rope.

He played his flashlight on it. It took several seconds to realize that the rope was part of a long ladder, undulating with the water.

The rope ladder from the other side. Nearly instantly, Jordan realized the implications. If the rope ladder had fallen from one of the ledges, there was no way down.

*Caitlyn!* He needed to get to the other side, to the base of the waterfall.

He grabbed Billy's life jacket just before Billy stepped into the water.

"Pick me up!" Jordan said. He trained his flashlight beam on an exit tunnel. "Run with me! There!"

## FORTY-NINE

Caitlyn was in the air. She felt it rush against her face. A roar in her ears from the waterfall.

And stabbing pain in her right shoulder from Mason's knife.

She'd seen the shift of his knife hand and had been

preparing to jump even as Mason took the first step toward her.

She shouldn't have answered when he said she wouldn't jump. She should have just jumped, as her instincts screamed for her to do, and coldly left him there to die. She had done enough, offering that they both could live.

But he was a killer and she wasn't, so she hesitated.

When his hand began to move, she'd finally leaped toward the chasm. Too late to avoid the knife, but enough of a shift that the knife struck her shoulder instead of the center of her chest, below the throat.

Now she was in the air, the spray of the waterfall reminding her that the water would slam her down if she ventured too close.

She banked away from it.

*Banked. As in soaring. Through the air.*

That's when she realized what was happening. The pain had distracted her. Until now, discovering the sensation of banking in the air, with the updraft of cool air holding her aloft, making instinctive moves that she couldn't have explained to anyone except herself.

Her arms were spread in the Iron Cross that she'd spent her entire life perfecting, and not even the embedded knife could diminish the strength in her locked joints and muscles.

Her outstretched fingers supported another incredible sensation. The ends of the wings that pressed against her arms, with tips that flexed as easily as moving fingers, subtly making adjustments to the flow of air.

*Her wings.*

She gloried in the sensation of freedom. The miner's light on her forehead gave ample illumination for what she needed, bouncing off the face of the rock as she approached in a slow, wide circle.

She banked again, riding the updraft.

The light glinted off the waterfall, showing scattered diamonds of moisture as spectacular as a shower of stars.

Another slight flexing of her wing tips and she soared away from the danger.

She felt no fear. Just amazing comprehension, an understanding of the trembling that had first taken place at the edge of the chasm, the urge to throw herself into the depths, an understanding of the ache for freedom she'd always felt on mountainsides with Papa.

This was her destiny. Where she belonged.

That hideous bursting of her back had been like stepping from life through death into life again. Even then, she hadn't quite comprehended what had sprung forth, folded inside the hunch, growing until her time had arrived.

But now she understood.

Her arms pressed against the wings, and her wings pressed against her arms, a fit so secure that by bringing her arms forward, her wings moved with them. It was a tentative movement, but she discovered that even this slight attempt gave her lift.

Another beat of her wings, levered by chest muscles that had become indefatigable through all the years of holding the Iron Cross. Another upward lift. She wasn't just riding the draft like a glider but was actually able to move at will.

It gave her a deep, unspeakable peace. She longed for open air, a place to swoop and dive and rise again.

Yet even as she gloried in the realization that this was who she'd been meant to become since birth, the pain in her shoulder grew.

She felt faint as she banked again to dodge the other side of the chasm. Edges of blackness crept in at her vision.

Her light showed another ledge with a rope ladder in place for her to descend. This would be safest. If she lost consciousness in the air, she was dead.

But she would be just as dead if she crawled onto the ledge and let the blood seep from the knife wound in her shoulder. Except that death would be the death of a creature of the earth. Not one born for the sky.

She banked away again.

At the bottom of the chasm was the river that Jordan had described, a tremendous flow of water that disappeared into the rock, flowing for a mile underground before it came out. It would sweep her to a different kind of death, where water filled her lungs and matted her wings.

But also at the bottom of the chasm was the second

rope bridge that Papa had promised, the one that would take her to the others.

If she could reach it, or reach the tunnel the bridge led to, she'd find the others. She didn't want to die now, not so soon after discovering this glory.

She blinked away the pain, concentrating on the beam of light that came from the coal miner's lamp. She didn't know how long she could fight the blurring at the edge of her vision. But she couldn't dive down. She didn't know the limits of what she could do with her wings, didn't know if she'd have the strength to pull out of a dive. And the river below was waiting to drag her into a different kind of darkness.

She circled and circled downward, her light showing the rock face, the fall of water, the rock face.

Each turn brought more weakness. The black edges continued to press into her vision. Then, dimly, she saw the rope stretched from one side of the chasm to the other, like a strand of web, shadows of the rope thrown onto the slickness of black water below it.

With a fierceness she didn't know she had, she willed herself not to fade into oblivion. Her conscious mind screamed to keep at bay the encroaching walls of death, and her subconscious flexed her wings where she needed to hold herself aloft, doing it as naturally as the act of breathing.

Then the rope bridge was looming in front of her light, suddenly upon her, and she nearly overshot it. In her weakness, and in the newness of flight, she didn't have the coordination to come down lightly and move her hands and arms separately from her wings to grab at the rope.

She tumbled into the bridge, entangling herself in the rope, nearly sliding through and off.

There was a horrible wrenching at her ankle again. This new sensation of pain was her last moment of awareness.

## FIFTY

Mason could not climb down from his ledge, but he could climb back to the top, where he'd dropped the rope bridge.

He kept his mind on the physical labor of pulling himself up. His cast rasped against the rope, and he welcomed the sensation as a distraction. He knew if he allowed himself to think of his position—in the dark, hanging on a rope ladder hundreds of feet above the bottom of a chasm—he'd go insane.

There was no hope downward, unless he jumped too.

That only left up.

He was panting when he reached the upper ledge. Slowly, he crawled forward. For a dizzying moment, his hand reached into the void, and his entire body shook with the adrenaline of his fear of heights.

He shuffled back, away from the drop-off, until his feet hit the rock wall behind him.

Like an old man, he rose on weak legs. He faced the rock wall and shuffled sideways, toward the waterfall.

Maybe there was a way behind it, a place were the limestone had worn away, like behind the waterfall where he first believed he'd captured Caitlyn.

A few steps later, he slid his foot into air and nearly toppled into the abyss.

With a sob, he pulled his foot back. Then crumpled to the ground in relief that he hadn't fallen. A snake wrapped itself around his thigh. He pushed it away but felt nothing in his fingers. He realized it had been a product of his fear, as if his nightmares were coming to life at the realization that he'd die on this ledge. It would be thirst that took him, and the thought of it made him lick his lips.

The waterfall was so close that mist hit his face. Yet he was unable to reach across the last few feet to that water.

He crawled back to the rope ladder. He found the two iron hooks, the two loops.

Then a thought hit him and jolted him with hope.

He could cut the ladder in half! He'd leave one loop on this hook, and with the matching half coiled around his body, he'd slide to the ledge below. He'd loop the other half at the hook below and slide down again. Then he'd be at the next ladder, and he could climb all the way down.

It would work!

He slapped his hip for his knife.

*Gone.*

He felt a snake curl around his belly. He screamed, pulled at it, but found nothing. He bit the inside of his cheek, trying to hold on to his sanity, and whimpered with frustration, remembering what hope had caused him to forget. He'd thrown the knife at Caitlyn.

All that remained was his backpack, holding the canister he'd intended to use for the harvest of eggs from her body. There was nothing to cut rope.

After the exertion of climbing the rope ladder, thirst had intensified to torment him. Now there was something else to torture him.

The offer that echoed in his mind. *Life for a life, or death for a death.*

If he hadn't been so determined to kill her, the knife would be in his hands. He'd be able to escape this horror of slow death, alone in the absolute black of hell.

Easy death was a mere step or two away, into the void. But he was too much of a coward for that.

He thought of hanging himself and had a vision of climbing back down the ladder and trying to wrap one of the rope rungs around his neck and letting go. But the fear of heights was too overwhelming.

If only he had kept his knife.

Snakes of terror seemed to crawl over his body. He imagined tiny snakes, worming into his ears, pushing at his brain.

He began whimpering again, almost reduced to catatonic fear.

The rope, the rope, the rope. If only he could find a way to cut it.

Crying, he began pulling the rope ladder up until there was enough of it to rest on the ledge beside him.

Whimpering, he lifted one of the rungs to his mouth.

He clamped his teeth on the rope. His mouth could barely get around it, and immediately the coarse strands cut through the edges of his lips and the taste of copper streamed onto his tongue.

Didn't matter. Didn't matter. Didn't matter. He was an animal. He would gnaw through it. This rung. The next. And dozens and dozens more. Yes. Yes.

More tendrils of terror and insanity curled through his brain. He fell on his side and curled into a ball, rope in his mouth.

Chewing. Chewing. Chewing.

## FIFTY-ONE

There," Jordan said. The beam of the flashlight showed Caitlyn's ankle stuck in the webbing of the rope bridge. Her head dangled only inches above the water.

Billy still cradled Jordan, like a child in his arms. They had thundered through a series of short tunnels to the base of the waterfall, Jordan giving Billy directions at every turn.

Billy set Jordan on his feet. He didn't need instructions.

When Billy stepped onto the rope bridge, it sagged with his weight. He wished he'd left the life jacket on, instead of throwing it off back in the other cavern.

Jordan kept the flashlight beam on Caitlyn. Her eyes opened.

"Don't move," Jordan urged Caitlyn. "Don't panic."

It was obvious that if she shifted slightly, her weight would pull her loose from the bridge. As it was, she was slipping incrementally.

Billy tried to tiptoe forward, but the bridge kept swinging. One of the slats that formed the floor of the bridge snapped. His right foot slipped through.

*Think,* Billy told himself, *think.*

If the slats couldn't hold his weight, he knew the rope could. That left one option.

He slowly pulled his foot loose and backed up the half step to the end of the bridge and found solid land.

"You've got to go," Jordan said. "She can't hold on much longer."

Billy grunted. He moved to the side of the bridge, squatted, and leaned his upper body precariously over the swift-moving water. If he fell in, he'd drown. It was too far to the open cavern on the other side, where Pierce and Theo and Gloria had been sent floating down the river in life jackets.

But he had no choice.

With one hand, he grabbed the lower rope of the bridge, where the slats were attached. He allowed himself to fall forward.

For a moment, the water threatened to suck him loose, an angry monster determined to steal its prey.

But Billy managed to secure his other hand on the rope. Now he clung with both hands. He scuttled sideways, hand over hand, toward the center of the bridge, his legs and waist in the current, dragging at him with malevolent power.

He dared a glance over at Caitlyn. She hung upside down, arms at her side, making no movement that would pop her loose from the rope webbing that held her by the ankle.

Hand over hand. Hand over hand.

As he got closer, she slowly reached for him.

They were inches away, pinned in the beam of light that Jordan held at the edge of the river, when she fell.

Billy gave it no thought. He let go with his right hand and clutched for her wrist. His fingers closed over her lower arm. Her body jerked as her feet fell toward the water.

She gasped and their eyes met.

Neither said a word. Billy was concentrating too hard on keeping his grip on her arm. And on the rope bridge with his other hand.

The current pulled too hard, and her arm began to slip through his fingers.

"No!" Billy roared. He'd never felt anger, not like this. He roared at the river as if it were a living creature. "No!"

Her wrist slid into his fingers, and he tightened his grip. But that was all he had. Her body was deep into the water. Almost to her neck. He only had one arm to pull her loose. If his grip on the rope bridge broke, both of them would be swept away.

"No!" he roared again. He fought the river, inch by inch, getting her closer and closer. Finally, her legs pulled loose, and the tremendous strain on his shoulders and arms lessened.

"Arms around my neck," he panted. He needed both hands to fight his way back.

She reached around with one arm, then the other. Billy never knew arms could feel so good.

He also knew the river wouldn't win now.

Hand over hand, he brought them back to safety.

The chopper was in the air. Brij and the others were all in plastic handcuffs, captured and transported.

Brij had never seen the valley from this perspective. He also knew it would be his last view of it. He had no doubt that he and the two dozen other Clan members would be sent to the factory. Some might be executed by stoning, but with such a large group, they would be valuable as slaves in the factories.

Brij wore a wan smile.

They'd sacrificed themselves to save the rest of the Clan, but it was a sacrifice with even more meaning. The survivors would be sent to the factories, a chance to be among the poor, the desolate, and the hopeless who lived there.

Caitlyn had helped the Clan more than she could imagine. She'd been a decoy, bringing soldiers to a decoy headquarters. Bar Elohim would believe he'd found a way to destroy the Clan's ability to remain hidden in the mountain.

But the others were safe and would continue what the Clan had already been doing for a generation. Eventually rumors would reach Bar Elohim, and in a few years, he might understand that he'd failed yet again.

In the meantime, it would be that much easier to help Appalachians reach Outside, where they had freedom of choice and belief. With Bar Elohim convinced the underground railroad had been dismantled, it would operate in far greater safety.

Far more than that, however, was the chance to end the desolation and hopelessness in the factories.

For years, Brij had been wondering how to smuggle faith inside, but Bar Elohim would be doing it for them, unaware that the choppers were the ultimate Trojan horse.


"You have wings," Billy said. He had his life jacket on again. His voice was filled with awe.

Caitlyn had spread them to let them dry after their time in the river. They were back in the cavern, downstream from where they'd nearly drowned at the rope bridge.

"I have wings," Caitlyn said, simply. They covered her arms as if wings and arms were one unit. Nothing seemed strange about it. As if this had been the destiny of her body and she'd finally reached it.

"Are you going Outside too?" he asked. Jordan sat in the wheelchair again, out of earshot, giving them privacy.

"Not by river," she said. "They'll be watching for me."

"Oh." Billy gave the implication some thought. "But you will be going Outside. Another way."

She nodded.

He was losing his breath again, the way it had happened the first time he saw her. Her face. Her eyes. He wanted to tell her how looking at her made him feel, but he didn't know if he could put it into words, not even for himself.

And he was big. Too big. Too slow. Too stupid.

She was exquisite. Beautiful.

He was a lumbering creature of the earth. She was of the sky.

He didn't deserve to even dream about her, so he said nothing. Only let that feeling of not being able to breathe grow and grow. He hoped he would remember this Outside.

"Good-bye," he said. "Theo's already gone into the river. Mrs. Shelton says she's going to be with us Outside. Will we see you again?"

What he didn't dare ask was something more direct. *Will I see you again?*

"William," she said, "thank you."

"William?"

"Stop calling yourself 'Billy,'" she said. "People call you that because they want you to stay like a little boy trapped in a man's body. Outside, they won't know who you were. Don't let them believe you are less than you are."

Billy nodded. He wanted to remember this too.

"Good-bye," she said. "I'll look for you on the Out-side. William."

He stepped into the current. Faster than he could have guessed, it took him into the passageway that led to freedom.

That was the final picture of Appalachia for him.

Her. In shadows. Wings outstretched. Beautiful.

*In the new millennium, when scientists completely understood the human DNA code, advances in medicine became astoundingly rapid. For the wealthy, embryonic screening eliminated every hereditary disease; embryonic stem-cell technology led to an industry of organ cultivation, and the extremely wealthy were able to extend their lives by purchasing new hearts and livers, custom ordered from a laboratory.*

*It didn't stop there.*

*Understand that at the one-cell stage, an embryo is much like an egg. The outer cell wall is like the shell. The nucleus at the center is the yolk, containing the DNA that programs the growth of that embryo. Soon, the one cell divides into two, then four, then eight, and continues to divide.*

*Different strands of DNA are coded to become active as cells begin to specialize. Scientists learned early to take advantage of this. They first learned to create flies that had up to fourteen pairs of eyes, simply by adding a snippet of DNA into the nucleus at the one-cell stage.*

*Because every cell contains the entire DNA code for that organism, any changes inserted into the nucleus at the one-cell stage will be replicated in the nucleus of every new cell created. Once the embryo matures to adulthood and reproduces, it will pass these changes to the next generation of its species through its off-spring. Thus biotechnology and the funds and the secret blessing of certain military agencies literally gave scientists the power to begin to reengineer the human species.*

*In your innocent childhood, you were unable to comprehend what science had given to you. And stolen from you because of the solitude and loneliness inflicted upon you with a single injection of a DNA strand into the single embryonic cell which became your being . . .*

They'd been waiting for Caitlyn's shoulder to heal from the knife wound and for a clear, moonless night, with wind coming off the eastern slope of the high ridge that overlooked the perimeter fence of Appalachia.

Unlike the climb a few weeks earlier near Cumberland Gap, on this night there was no mystery in climbing to the tree-stunted top of this mountain. Caitlyn knew exactly where they were headed and why.

During the ascent, the silence between Caitlyn and Jordan was as strained as it had been since Billy had pulled her from the river. The wind helped them up the western side of the mountain. It wasn't until they reached the narrow ridge that its force seemed malevolent, with a strength set on pushing them into the abyss, down into the orange glow of lights that marked the perimeter fence, a long line snaking around the base of the mountain and disappearing miles away.

It also seemed as if the wind tugged at Caitlyn's soul. A wind much colder than this summer air. During all the days since the pursuit had ended in the waterfall cavern, days without the adrenaline of fear to distract her, she'd endured long, long hours with the words of Jordan's letter to haunt her.

*"We had agreed—the woman I loved and I—that as*

*soon as you were born, we would perform an act of mercy and decency and wrap you in a towel to drown you in a nearby sink of water."*

He stood silently beside her. She had no doubt what he wanted. Absolution from her. A single word of forgiveness or love.

They were poised at the moment of separation. On the other side, she might never see him again. She could sense how badly he wanted to speak.

An abyss stretched in front of them. One also lay between them. The numbness that Caitlyn used so effectively for survival against Mason Lee would not leave.

"The letter you gave me near Cumberland Gap, it doesn't tell the whole story, does it?" Caitlyn asked.

Jordan's legs were braced against the wind, and he steadied himself.

When he didn't answer or even look at her, she continued. "You led Mason away from me and expected to die or to be put in a factory. Even then, you avoided all of the truth in the last words I might get from you."

"Yes. There is more."

She couldn't see his face. It was too dark. On a moonlit night, or one with a low cloud bank reflecting the orange lights, the chance that a guard looking upward might see her outlined against the sky was too great. Tonight was perfect for escape.

"Even now . . . are you going to keep it from me?"

"Since the river, each morning I would tell myself that 'Today is the day I will tell her the rest.' But I could never find the right moment. Or the courage. We seem like strangers. When you look at me, all I see is a silent accusation. When I tried to talk to you, I mean *really* talk to you—you'd find an excuse to change the subject."

"I've had a lot to think about." The numbness now felt like ice. "I'm sure you can understand that."

"I could see the transformation coming. I had to get you out of Appalachia. But if you went by river, the Outsiders waiting to help would have turned you over to the government. You would have been caught."

He gestured at the abyss in front of them. "The only way out was this."

"You could have brought me here. You could have explained what was happening to my body. You could have helped me fly over the fence without using me as a decoy."

Caitlyn shuddered at an image of Mason Lee and the knife poised over her belly. It had been the evil as much as the threat that terrified her.

"Don't you think I agonized over that? The risk to you against the certainty that the Clan would eventually be destroyed?"

"You hid all of that from me." She'd wanted to voice this accusation since surviving the waterfall. It seemed to explode from her, as her wings had.

"The risks for you to reach Brij were meant to be minimized by my capture. I had the information for Mason on a vidpod in my pocket. He was supposed to take it to Bar Elohim so they could set up a trap for you in the valley. I was the one at greatest risk. Not you. I was prepared to die."

"Even that was selfish. You could have told me."

"And what would you have done with the knowledge?"

"You made me a decoy. You and Brij talked of freedom, but you didn't give me a choice."

He tried to touch her shoulder, but she stepped away. "You learned of it when you reached Brij. You didn't go into the mines without knowing you were the decoy."

"How could I refuse at that point?"

"Others would have." He was shaking. It took her a moment to realize he was weeping noiselessly.

She wanted so badly to let go of her pain and anger and comfort him. But she couldn't. The betrayal had been too great.

"Finally, tears for what you did to me?"

"Bar Elohim was going to destroy—"

"No! What you did *to* me." Only a couple of feet separated them, but to Caitlyn, the abyss seemed infinite. "Do I need to show you my wings to remind you?"

Despite the dark, she could see him fight to get control of his emotions. "I've lived with it every moment since you were born. I knew watching you leave would be difficult, but my heart didn't understand it until now."

Caitlyn felt like her own face was as cold and rigid as the bare stone of the precipice. "I'm so angry. I wish I wasn't, especially now. I want it like it was between us."

"It can't be the same. You have to go over the fence. You have no future in Appalachia."

"I want it like it was before I knew that you were the one who did this to me." She prayed he would deny it, but only the wind across the rock made any sound.

"I know what Mason wanted from me." She'd had days to think about the letter. About the silver canister. She became almost savage. "My eggs. He wanted to cut me open and harvest my eggs like I was an animal. That's what they wanted from me. The Outside. My eggs."

"Enough." His whisper was barely audible above the sweeping wind.

"Am I right?"

"The research used was destroyed. You are all that remains. Your genetic code would almost be enough to bring the project back to where it was. With eggs, all it would take is fertilization and surrogate mothers."

"And more freaks would be born?"

"Caitlyn . . . we have all been designed to soar with angels. Our souls will someday leave the prisons of our bodies and return home. In one way or another, God allows us to fly."

"Do you know how you sound?"

"I don't know how I sound. But I feel like a broken man."

"Would you prefer to be a broken angel? When I was born, you *should* have drowned me."

"Caitlyn . . ."

She knew how badly she was hurting him. She couldn't stop herself. She wanted to flail, to strike out. Anything to lance her own pain.

Jordan reached out for her again. She took another step away. "You couldn't tell me who I'd become, because then I'd ask how you knew. Because you were the scientist who did this to me. Are you going to deny that?"

"You know what's waiting for you on the other side and how to get there," he said. He seemed calm again, the Papa of strength that she so desperately wanted to love without reservation. "Once you have the surgery, you won't be—"

"Should I say it again? A freak."

"You have no reason to forgive me. Just know this. I love you as big and forever as the sky. That will never change."

Their childhood game.

This was the moment she could erase all the anger. Just one word would do it.

*Papa.*

Instead, in cold, blind anger, she leaped into the abyss, stretching out her arms and wings, letting the wind pull her away.

Her memories of flight in the waterfall cavern had seemed like a surreal dream, blurred by the terror inflicted on her by Mason Lee.

But here it was again. The instinctive adjustments of her wings, so like the hawks she had watched with such envy as a child. She too trusted in the same fabric of nothingness that let them soar.

She exulted in fierce joy, and in that moment, far above the ground, weightless, flying, she realized that this was her destiny. In the womb she'd been designed for this freedom.

That joy and that flash of realization shattered the numbness, tore away the anger, let the love warm her again.

"Papa," she cried.

Then the backdraft rushed against her, carrying her away, and it was too late to turn back. Caitlyn was over the fence.

# ACKNOWLEDGMENTS

Shannon, thank you for the passion and keen insight and frank but enjoyable discussions that you brought to Broken Angel.

## Center Point Publishing
600 Brooks Road ● PO Box 1
Thorndike ME 04986-0001 USA

**(207) 568-3717**

**US & Canada:**
**1 800 929-9108**
www.centerpointlargeprint.com